AF377900

———————

Mondrala Press wishes to thank all its friends, fans, patrons, and
investors for making this book possible, and especially:

Ms. Randa Dumanian
Mr. and Mrs. Karol and Dagmara Maziukiewicz
de domo Sowul

without whose enthusiasm and open hearts this book
could never have happened.

———————

Thank you for reading with me!

My micro-publisher, Mondrala Press, publishes English translations of great Polish books—books with a track record of international critical and commercial success but which, for political reasons, have never been published in English. And now, finally, they are!

I have grown up reading these books and I have been telling my American friends about them all my life. And my American friends have always asked: "When will you translate them so we can read them, too?"

And now, finally, I am doing it and I am delighted that I can finally share these books with you.

To see my newest titles, or to subscribe to my news, or just to say "Hi!" please visit:

WWW.MONDRALA.COM

THE GREATEST BOOKS YOU HAVE NEVER HEARD OF

MR WHEELS

AND

THE MYSTERIES OF THE CITY OF COPERNICUS

BY

ZBIG NIENACKI

TRANSLATED BY
TOM PINCH

MONDRALA
PRESS

TABLE OF CONTENTS

An Important Note:
On the Spelling of Polish names

In this book, I use a phonetic spelling of Polish names.

Some of you may be familiar with the Polish script and may be surprised that I write "Helmno" instead of "Chełmno" or "Wooj" instead of "Łódź."

I do this because I have discovered that people unfamiliar with Polish script cannot pronounce these names, and because they cannot pronounce them, they cannot keep them straight. One of my readers put it best: "I can't keep track of who is who because they all have long names, and most start with an S."

Now, phonetic transcription of foreign names is a matter of course. Translators of Tolstoy write *Trubetskoy*, not *Трубецкой*. Translators of Chinese write *Li Bai*, not 李白. So, why not write *Helmno* instead of *Chełmno*? No spelling convention should ever stand in the way of a good book, right? As a translator and editor, I have the duty to make my books readable and fun, and I find that this phonetic spelling helps my British and American readers.

But for those of you who are familiar with the Polish script and would prefer to see it in this book, contact me via www.mondrala.com. We are preparing an edition of this book with Polish spelling.

From Your Translator:
The Teutonic Knights and their Legacy

If you read volume 1 of this series (*Mr. Wheels and the Templar Treasure*), you are familiar with the Teutonic Knights, an order of warrior monks born, like the Templars, in Palestine during the Crusades. The order went on to play a very important role in Eastern Europe. The Knights arrived on the Baltic to defend local Christians against pagan Prussians. But then they went a step further: they wiped out the Prussians and created their own independent state; and then went on to have further territorial ambitions—in Poland and in Lithuania. To this day, their massive castles and churches dominate the landscape of northeastern Poland.

After a century of wars, the victorious Polish-Lithuanian Commonwealth broke up the Teutonic state, absorbed half its territory, and made the rest its feudal subject. But that was not all: the ecclesiastical state run by a military religious order became a private dukedom owned by the nephew of the King of Poland.

150 years later, this entity would declare itself the Kingdom of Prussia and go on to participate in the Partitions of Poland, and, eventually, reunite Germany and become its largest federal state.

The legacy of fraught ethnic relations between Prussia's German and Polish settlers would reverberate down the centuries and culminate in the destruction of the Third Reich and the complete expulsion of Germany and Germans from the former Prussian territory.

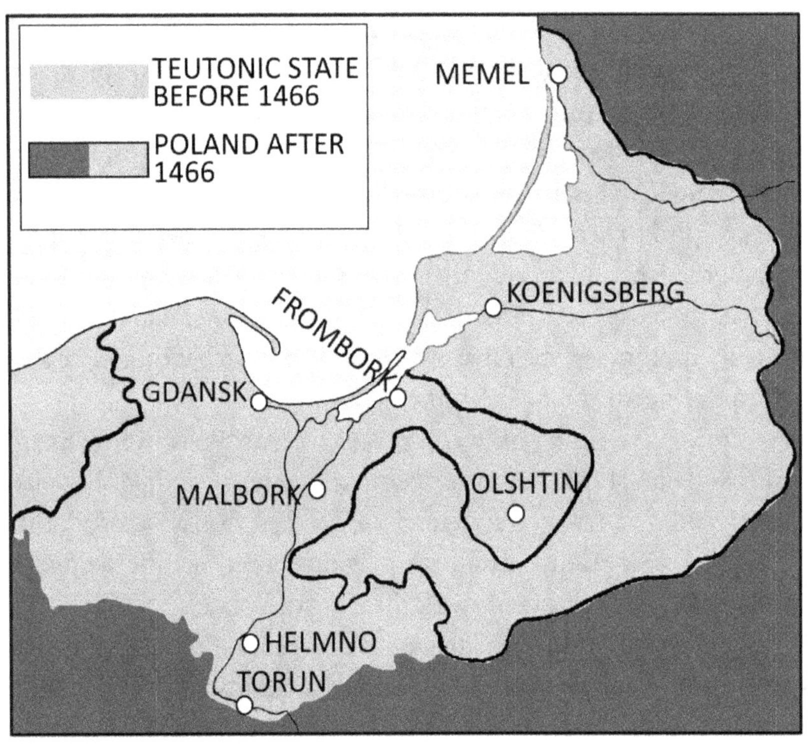

The Break-up of the Teutonic State in the Peace of Torun (Thorn) 1466

Much of the state, including Gdansk and Frombork, was absorbed by the Polish Commonwealth. The rest was "privatized" in 1522.

CHAPTER 1: THREE PRICELESS COINS

After my return from the Loire. A new assignment. Who shall be in charge of the riddles of Frombork? Colonel Koenig's first cache. Three priceless coins. A mysterious couple. What the investigation has revealed. Code-name "The Ducat of the Elbow-High."

I returned from a month-long vacation in France and barely had time to resume my usual duties at the Ministry of Culture when I was summoned by Director Marchak, my immediate supervisor.

Gone were the days of my work in provincial museums, when I dabbled in solving historical puzzles and searching for cultural treasures lost during World War Two. Nor was I the curator of a small museum in the countryside any longer. I now had an apartment in Warsaw and a full-time position at the ministry. Officially, I was only a humble clerk in the Department of Museums and Historic Preservation, but in reality, I was a detective for special assignments. No, I was not guarding display cases or chasing burglars through museum halls (though, unfortunately, such incidents do occur quite often). My job involved cases that sometimes had no apparent characteristics of a crime at all and yet could expose our country to significant cultural losses. For example, I often visited stores to observe transactions and to ensure that valuable artifacts (whose worth was sometimes not known to the seller) did not fall into the wrong hands. I also observed the activities of various antique and art dealers.

I had plenty of work; the work of protecting the antiquities is full of surprises and puzzles. Those who follow the press might remember the sensational news about the discovery of an El Greco painting in a small country church; of a Lucas Cranach painting found in an old attic; and the affair of the priceless stained glass window. I was involved in all these matters as an appraiser for my department. My work also included the search for art collections lost during World War II. My activities and my numerous adventures on the job could fill many pages.

And if I find the time, I will also describe my stay in France, where I had been invited by Karen Petersen, the daughter of famous treasure hunter, Captain Petersen. Throughout July, Karen and I were engaged in solving the mysteries of one of the most beautiful castles in the Loire Valley. We experienced many dramatic and fascinating adventures worthy of a separate book.[1]

But by now, I had returned to Poland. It was the first of August and the first day of my work after the summer vacation.

"I've been eagerly awaiting your return," said my supervisor, Director Marchak. "I have a new and very important task for you."

"I can guess what it is," I replied. "It involves the riddles of Frombork?"

The city of Frombork on the map of Poland

"Oh, you have heard about this? But you only arrived from France yesterday."

"The French press wrote about it. Anything connected with the city where Copernicus made his great discoveries interests the

---

[1] See *Mr. Wheels and Phantomas* (upcoming)

world. I wish to assure you that I will take on the riddles of Frombork with great enthusiasm."

Director Marchak shook his head.

"Unfortunately, I must disappoint you there. Your colleague, Dr. Parsley, has been in charge of the Frombork business for three weeks now. He has already found one of the three hiding places where Colonel Koenig had hidden the art he had stolen in Poland. We have recovered priceless works of art, Mr. Thomas, and therefore, I see no reason to take the Frombork business away from Dr. Parsley and hand it to you."

"I haven't heard anything about the discovery of Koenig's cache."

"We have kept it under wraps. There was way too much hype about the discovery of Colonel Koenig's corpse and the map showing his three caches. We don't want amateur treasure hunters to descend on Frombork. After we locate all the caches and recover all the treasures, we will hold a press conference. But for now—radio silence! For your information, though, Dr. Parsley has discovered one of the caches, and its treasures are in the basement of the National Museum. If you want to see them, contact the director; he will probably agree to show them to you."

"*Hm...*" I grunted sadly.

"Do not *hm,*" Director Marchak said. "I dislike it very much when you *hm.* I know that there is a lot of animosity between you and Dr. Parsley. He has repeatedly complained that we give you all the most interesting cases and leave him in the shadows, unable to demonstrate his detective talents. And I confess that I was glad that you were abroad when the Frombork business came to light because I could assign the case to Dr. Parsley with a clear conscience. And it was a good thing, too. I am very pleased with his work. He has already found the first cache."

I solemnly placed my hand to my heart.

"I declare, Director, that I will not meddle in the mysteries of Frombork. Dr. Parsley can work peacefully without fear of my interference. And now, I look forward to the task you will assign me."

"Well, alright, then. Let us get down to business," agreed Director Marchak, opening his notebook. "As you know, Mr. Thomas," he said, "we monitor purchases made by Polish museums, and we strive to be fully informed of these purchases, especially if they involve objects of great value. Well, over the past week, I've received the following reports from three different museums in three different Polish cities. First, the museum in K. has acquired from a private collector a *Gnezdun civitas*. The museum in L. acquired the denarius of Meshko I..."

Meshko I (Mieszko I) (ca. 960-992)
The first historically documented ruler of Poland. His decision to accept baptism in AD 966 placed Poland off limits for slave-hunting by Christian rulers. Here: a drawing by Yan Mateyko (Jan Matejko).

"What?" I sprang up from my seat.

"Yes, yes, please. The denarius of Meshko I. And sit down, Mr. Thomas," said Director Marchak. "Sit down and hold on tight to your seat because this is not the end of the revelations: an anonymous collector offered the *bracteate* of Yaksa to the museum of Wooj."

"What!?" I exclaimed, not believing my ears. This time, however, I did not spring up but held firmly onto my chair.

"Yes, Mr. Thomas," continued Director Marchak. "I share your amazement. In a single week, the numismatic market saw some of the most interesting and oldest Polish coins appear all at once. What is more, although all the specimens were simply priceless due to their rarity, the sellers offered prices that were not exorbitant—even if they reached tens of thousands of zloty."

WOOJ (ŁÓDŹ)

Wooj is the fourth largest city in Poland, home of its textile and film industries, the setting of the great Reymont classic The Promised Land, and the hometown of both Zbig Nienacki and—of Mr. Wheels. Here: a seal from 1577 with the coat of arms of Wooj.

"Unheard of!" I could not contain my amazement.

"Each of the museums mentioned jumped on the unique opportunity offered and made the purchase quickly, without special formalities. It was only here, in the department, as we received information about these purchases, that anyone grew uneasy."

"Was the seller one and the same person in each case?"

"That's just the thing. No. The museum in K. bought the denarius of *Gnezdun civitas* from a man. The museum in L. bought the denarius of Meshko I from a woman."

"Usually, with this type of transaction, there is a bill of sale showing the personal details of the seller," I said.

"And there you have it, Mr. Thomas. We investigated the matter. It turned out that in every case, the seller was a proxy."

"What do you mean?" I asked.

"The transactions took place as follows: first, there was a phone call to the museum. An anonymous man offered to sell a priceless coin and set a meeting at a cafe to view the item. When asked where he got the coin, he replied: *I will not answer any questions. Do you want to buy? If not, goodbye.* Since they were unique specimens and the price was relatively low, every museum wanted to buy. At any rate, the seller has no obligation to disclose the provenance of the goods. He can always say: *I found the coin in an old trunk in the attic,* and who will prove that this was not the case?

"So. The transactions were consummated: the proxy collected the money and then went back to the actual seller. He handed over the money and received a commission of one thousand zloty. According to the descriptions these proxy sellers gave us, the actual seller was a different person in every case: sometimes an elegant lady, sometimes an elegant gentleman."

"Which doesn't mean it wasn't a group acting together," I said.

"Of course. It is almost certainly the work of several people. After all, it can't be a coincidence that as many as three unique coin specimens were offered for sale in one week."

"Have you notified the militia?"

"Yes, thanks to the militia, we learned that the sellers of the coins were proxies and that someone else was hiding behind them. Of course, this is suspicious but it does not warrant a formal investigation and certainly not the involvement of law enforcement agencies. It is just not a crime. Anyone in Poland has the right to sell some old antique coins in his or her possession as he likes within the country. Of course, it is rather suspicious for someone to send someone else in his place and then pay him a commission, but such a seller can always say that he has many other coins for sale and doesn't want to be pestered by numismatists. You know how it is with those coin collectors. When they find out that someone has a big collection, they start to pester him, ask to view the collection, exchange, sell, or buy, and so on. So, such a person may justifiably prefer to remain unknown. It certainly looks suspicious, but it doesn't make him a criminal. And in this case, no one has reported these coins as lost, or stolen, or missing. So, the specimens sold to the museums are not, as far as we can tell, the proceeds of a crime, and therefore, there are no grounds for a formal investigation. They may have been accidentally found somewhere. After all, quite a few collections of various kinds were lost during World War II. And one should only be glad that the anonymous finder, instead of hiding his precious coins in some safe or bank vault where they would never be seen by the public, offered them to the museums for an unaffordable price."

"Maybe the seller had no idea about the value of the goods he offered?"

"That doesn't seem the case. In his telephone conversations with museum curators, the man described the coins professionally and said that they were priceless but that he was aware of the modest financial resources available to the museums, which was why he proposed such a low price. He explained further that he did this because he wanted these coins to end up in museums and not in private hands."

"This seems like a very patriotic stance."

"Yes. And that is another reason we don't see the need to involve the militia. Instead, we assign this business to you."

I thought for a moment.

"How do I get on the trail of this mysterious someone?" I asked.

"As I said, the museum in Wooj received a proposal to buy the *bracteate* of Yaksa, issued by Yaksa, the prince of Kopanitsa, about AD 1210.[2]

This time, the offer was made by a woman. She proposed to make the transaction at the *Honoratka* cafe tomorrow at 8 pm. The curator of the museum is supposed to meet her and bring the money in cash. The mysterious woman said she knew the curator by sight and

---

[2] Yaksa of Kopanitsa (Jaxa of Köpenick) (flourished 1151–1157) was a prince of the West Slavic Sprevan Principality of Copnic (Kopanitsa). He was an opponent of Albert the Bear during the formation of Brandenburg in 1157. Kopanitsa was a Slavic state located more or less on the site of today's Berlin. It was captured in the early 12th century by the German-speaking Margraviate of Lusatia. Today, it is Köpenick, a suburb of Berlin.

would approach his table to talk to him. She would hand him the coin and collect the money. So, Thomas, I suggest you go to Wooj tomorrow and appear in the cafe a little before 8 PM and see the lady for yourself. The rest is up to you."

"And should I allow the transaction to proceed?"

"Oh, yes! This is a priceless coin, and she only wants thirty thousand zloty for it. Just see what you can learn; perhaps follow her or speak to her. I leave this up to you. And for future reference, in case we need to speak in code, I give this case the code name of...."

And just at that moment, the phone on Director Marchak's desk rang.

"Yes, this is Marchak," he said into the earpiece.

After a moment, an expression of astonishment arose on his face. Then he shouted into the phone:

"What?! You want to sell me the golden ducat of the Elbow-High?

"But this must be a joke! The Elbow-High ducat is unique! There is no other coin of that issue. There has never been one, as far as anyone knows. What's that? You say that you have a second coin?"

Tiny drops of sweat appeared on Director Marchak's forehead. His fingers, tightly clenched on the handset, turned white.

"Ma'am, I agree to all your conditions!" he practically yelled into the phone. "Please tell me where and when we can meet. Yes, I will bring the money, but you must first show me this coin. I do not believe it exists. No one has ever seen another example of the ducat of Vladislav the Elbow-High... What? You will call me back?... Hello! Hello?" cried Director Marchak into the phone.

But he called out in vain. The woman had hung up.

Director Marchak slumped into his chair and sat there speechless for a long time. Then he said quietly, as if out of all energy, "I give this case the code name *The Ducat of the Elbow-High.*"

And he added pleadingly, "Mr. Thomas, you're my only hope."

Vladislav Lokietek (Ladislaus the Elbow-High) 1260-1333

Nicknamed for his small stature (an elbow being a measure of distance equal to about two feet), he was born a ruler of a tiny principality in central Poland. He ended a period of 120 years of civil wars by reuniting the country under his rule in 1320 and fighting off a joint Czech/ Teutonic invasion in 1331. Here: a drawing by Yan Mateyko (Jan Matejko).

CHAPTER 2: ENTER THE EVIL GENIUS

National treasures. The numismatic Yetis. Trouble with Prince Yaksa. Villains or collectors. My secret mission. In Honoratka. Enter the Evil Genius. Batura answers some questions. The gauntlet is thrown. One-zero for Batura.

The following day, I drove to Wooj. I made the journey in my vehicle because I felt that I had to be prepared for all eventualities when trying to establish the identity of the mysterious lady willing to sell the *bracteate* of Yaksa. The circumstances of the case, and above all, that strange phone call to Director Marchak, made me think that I was in for a difficult challenge. So, did I regret that I had not been assigned the Frombork case of treasures buried by a Nazi thief? Well, that case sounded fascinating, to be sure. However, I felt certain that the codename *The Ducat of the Elbow-High* was equally likely to electrify public opinion.

The road to Wooj is wide and straight, easy on the driver. My trusty vehicle carried me safely, and I knew it would not give me any unpleasant surprises. During my stay in France, as a reward for my participation in unraveling the mysteries of the castle on the Loire, Captain Petersen had bought a new engine for my vehicle and new tires from the Italian company Pinin Farina. The total cost could have bought me a new Peugeot. But I didn't want to part with my vehicle, which had carried me through all sorts of dangers so many times. I treated it as my best partner and friend. Equipped with a new engine and new tires, how could it fail me?

As I drove it on the good road to Wooj, I reflected on the task I had been assigned by Director Marchak. I knew I had to execute it carefully, with the greatest possible tact, for who could know whether some famous collector was not behind the transaction? However, national treasures were at stake, and it really did seem necessary to learn where they had come from.

National treasures! When people hear this term, they imagine huge museum halls hung with tapestries, paintings by old masters, crown jewels, weapons, and magnificent furniture. But these particular national treasures, the provenance of which I was to discover, could be hidden in a child's hand. Why, the fist of a newborn was large enough to contain all three. None of these rare and priceless coins exceeded the size of a grown man's fingernail, and none was much thicker than a fingernail. Yet these tiny objects are guarded in our museums as carefully as our gorgeous tapestries and our magnificent paintings. And they are guarded like this because they were just as important in the history of Our Nation. They are mentioned in many books and textbooks—but you will never find them in any sales catalog because—they do not have a price.

Do you now understand why, when I heard the first words of Director Marchak, I sprang up from my seat and listened to his story with amazement?

Consider the denarius of Meshko I: the first Polish coin ever. Until then, the Polish people had either used barter, or Arabic, or even ancient Roman coins. Or, sometimes, lumps of silver. But then Meshko I issued his denarius—probably soon after he accepted baptism in AD 966, and now, for the first time ever, Poland had its own coinage—just like France, or Bohemia, or Germany did. Back in those days, a coin featuring the name of its ruler was a visible sign of the country's sovereignty, proof of its existence—not only to his own subjects but to everyone who ever accepted the coin in payment.

Have there been many of these coins? Experts calculate that the denarius of Meshko I was minted in twenty or thirty-five thousand copies. How many of these coins have survived to our time? There are forty-seven known specimens. But the fact that this coin has not been offered for sale at any major auction in a century is a testament to its extreme rarity. That little coin is more than a thousand years old—it is as old as the Polish State. It is made of silver, has a diameter of twenty millimeters (about three-quarters of an inch), and weighs only 1.97 grams (or 1.7 pennyweight). On the obverse, it shows a crowned eagle (or, possibly, a chicken) and the distorted name of the ruler. On the

reverse, it has a simple cross, and in the four corners of its arms—four
spheres

The denarius of Meshko I
*It has since been proven to have been issued not by Meshko I but by his
grandson, Meshko II.*

And this particular denarius was now sold to the museum in L.!

But even more electrifying was the sale to the museum in K. of
a denarius with the inscription *Gnezdun civitas*.

Gnezdun civitas

Among Polish coins, this one ranks second only to the coin of Meshko
I. The denarius with the inscription *Gnezdun civitas* was minted on
the orders of Boleslav the Brave to commemorate the famous Congress
of Gnezno in the year 1000. Its value, however, exceeds that of the
Meshko denarius, for it is unique: only a single copy of it is known to
exist. This copy is held by the Emeryk Chapski Museum in Cracow.

Chapski was a rich landowner who put all his vast wealth into his collection of Polish coins. On his deathbed, he donated the collection to the Nation, and it can still be seen in Cracow today.

Rumor has it that a second copy of the *Gnezdun civitas* has once existed—found in a treasure hoard unearthed in Rihnov in Vonbzhezhno County. Supposedly that copy then entered the Cracow collection of the famous banker Bohenek in or about 1863 but later disappeared without a trace. Before World War II, the well-known numismatist Felix Mojinski of Warsaw claimed to own it. But numismatists are like anglers, they are fantasists, and not everyone believed him.

Gnezdun civitas is even smaller than the Meshko denarius. It has a diameter of eighteen millimeters and weighs 1.68 grams. The obverse shows a man in a diadem with a necklace of pearls. The reverse shows the familiar cross with four bullets and the inscription *Gnezdun civitas.*

And now, a second copy of this denarius was sold by a mysterious someone to the museum in K. for (only) seventy thousand zloty! Where had that copy come from? How did it find its way into the hands of this mysterious someone?

Do you now see why this event has excited Director Marchak? And then, to top it off, as if these revelations were not enough, the museum in Wooj notified Marchak that a *bracteate* of Yaksa, the prince on Kopanitsa, was now on the market!

Bracteate of Yaxa of Kopanitsa

A *bracteate* (from the Latin *bractea*, meaning 'wafer') is a coin so thin that it can only be minted one-sided because the negative of the stamp shows up on the other side. It is difficult to say exactly how many *bracteates* of Yaksa survive in the world—in any case, there are very few; only a few museums have it in their collections. This coin is extremely interesting not only because of its rarity but also because of the person of Yaksa, the prince who had minted it. According to historians, the Slavic prince Yaksa had his seat in Kopanitsa in the early twelfth century—more or less where Berlin stands today, or more precisely, its Köpenick district.

A map of present-day north-east Germany about AD 1100
showing the names of the Slavic tribes (Obodritii, Veletii, Stodoranii, Sprevanii, etc.) and their strongholds (Brandenburg on the Havel, Köpenick). These nations have eventually been "ethnic cleansed" by the Germans.

This Yaksa fought hard against the German margraves during his reign, especially Albert the Bear, for the control of the principality of Brenna, which later received the German name of Brandenburg.[3] Yaksa was able to seize Brenna first, but Albert pushed him out in AD 1157. What happened to Yaksa afterward is unknown. Some say he died in exile in Poland.

The *bracteate* minted by Yaksa has a diameter of eighteen millimeters and weighs only 0.83 of a gram. It shows the bust of a bearded prince holding a sword in his right hand and a palm branch in his left. The background is decorated with three stars and the inscription *IACZA DE COPNIC*.

This thin coin once caused German nationalists a lot of trouble: that the city of Berlin had once been a Slavic capital simply could not be accepted by them. The Nazis searched for the coin in all Polish museums and private collections in order to destroy it and thus erase from memory the fact that a Slavic prince named Yaksa once dared to have a stronghold in today's Köpenick district of Berlin.

And now, a mysterious woman offered to sell this coin to a museum in Wooj. How did it end up in her hands? Who was this person who possessed such a priceless coin?
And what to make of the astonishing phone call to Director Marchak about the gold ducat of Ladislaus the Elbow-High? If the woman caller had not been lying, another revelation awaited us, even bigger than the sale of the denarius *Gnezdun civitas*. The one hundred thousand zloty the woman demanded was nothing compared to what she would have received at a foreign auction. So maybe there really was someone honorable behind these sales who simply found himself or herself in financial difficulties and was willing to part with some specimens of his or her collection for a price affordable to museums?

Still, a second copy of the Elbow-High ducat?

No, it was too fantastic.

You should know that for many years, scholars believed that Poland had never had any gold coinage before the sixteenth century. Only the year 1847 changed this opinion.

That year, in Bosnia, near Cracow, a local goldsmith bought a

---

[3] The future parent of the Kingdom of Prussia.

gold coin discovered in the ground by municipal workers digging to lay sewage. He earmarked it for melting down and was about to throw it into the crucible when it came to the attention of a visiting numismatist, a landowner named Nejelski from nearby Senjeyovitse. He bought the gold coin for six guilders. The coin turned out to be a gold ducat of Vladislav the Elbow-High, most likely minted to commemorate his coronation in the year 1320.

Then, Emeric Chapski brought the ducat and bequeathed it, along with the rest of his vast collection, to the National Museum in Cracow, where it remains to this day. It is the only copy of this coin in the entire world.

Precisely because of its rarity, there is a dispute among numismatists as to whether the ducat was a circulating coin or simply a commemorative medal minted on the occasion of the coronation. In the latter case, only a few, or at most, a few dozen such coins were ever minted.

One specimen! Think about it! How many collectors around the world would give up a fortune to acquire such a specimen?

In the world of numismatists and collectors, rumors arose from time to time that someone, somewhere, had seen a second copy of the Elbow-High ducat. Even newspapers reported such stories sometimes. But museum professionals only shrugged their shoulders. The existence of a second copy seemed like Yeti, the Himalayan Big Foot: much talked about but never seen. This person or that person claimed to have seen it, but no one has ever produced any tangible evidence.

And now, a mysterious lady was offering to sell a second copy of the golden ducat to Director Marchak! Was it a joke? Did a second copy really exist?

The whole situation seemed very complicated, and only my role in it was simple. I was supposed to discover where these rare Polish coins came from. The instructions I received from Director Marchak greatly narrowed my scope of action. I was to get on the trail of the mysterious seller, but I was not allowed to impede the transaction. I was only to witness the act of purchasing the *bracteate* of Yaksa.

I had plenty of time. First, I contacted the custodian of the numismatic cabinet in Wooj, Mr. A. G., a great expert on all matters related to Polish coins and the author of many works in this field. We agreed that we would go to *Honoratka*[4] separately. We would sit at different tables, the custodian would make the transaction, and I would remain an observer. Then I would tail the lady who sold him the *bracteate*.

I found myself in *"Honoratka"* half an hour before the appointed time and took a table near the door. Everyone who entered or left the café had to pass by me. It's a small cafe: one small room with a dozen tiny tables. In the evening, it was usually frequented by people from artistic circles, mostly from the world of film, since Wooj is the home of Poland's largest film studio. And in the evening, you could see lots of girls and boys from the art school there. The cafe is famous for its excellent coffee and excellent tea, great cheesecake, and tasty apple pie. Most of the regulars know each other personally or by sight. An old-fashioned cuckoo clock keeps the time.

The custodian of the numismatic cabinet came in at ten to eight. He sat down two tables away from me and, to while away his wait, leafed through some scholarly journal.

When it struck eight o'clock, the custodian was flipping through a scientific journal, and I was keeping my eye on the door, expecting the mysterious lady to open it any minute.

And the door did open, but instead of the lady, my former college friend, Valdemar Batura, walked in. He looked around the café, spotted me, and bowed politely. He then approached a phone on the buffet, dialed a number, and talked to someone briefly. One would have thought that he had entered the café only to use the phone.

Having finished with the call, Valdemar Batura took off his coat, hung it on a hanger, and walked over to my table.

"Good evening, dear Thomas," he said. "What are you doing

---

[4] *Honoratka* was an iconic café in Wooj between 1947-1975, and the favorite meeting place of the cultural elite of the city. There are ongoing efforts to revive it and a commemorative plaque has been placed on its former location.

in Wooj? We haven't seen each other for a thousand years. May I join you?"

"By all means," I replied politely. I had already figured out that the mysterious lady would not come to the meeting with the custodian. The presence of Valdemar Batura made this clear.

Who was Valdemar Batura? A slender, medium height with smoothly combed dark hair, he had a face as delicate and as beautiful as a woman's. He once had sported a refined small mustache but was now cleanly shaven.

He had been a star student in college. He was considered, and not without reason, to be the most talented student in our year. He possessed a tremendous amount of knowledge in history and art history, and at the same time, like me, he had the investigative instinct. While still in our senior year, we solved some interesting historical puzzles together and detected the forgery of a famous painting.

Then, our paths diverged. We started working in provincial museums. I soon learned that Batura had left his post, and his name became well known in the antique dealers' circles, not only in Poland but also abroad. Batura traveled abroad several times a year: to Italy, England, and West Germany to, as he claimed, further his study of architecture. In reality, he was probably involved in the antiques trade. He was very successful, dressed elegantly, and always had a state-of-the-art car. He was very shrewd, he only took up business where the line between legality and crime was vague, and so far, he had only once—and that was because of me—fallen afoul of the law. However, he had been sly and was never arraigned for the crime, but only for a minor incident related to it. You see, he had attempted to rob a huge collection of priceless Masonic antiquities but all that was ever proven against him was the breaking of a few floorboards of an old mansion.[5]

As for me, I have always considered Batura an extraordinary mind, a great connoisseur of antiquities and works of art, and an excellent detective. If only I had had a friend and an ally in him, I am sure that none of my great puzzles related to lost collections would

---

[5] See *Mr. Wheels and the Mystery of the Palace* (upcoming)

have remained unresolved. But Batura was very fond of money, exquisite clothes, and a lavish lifestyle, for which his modest salary as a museum worker could not provide. And therefore, he was not my ally but my opponent. And he was an uncommon opponent, an individual of extraordinary intelligence and cunning and grace.

As soon as he entered *Honoratka*, I knew that the deal was off. His appearance here could not be a coincidence. Obviously, he was behind the sale of all those rare coins to our museums.

"Will you have a cup of coffee?" I asked politely.

"Of course," he replied with a smile. "That's why I came to the cafe."

"Is that so? Didn't you come here to check if the custodian had arrived and whether it was safe to proceed with the transaction? And then, when you saw that I was here, didn't you call off the whole thing and signal to the woman who was supposed to do the transaction not to come? Yes? No?"

"What are you talking about, Thomas? What transaction? What woman?"

"Well, I don't know her, you do," I replied. "But you have the *Bracteate of Yaksa*."

"*Bracteate of Yaksa*? Dear Thomas, you must be joking. That's a very rare coin, and as you know, I am not a collector."

"Really? So, you do not own the *Elbow-High Ducat,* either?" I asked, ignoring his evasions.

He sighed heavily.

"Thomas? Hello? Do you really think a second copy of that ducat exists?"

"Imagine this, Valdemar! A woman telephoned Director Marchak yesterday, offering to sell him this very ducat. For a mere hundred thousand zloty. What do you think? Isn't it a prank?"

Batura paused in thought, and I watched him carefully, thinking that his response would tell me everything I wanted to know, for if he made fun of the situation, he was likely not involved. But if he took it seriously, it would confirm his connection to the business.

"A second copy of the Elbow-High ducat?" Batura pondered

aloud. "Such a joke wouldn't go far. Who would ever believe it? But then again, there have long been rumors of the existence of a second copy. Maybe the person owns it and wants to sell it to you? A hundred thousand isn't much for such a rare coin."

"Why ask a hundred thousand and not a million?" I pressed.

"How should I know?" He shrugged. "Maybe the seller is a realist? Maybe he knows that our museums do not have huge budgets? They might afford an Elbow-High ducat for a hundred thousand, but not for a million."

"So why not sell it abroad? The seller would get enough money to live comfortably for years. Smuggling the ducat would be easy; it's as thin as paper and as small as a fingernail."

"I don't know, Thomas," Batura shrugged again. "You're asking me to read someone else's mind."

I wasn't giving up.

"What about you, Valdemar? If you had the Elbow-High ducat, wouldn't you rather sell it abroad for a hundred thousand dollars rather than give it away for a hundred thousand zloty?"

Batura shook his head.

"Now you wrong me, Thomas. I know that you think that I'm a scoundrel because you see every artifact as a national treasure, and I dare to trade in such things. But it's not that simple. Sure, I deal in old oil lamps, sabers, and armchairs, but that doesn't mean that I'd sell something priceless, like a second copy of that ducat abroad. I'm a patriot, too, Thomas, just in a different way. And believe me, if I knew someone who was trying to sell a priceless relic to foreigners, I would report them to the Authorities. That does not mean I will stop dealing in antiques, but I will never be a scoundrel."

Sincerity rang in his voice, and I couldn't help but respect him for it. Out of the corner of my eye, I saw the custodian growing impatient. Unable to wait for the mysterious woman any longer, he folded his journal, paid for his coffee, and left the café. Like me, he must have concluded that the mysterious woman was not coming and that the transaction was off.

For a moment, I considered ending the conversation with

Batura to follow the custodian and discuss the new situation. But I decided to stay because I thought that I might learn more by staying. If I could confirm that Batura was behind the coin sales, my task would be as good as accomplished. Besides, I could call the custodian later and arrange another meeting if the woman contacted him again.

"I'd like to believe you," I said to Batura. "And there's no reason for me to hide from you the purpose of my presence here in Wooj. Recently, several of our museums were offered some very rare Polish coins: the denarius of Meshko I, the *Gnezdun Civitas*, and the *Bracteate* of Yaksa of Kopanitsa. And, if the last phone call was not a hoax, the golden Elbow-High ducat."

"Did the prices seem excessive to you?"

"Oh no, they were quite reasonable. That's why the denarius of Meshko I and the *Gnezdun Civitas* have been purchased. Today, here, a third transaction was supposed to take place: the purchase of the *Bracteate* of Yaksa. But the woman offering it didn't show up. Instead, you did."

"I see. So, you suspect me of being involved," he nodded.

"All the previous transactions were handled by intermediaries. Someone else is behind them. You, of course," I said.

Valdemar laughed.

"Surely, you are joking, Thomas. Do you think I've suddenly dug up some treasure?"

"No, I don't think so. Among all the coins that our farmers plow out of the ground from time to time, there may be a rare one, sometimes. It is hard to believe that a treasure that included the denarius of Mieszko I, and the *Gnezdun Civitas*, and the *Bracteate* of Yaksa, and the Elbow-High ducat was happened upon accidentally."

"So, you think I stole the coins somewhere?"

"No. I think you came into possession of a very interesting old coin collection lost during World War II. And I appreciate that you're offering them to our museums instead of selling them abroad."

"But you are not really sure I am behind this," Vademar said.

"Tomorrow, I'll know exactly where these coins have come from. Our department has records of all major collectors and their collections, both pre- and post-war. Not many collectors owned the *Bracteate* of Yaksa."

I was bluffing. Our records were sparse, and many private collectors kept their collections secret. But did Batura know it?

"I don't see the point of your investigation," Batura said. "Even if you're right, and these coins do come from some collection you can identify, could it not be that the collector is simply selling off some duplicates?"

"I doubt anyone owned two *Gnezdun Civitas* or two Elbow-High ducats."

"Or maybe the collector lost his collection during the war, and it ended up in someone else's hands? Many people were forced to part with their most valuable items during the war. Didn't people trade Rubens' paintings for a piece of bread back then?"

"Yes. It is true," I agreed. "And we don't want to delve too deeply into those complicated war-time transactions. But when we acquire priceless relics, we need to know their origin. My investigation isn't about uncovering some conspiracy or catching a gang of criminals. We just need to know where these coins are coming from. Maybe this 'someone' has more valuable coins and is selling them to us one by one. Perhaps we can contact him and purchase the entire collection? Not all our museums have numismatic cabinets."

"And you think this 'someone' is me?" Batura asked.

"Yes," I replied. "But one thing puzzles me: why would this 'someone' offer several priceless coins in such a short period? Surely, he would know it would raise suspicions."

Batura laughed and replied, "Maybe he needed the money? Or maybe he thought you'd still be in France and that Director Marchak would hand the case to Dr. Parsley?"

"Thanks for the compliment," I said dryly.

The clock in *Honoratka* chimed nine. It was time to end the conversation and return to Warsaw. I excused myself and went to the phone. I called the custodian's private apartment.

"What happened?" I shouted into the receiver, unable to believe what I heard.

As the custodian was on his way home, just as he was about to enter his apartment building, a man approached him, claiming to have been sent by the woman-seller who had fallen ill and was unable to make it to the café. The man explained he had the *Bracteate* of Yaksa with him and was ready to proceed with the transaction. The custodian, following his orders, invited the man inside, verified the coin's authenticity, recorded the man's details, and paid him the agreed sum. Just moments ago, the man—another intermediary, by the sound of it—had left the custodian's apartment.

"I'll be there shortly," I said and hung up.

I returned to the table where Batura still sat. I looked at him grimly.

"This time, you've won," I admitted.

"Did something happen?" he asked, feigning ignorance.

"The custodian has just purchased the *Bracteate* of Yaksa. So, everything is in order. But I don't like being played for a fool. I believe you've challenged me. I accept. There will be a rematch."

I shook his hand. Despite everything, I couldn't help but admire his cunning. After all, by respecting our opponents, we show respect to ourselves.

CHAPTER 3: THE GREAT COIN CAPER

The Mysteries of Colonel Koenig. A treasure hunt. Dr. Parsley's extraordinary finds. A lesson in calculus: the story of a rich man, a cross of diamonds, and a thief. The great coin caper: how to steal without making things disappear. The fate of the second and third caches. A mystery unfolds. Leaving for Frombork. My Journey.

The following day, in Warsaw, I found a letter in my mailbox—it was a letter from my young friend, nicknamed "Bashka" ("Betty") because of his strikingly feminine beauty. He wrote:

Dear Mr. Thomas,

If you're back from France, please jump in your car immediately and come to Frombork. I'm staying at Boy Scout Camp No. 2 on the Vistula Lagoon, where I've been since late June because of the 'Frombork 1001' action— we're cleaning up the city of Copernicus.[6] You might have heard of the Frombork mystery through the press, but I'll describe the story here, as the press has left out a small but significant detail, and the discovery of a cache of treasures hasn't been publicized because it is kept secret by Dr. Parsley.

That detail is this: my unit—while clearing rubble from a ruined tenement near the port—stumbled upon a human skeleton dating back to the war. The remains of a Nazi uniform were still on the skeleton, and next to it, we found a tin can with well-preserved documents belonging to a certain SS Colonel named Gustav Koenig. We later learned

---

[6] After World War II, Moscow prevented Poland from participating in the Marshall Plan, meaning that as late as 1971 (when the action of this novel takes place), rubble of World War II was still present in many towns. Various youth organizations were used to clear it in "volunteer campaigns."

that Koenig had been the commander of a special unit responsible for looting artworks from Nazi-occupied countries, especially Poland. It's no surprise that the authorities were very interested in our discovery. Initially, we were kept in the loop, but when Dr. Parsley arrived, he dismissed our help and forbade us from interfering in the business.

In addition to his military papers, Koenig had by his side a curious, carefully folded piece of paper, something like a map. I made a copy of it—a stroke of good luck as it happens because Dr. Parsley would probably not let me take a second look now. The document looked like this: at the bottom was the inscription: Frauenburg 11.II.45. Frauenburg is, of course, Frombork. The entire document was in German, and I translated it into Polish, but I left the original Teufelb in, as translating it as "Devil B" doesn't make any sense, does it?

It seems that this document was written in Frombork on February 11th, 1945. That date is significant, as it marks the beginning of the Soviet offensive from the nearby Tolkmitsko. The offensive eventually took Frombork. Thus, this document was written on the day Frombork's fate was sealed. You probably know how fiercely the battle was fought; the story of the Branievo bridgehead, the tragedy on the Vistula Lagoon, and the heavily fortified Nazi resistance points.

Now, anyone who sees Koenig's document will immediately recognize it for what it is: a map to hidden loot. Koenig got stranded in Frombork, along with his spoils, and was likely hoping to escape by sea. However, with the ice on the Lagoon shattered by bombing and the Soviet offensive underway, Koenig decided to hide his loot in three different locations and drew a map which only he could understand. Since the map was created in Frombork, the treasure must be hidden here.

Because you were away in France, I tried to decipher Koenig's map myself but failed. Then, Dr. Parsley, your colleague from the Department of Museums and Historic Preservation, showed up. I didn't think much of him. He expressed disdain for you. But surprisingly, he found the first cache within a week. The explanation of the first puzzle turned out to be simple. The rectangle with crosses marked a cemetery, "H.A." stood for "Haupt Alee," meaning the main avenue in the cemetery, and "37R" indicated the grave number and the right side of the aisle, as "R" stands for "Rechts" in German, meaning "right." Sure enough, the hiding place was under the slab of the thirty-seventh tomb on the right in the central alley of the cemetery.

However, we weren't present when the tomb was opened because Dr. Parsley did it at night to avoid causing a sensation. The items found were immediately taken to Warsaw, and nothing was mentioned in the press—the idea was to prevent a flood of curious people that might hinder the search for the remaining caches. But it's been two weeks since the first discovery, and Dr. Parsley has found neither the second nor the third cache. He's dug in several places but with no results. When I told him that you'd soon return from France and might come to Frombork, Dr. Parsley got angry and accused me of spying for you. He insists he'll find the other caches by himself, but I think he just got lucky with the first one. So, I'm writing to ask you to come to Frombork and help solve the mystery.

A hearty handshake,

Bashka.

I read the letter several times, then studied the copy of Koenig's drawing, then called the director of the National Museum to ask if I could see the treasures Dr. Parsley had found. The director and I have known each other for a long time. I believe he appreciates my detective skills and the fact that I've dedicated them to protecting cultural relics. He has done a lot to safeguard our national treasures himself and is a staunch opponent of dishonest antique dealers and of anyone trying to export our heritage abroad. If it were up to him, he'd likely ban the trade in antiquities altogether and turn every old castle and palace in Poland into a museum.

Thanks to our rapport, within an hour, I was able to examine in the basement of the National Museum the treasures discovered by Dr. Parsely. I must admit, Parsley's discovery impressed me, and I even felt a twinge of envy. In Koenig's first cache, he found twelve paintings by famous Polish and Dutch painters looted from the Warsaw Ghetto. They had preserved well in the tomb. Also, there were four well-preserved 17th-century icons, likely stolen from a museum in Kyiv. If this hypothesis proves correct, they'll be returned to Ukraine, as there's close cooperation in this area between our countries.

Also in the cache, Dr. Parsley found thirteen wooden Gothic and Baroque sculptures stolen from various churches, as well as two gold church monstrances. The experts from the National Museum were working to determine where these items were looted from.

Finally, there was a magnificent collection of 147 Polish coins, spanning the spectrum from early medieval to late Enlightenment periods. These had likely belonged to a private collection, possibly obtained after murdering the collector or sending him or her to an extermination camp.

"Before the war, a well-known numismatist from Warsaw, Feliks Modzhynski, owned a beautiful collection of Polish coins," the custodian accompanying the director and me explained. "We think that this might be part of his collection. That collection had included over 1,200 Polish coins."

"And what happened to Modzhynski?" I asked.

A monstrance

*Also known as an ostensorium (or an ostensory), this is a vessel used
in Roman Catholic, Old Catholic, High Church Lutheran,
and Anglican churches for the display on an altar of some object of piety,
such as the consecrated Eucharist (the host, or the missal bread).*

"He was arrested shortly after the Nazis took Warsaw and sent with his
entire family to a concentration camp where he was murdered. The
fate of his collection remains unknown, but those who arrested him
likely stole it. Perhaps the robbers divided the spoils, and Koenig ended
up with this portion of the coins. Or perhaps Koenig bought this
collection from some Gestapo officer."

"How many coins are there?"

"Exactly one hundred and forty-seven," the professor replied.

I took out the letter I had received from Frombork that
morning.

"There should be one hundred and fifty coins," I said.
"Koenig noted that he hid that many coins in the tomb."

"Well, yes, there were one hundred and fifty, but we discarded
three worthless German pfennigs."

"How did those three pfennigs end up among the most

valuable Polish coins?" I wondered out loud.

"That's something only Colonel Koenig could explain, but he's no longer around to answer us," the professor said.

"And how certain are you that this collection is part of Modzhynski's collection?" I asked.

"There are several unique coins here, such as a special edition of the 'Fight with the Dragon' denarius.[7]

It's well-known that Modzhynski was the only collector to own these coins, and since they were found in Koenig's cache, the conclusion seems almost certain. Here, take a look at the complete inventory of the coins from the tomb," the professor handed me a large sheet listing all one hundred and forty-seven coins.

I scanned the inventory but didn't find what I was looking for.

"The *bracteate* of Yaksa of Kopanitsa is not here. Modzhynski was known to have had it in his collection. Also missing are the denarius of Mieszko I's and the *Gnezdun Civitas.*'"

The professor shrugged.

"Modzhynski's collection had over one thousand two hundred Polish coins. It's hard to say how many were lost forever. The fact is, Koenig had only one hundred and forty-seven Polish coins because that's all that was found in his stash. The *bracteate* of Yaksa, Mieszko's denarius, and perhaps many other valuable coins are missing."

I nodded in agreement with the professor's reasoning, but I remembered that the museum in Wooj had recently acquired a *bracteate* of Yaksa, and other museums had purchased a denarius of Mieszko I and a *Gnezdun Civitas.*

After thanking the director and the custodian for showing me the treasures, I headed to the Ministry of Culture to see Director Marchak. He must have already been informed about the events in Wooj because he received me coolly.

"What happened?" he asked as soon as I entered. "You were sitting in a café, sipping coffee, while this mysterious lady sold the

---

[7] Issued by Duke Boleslav the Wrymouth about AD 1136.

bracteate of Yaksa to the custodian somewhere else. You didn't even catch a whiff of her perfume, let alone track her down."

I smiled, which only irritated Marchak further.

"And you were so confident," he grumbled.

"And yet, you're mistaken," I replied.

"Mistaken about what? The curator of the Wooj Museum already gave me a full account of the events over the phone."

"But has he told you with whom I was sitting in the café?"

"No."

"Too bad. That would have explained everything to you. I met Valdemar Batura in *Honoratka*."

"Batura?" The director looked at me in disbelief.

"Yes. I'm certain he's behind all these sales of priceless coins to our museums. So, there's no point in searching for the mysterious lady anymore."

"Batura!" Marchak muttered thoughtfully. Like me, he knew all too well the cunning, intelligence, and knowledge of Valdemar Batura. Our paths had crossed before at an old manor where some Freemason artifacts had been hidden. At the time, Director Marchak clashed with Batura and realized he was a formidable adversary.

"Where did he get these coins?" Marchak wondered aloud. "I'd bet anything that he acquired them through some fraudulent means. Damn it, such coins don't just appear on the market! You must get to the bottom of this!" The director pounded his fist on the desk, his face flushed. "I suspect there's some huge villainy behind this. We can't let ourselves be outsmarted by Valdemar Batura. Or anyone."

"No, Mr. Director, we cannot," I said. "That's why I'm requesting your permission to travel to Frombork."

Marchak looked at me with astonishment.

"To Frombork? Dr. Parsley is already operating there!"

"But that's where the solution to this riddle lies," I insisted.

Director Marchak began waving his hands angrily.

"Anything but that. No! Never! Do you think I don't know what you're up to? You're jealous of Dr. Parsley's success. No, Mr.

Thomas. Frombork has nothing to do with this. I'd sooner send you on a business trip to Patagonia. What will Parsley think? That I don't trust him?"

"But I have to go to Frombork," I repeated stubbornly.

Then, I lit a cigarette and waited for Director Marchak to regain his composure.

It took a while, but eventually, the director's face regained its normal color, even though his eyes continued to look at me sternly. His voice, too, remained firm.

"I'm listening," he said quietly but ominously.

I took a puff and began.

"Let's start with a lesson in calculus, Mr. Director."

"I'll have no jokes here!" The director slammed his hand on the desk again.

"This is no joke," I insisted, pulling a letter from my pocket. "Mr. Director, our colleague Dr. Parsley found the first of Koenig's three caches in Frombork. According to Koenig's map, he had hidden twelve paintings in the tomb. How many paintings did Dr. Parsley find?"

"Twelve," Director Marchak replied, growing suddenly curious.

"Koenig had four icons. How many icons did Dr. Parsley find?"

"Four."

"Koenig had thirteen sculptures. How many sculptures did Dr. Parsley find?"

"Thirteen," Marchak replied, but this time, he shrugged.

"Koenig also had two monstrances, and Dr. Parsley found two monstrances. In addition, Koenig hid one hundred and fifty coins in the tomb. How many coins did Parsley find?"

"One hundred and fifty."

"No, Mr. Director. Subtract the three worthless German pfennigs. That leaves one hundred and forty-seven Polish coins."

"Well, OK, for the sake of argument. And what's your point?"

"How many coins has our mysterious 'someone' sold to our museums in recent days?"

Director Marchak extended his hand and began counting on his fingers:

"The denarius of Mieszko I is one. The *Gnezdun Civitas* makes two. And the Yaksa *bracteate* is three. Three," he concluded.

"What a coincidence! Three coins! And exactly three coins are missing from the total of one hundred and fifty in the hoard Dr. Parsley found. For that's how many coins should have been found in Koenig's stash," I said triumphantly.

Director Marchak squinted at me.

"You forget about the Elbow-High ducat, which I was offered yesterday. That makes four coins. Your math is off."

This time, it was my turn to shrug dismissively.

"I believe the Elbow-High business was nothing but a clever ploy to disguise the real number of coins on the market, which was three. There is no second copy of the Elbow-High gold ducat. If this mysterious someone indeed had such a copy, he or she wouldn't have called you but would have offered it to a specific museum, as they did before with all the other coins. I'll bet there won't be a second phone call about this ducat. So, let's stick to the facts. And the fact is that our museums have been sold three valuable Polish coins. And that three coins are missing from the Frombork tomb."

Director Marchak looked at me as if I were insane. Then he pounded his fist on the desk again.

"What kind of nonsense is this, Thomas? There were one hundred and fifty coins in the tomb, not one hundred and forty-seven. One hundred and fifty, do you hear?"

"One hundred and forty-seven," I replied.

"One hundred and fifty!" shouted Director Marchak.

"One hundred forty-seven," I repeated politely.

"One hundred and fifty!" Director Marchak's voice rose, his face turning purple once more.

I sensed that if I said "one hundred forty-seven" again, he might order me out of his office. With a heavy sigh, I pulled a sheet of paper from my notebook and drew a large cross on it.

"Would you allow me to pose you a little riddle?" I asked cautiously.

For a moment, it seemed to me that Director Marchak might lose his temper completely. But he managed to control himself, even though his whisper was filled with menace.

"I am a very busy man, and I don't come to this office to listen to riddles from my employees."

"Yes, Mr. Director," I nodded politely. "But just this once, please make an exception. Here's the riddle. There was once a wealthy man whose wife passed away. He erected a magnificent monument to her in the cemetery, which included a cross encrusted with diamonds. This is what the cross looked like, and here's how the diamonds were set."

Marchak, now more curious than angry, leaned forward.

"This wealthy man feared for his diamonds," I continued, "so he came to the cemetery every day to count them. He counted eleven diamonds from the bottom to the top, eleven from the bottom to the right arm, and eleven from the bottom to the left arm. Is that correct, Mr. Director? Have you checked?"

Marchak counted the diamonds on the cross with the end of his pen.

"That's right. Eleven each way."

"But a clever thief came along and stole two diamonds. Yet the rich man never noticed. He still counted eleven diamonds from the bottom to the top, eleven from the bottom to the right arm, and eleven from the bottom to the left arm. The number of diamonds matched, but two had been stolen."

"But that's impossible!" Director Marchak shook his head. "It couldn't still be eleven if two diamonds were stolen."

"Allow me to explain. The thief took one diamond from each arm and moved the first diamond from the top to the very bottom of the cross. Now, count again, Mr. Director. From the bottom to the top: eleven. From the bottom to the end of the right arm: eleven. And the same to the end of the left arm. Yet, two diamonds are missing."

Marchak clapped his hands, impressed.

"A great riddle! I'll share it with my son tonight."

But then, just as quickly, his expression turned serious again.

"But what does this have to do with our case?"

I lowered my eyes humbly.

"I forgot to mention, Mr. Director, that the thief's name was Valdemar Batura, and the rich man was Mr. Marchak."

I braced myself, expecting the director to yell at me in fury. But instead, he responded differently. He spoke calmly but with a sharp edge in his voice.

"Prove it, my friend."

I took a deep breath and explained:

"Colonel Koenig hid one hundred and fifty coins in the stash. I believe that three coins were stolen from that cache, but no matter how you count, it still appears as though all one hundred and fifty coins were found, and everything seems in perfect order."

"Well?" the director growled.

"Colonel Koenig was a thief, but he wasn't a fool. Why would he include three worthless German pfennigs in his cache? He intended to conceal one hundred and fifty priceless Polish coins, yet only one hundred and forty-seven were in the cache."

"There were one hundred and fifty coins!" Director Marchak groaned in frustration.

"So, you still want to be the rich man who, no matter how he counts, always gets eleven? Someone stole three priceless coins and replaced them with worthless pfennigs. And he then offered the priceless coins to our museums."

Director Marchak took several deep breaths, calming himself. I could tell that from that point on, our conversation would become much more serious. Director Marchak was a smart man. He might not have had the instincts of a detective, but that's why he had people like me and Dr. Parsley. His wisdom lay in the fact that if you approached him with solid arguments, he wouldn't stubbornly cling to his own opinions. He would listen, allow himself to be persuaded, and let us act—taking responsibility for our failures, of which we had no shortage.

"Do you suspect Dr. Parsley?" he asked. "Do you think he's exchanged priceless specimens for worthless pfennigs?"

"No, Director. Dr. Parsley is an honest man through and through. While my professional envy might lead me to question his detective skills, his integrity has never been in doubt. I believe someone else has beat him to the cache. Someone else opened the tomb before him, took three of the most valuable coins, and replaced them with worthless pfennigs."

"Why didn't they steal one of the paintings? Or an icon? A monstrance or a statue?"

"Because the thief wanted the number of items found in the tomb to match the number listed in Koenig's plan. He would have had to swap one painting for another, one icon for another icon, one monstrance for another monstrance. And suitable replacements for these things can be hard to find. The thief would have had to replace each painting with another painting, perhaps one of low value but at least old. Same with monstrances and icons. But coins? And three out of one hundred and fifty? No one other than me seemed bothered by the three pfennigs in the collection, they seemed like a small detail, a footnote to the affair. It is clear that the thief we're dealing with is someone who avoids direct confrontation with the authorities. If he steals, he does it in such a way that no one can prove his theft. So, I firmly believe that we're once again dealing with Valdemar Batura."

"Why did he take only three coins and not the entire collection?"

"What would he do with the whole collection? His theft would be immediately noticed, and we would immediately know that one hundred and fifty coins were missing. Batura, as you know, is the kind of man who can be satisfied with a smaller loot as long as he can't be caught. He took three of the most valuable coins and planted worthless pfennigs in their place, hoping that no one would notice the theft and that he could then sell the coins without raising suspicion. He was brazen enough to offer them to our museums, making over a hundred and fifty thousand zloty in proceeds. And that's bad. But the true stakes are much higher, Director. There are still the second and third caches to go.”

I took out of my pocket the letter from Frombork, glanced at it, and continued:

“Koenig’s second stash should contain four miniatures, a porcelain table service, twelve candlesticks, and five chalices. If you were to repeat the same trick with this collection by swapping valuables for items of lesser value, what would you target?”

The director thought for a moment, pondering aloud:

“It would be difficult to swap the miniatures—where would you even find replacements? Handling porcelain might not be easy either. The easiest items to swap would be the candlesticks and chalices.”

“Exactly, Mr. Director. But the candlesticks are likely out of the question because they were probably made of silver and, therefore not very valuable. That leaves only the chalices. We can assume that Koenig had valuable mass chalices made of gold and set with precious stones. But what if Dr. Parsley finds five silver cups in the second cache instead?”

“We’ll all be surprised to learn that Koenig was looting second-rate stuff.”

“But you won’t have any suspicions, will you?” I picked up. “You see, it’s not at all difficult to get cheap old silver goblets. You can find them in Desa stores, and for a relatively low prices, too. Just exchange them for gold, and you’re home.”

“And the third cache?” Marchak asked. I took another look at Bashka’s letter.

“He won’t steal the infula or the four reliquaries.

“But this cache will contain ten rubies. Nothing easier than replace them with artificial, fake rubies. It’s not hard to find artificial stones in jewelry stores. And we will all think that it was Koenig who had somehow got tricked.”

There was a moment of silence. Director Marchak considered my argument. I added:

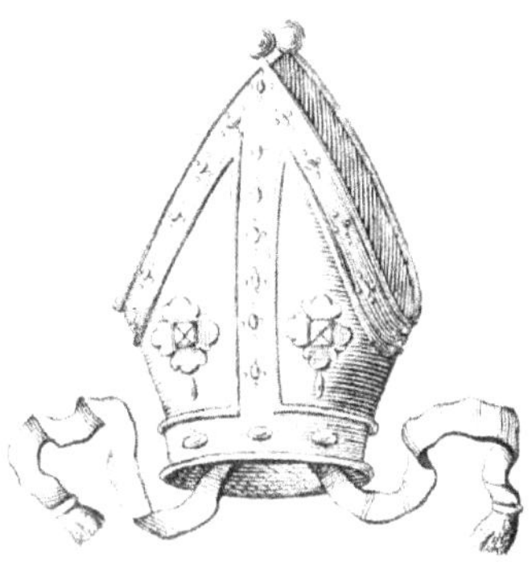

Infulae *are the ribbon's of a bishop's mitre.*

"Fortunately, the thief does not yet seem to know where Koenig's second and third caches are. He is still looking for them."

"And maybe Parsley will beat him to it," Marchak was pleased.

"Yes," I agreed. "Besides, what I am saying remains in the realm of hypotheses."

"We have to consider Parsley's feelings," director Marchak agreed with visible relief. "Parsley is very ambitious. If I send you to Frombork as his aide, he will consider it my vote of no confidence in him and will suffer terribly. He is an extremely sensitive man."

"And yet I should go to Frombork," I said. "The coin investigation is ponting there."

Saddened again, Director Marchak considered the matter. Then his face beamed suddenly.

"I have an idea!" he called out cheerfully. "We need a new, comprehensive guide to Frombork. Several groups of scholars have been working there—archaeologists, historians, even astronomers. Someone should get acquainted with the results of their work and develop a new tourist guide, taking into account new findings about ancient Frombork and about Nicolaus Copernicus's life there. So, let's make this your official assignment, so to speak.

"But your real assignment, I say, continues to be to clear up the mystery of this inexplicable appearance of all these priceless coins. You are going to Frombork because that is where the clues of that case lead you. After all, it sometimes happens in detective work that cases conducted in two different places, seemingly independent of each other, nevertheless lead to the same source and overlap. Parsley is tasked with discovering Koenig's stash, while you are tasked with explaining the case of the priceless coins. If you two can arrange cooperation, all the better. If not, well, then you have to act separately," concluded Director Marchak.

CHAPTER 4: THE ANIMAL TAMER

The mystery of the box of chocolates. Will I take an animal tamer? Maestro Cagliostro and his amazing menagerie. The nightmare journey. A man who keeps lying. Concerning the arcane knowledge. What happened at lunch. Where the snake was. My new, strange assistant.

On the morning of the fourth of August, I pulled up in front of the Ministry of Culture to set off on my business trip. I had a bag with my personal belongings and camping gear in the car. I was determined to set off immediately after completing the formalities at the ministry.

In the director's secretary's office, I found Mrs. Zosha, the secretary, smiling radiantly as usual. She was a person of a certain age and rather rotund, for she was very fond of sweets. As I entered the room, I saw her taking out a chocolate from a huge box of chocolates lying on the desk in front of her. She did this carefully, with two fingers, like an entomologist lifting a beautiful butterfly out of her collection.

"Your business trip papers are ready," she said and handed me my papers with her left hand since, in her right hand, she was holding a chocolate.

"I thank you very humbly," I bowed low because, while it is generally a good policy to live in harmony with one's Director, it is a critical mistake to come into conflict with his secretary.

"But I have a request for you, Mr. Thomas," Ms. Zosha bestowed a radiant smile on me and nudged the open box of chocolates in my direction. "I got a call from our live events department. And they have a request. Would you take a certain very nice artist with you to Frombork? The artist will be giving a performance for the Boy Scouts, and he can't travel by train."

"Did he lose his ticket?" I asked.

"Ah, no, Mr. Thomas," Mrs. Zosha looked at me with

disapproval. "Obstacles of a technical nature, so to speak, prevent him from taking the train."

"And what kind of artist is he that trains do not serve him?"

"This is a special request from the events department. Apparently, he's a circus performer," Ms. Zosha replied uncertainly.

"And what prevents him from taking the train?" I insisted in the most angelic way I could master.

She glanced helplessly at the open box of chocolates and nudged it a little more in my direction. It did not exactly require a detective's perspicacity to realize that Mrs. Zosha had been corrupted by the artist, who, presumably, wanted to save himself the cost of the railway ticket and preferred to travel in someone else's car.

"He's carrying some *animals*," she whispered and bit into a chocolate.

"Elephants? Giraffes? Tigers?" I was horrified. "Is he a tamer of wild animals?"

"Oh, what nonsense, Mr. Thomas," she laughed. "He is probably an illusionist. He has a white bunny. You understand, the kind you pull out of a hat."

"Forgive me, Mrs. Zosha, but as far as I know, rabbits are allowed on trains."

"Yes, except that he also has.... white mice, too."

"Mice?"

"Yes, and... a colubrid. That is—a snake," said Mrs. Zosha, and she shuddered a little.

"And I'm supposed to take all his menagerie to Frombork?"

"But where is the harm? Don't you have room in your car?" she asked, glancing at the open box of chocolates. I realized I would never be able to dodge the illusionist—the bribe had been too powerful, the chocolates too delicious.

Resignedly, I waved my hand.

"Very well, let's have this circus performer. Only right away because I'm ready to leave."

She hastily swallowed the chocolate.

"He is waiting in the hall. You will easily recognize him because he has a black beard…"

I took my papers, kissed Ms. Zosha's chocolate-scented hand, and went out into the hall. The illusionist immediately caught my eye. He had a beard and was standing next to ten rectangular boxes piled up, one on top of the other on the floor.

He was about thirty and extremely handsome: handsome, swarthy, with a kind of North American Indian face with dark, penetrating eyes.

"Are you the fellow I am supposed to take to Frombork?" I asked.

"That's right," he bowed politely, almost in half, as he probably did before his audience when his performance was over.

"My name is Thomas," I extended my hand to him.

"And I am Giuseppe. That it is to say, Frank," he said.

"Er… So, is it Giuseppe or Frank?" I asked just as politely.

"Well, I labor under an artistic pseudonym: Giuseppe Balsamo, count Cagliostro," he explained.

In my life, I have had to deal with all kinds of people. And here, finally, was my chance to shake hands with Count Cagliostro himself, a man who had once stirred a great brouhaha across Europe, Warsaw included. Admittedly, that happened more than two hundred years ago, but that was all par for the course since Cagliostro was said to be immortal and have been as ancient as the pharaohs of Egypt.

"I've once read a Dumas novel about you," I declared with great unction.

"Ah, that was about my predecessor," he shrugged his shoulders dismissively.

And then he leaned forward, picked up four of his packages, and put them in my hands.

"Please help me carry the lot to the car," he said warmly.

"God forbid, is there a *snake* in any of those packages?" I asked with some concern because I don't like creepy crawlies. "If you are so kind, I would prefer to carry a bunny."

"Ah, no. I carry Peter with me at all times," replied Maestro Cagliostro, reaching with his hand into the inside pocket of his coat. (For I forgot to mention that Maestro Cagliostro was not wearing a jacket but something long and black, a kind of cross between a wizard cloak and an evening frock coat. And from the inner pocket of it, he now pulled out a black snake.

"This is Peter," he declared. And he added:

"Peter, be nice to Mr. Thomas."

I don't know anything about snakes, and I certainly don't know if they can be nice. This one wrapped itself around his master's neck. I prudently took a step back.

"And here are my mice," Cagliostro reached into the other inside pocket of his cloak-frock-coat. A second later, two white mice were marching up the lapels of his strange garment.

"*Hm, hm,*" I grunted disapprovingly. "I prefer not to ask what you have in your other pockets. I think it'll be best to just go down to the car."

The whole scene took place in the august halls of the Ministry of Culture, where you generally meet nice, elderly, very cultured ladies. At one point, I got the impression that one of these ladies nearly retched at the sight of the snake and the two white mice as we passed her by.

Cagliostro must have noticed it because he jammed the snake into one pocket, the mice into the other, and we hurriedly left the historic edifice.

We placed most of the packages in the back seat; Cagliostro sat next to me, placing one package on his knees.

It turned out that the package he had in his lap was a cage wrapped in wrapping paper. He opened its little door, and a rabbit's nose peeked out.

"A very nice creature," I declared.

Cagliostro breathed a sigh of relief.

"And I was already thinking that you do not like animals."

"For me, a snake is not an animal," I replied firmly.

"Well, it does belong to the *animal kingdom*," he replied.

"I prefer plants," I said bitterly, although the bunny was sympathetic.

I was reminded of a popular song about a bunny, and, humming it under my breath, I took off.

> *Has anyone seen my bunny in the street?*
> *A bunny in the street?*
> *A what?*
> *A bunny in the street!*
> *Ho, ho, ho, ho, ho, ho, ho.*
> *A bunny in the street!*

I decided that Maestro Cagliostro was alright—perhaps because the sight of my vehicle did not elicit his derision or even the slightest remark. For a moment, I even had the suspicion that he had magically sensed the powerful engine inside my beast, which otherwise, truth be told, resembled a cross between a dugout canoe and a tent on wheels.

But wait! Did I suddenly believe in magic?

I will now try to describe my journey in the company of an illusionist, a bunny, white mice, and a snake.

The day was sunny, cloudless, and warm. The international highway E21 allowed me to step on the pedal. We passed forests, fields, towns, and villages, yet nothing of the charms of that long car ride survives in my memory.

Cagliostro settled comfortably in his seat and immediately fell asleep. Almost immediately, two white mice carefully peered out from the pocket of his frock coat and snuck out onto his lap. A minute later, a snake stuck its evil head out from his other inside pocket. It looked at sleeping Cagliostro, it glanced at me, it glanced at the mice. Finding that its maestro was soundly asleep, it crawled out of the pocket and, if I'm not mistaken, attempted to devour one of the mice. The mice bolted for the back seat, and the snake slid from Cagliostro's lap into mine, curled up in a ball, and fell asleep.

I nearly caused an accident twice. Really, it's hard to drive with a snake in your lap and mice rummaging about your back seat.

Finally, I couldn't stand it any longer. I nudged the maestro on the shoulder. He woke up.

He must have understood the horror of the situation immediately, for he took the snake from my lap and put it in his pocket again.

"I would rather you stayed awake," I said.

"Alright. Let's talk then," he said.

But what is there to talk about with a maestro of black magic?

Still, as I was the host in the car, it was up to me to suggest the topic of conversation. I didn't think the preservation of historic monuments or issues relating to fighting dishonest antique dealers could interest him. So, I tried a different tack.

"Did you study the arcane knowledge for long? And at what university?" I asked.

He responded with a question:

"Are you an idealist or a materialist?"

"A materialist."

"So, you do not believe in miracles and arcane knowledge?" he asked.

"It's all dexterous fakery, isn't it," I said frankly.

He did not take offense.

"Everything is an illusion," he made an indefinite movement with his hand as if letting me know that this illusion included my car, myself, and the whole world around us.

"Living in this world of illusion, I stopped distinguishing between falsehood and truth. Besides," he added with a touch of sadness, "I almost always cheat. This is a professional bent. Usually, when asked where I acquired my secret knowledge, I answer: 'in India' or 'from Tibetan monks.' But you—I will answer you differently: I graduated from the Sorbonne."

How to talk to a man who programmatically, on principle, lies? So again, we drove in silence, which made the creatures in the frock coat think that the illusionist had fallen asleep. I saw the snake's head leaning out of his pocket again.

"Be a nice boy, Peter," Cagliostro admonished him, gently stroking the snake's head with his finger.

As for me, I preferred to listen to lies rather than to hold a curled-up snake in my lap, and I observed with some concern that the maestro began to show signs of drowsiness again.

"There are young people waiting for your show in Frombork?" I asked.

"I don't know," he shrugged his shoulders." I broke my contract with *Estrada* because I had an argument with the director. To be honest, I'm not doing well lately. I don't have permanent employment. But young people like magic arts, that's why I hope I will be able to organize some shows for the Boy Scouts in Frombork."

"I didn't realize Boy Scouts were fans of arcane knowledge," I marveled.

He shook his head.

"Boy Scouts are the most important customer base for illusionists," he stated. "There is no proper Boy Scout campfire event without a magic show. My demonstrations for the scouts will be combined with teaching all sorts of tricks. Of course, the simplest ones because, you understand, some of them require years of training. And you, Esteemed Sir, what takes you to Frombork?"

"Me?" I was surprised. "Didn't Ms. Zosha inform you that I am involved in the preservation of historic monuments?"

"My, my. And you are protecting them? With your own body, so to speak? Take a bullet for the castle?" he looked at me intently but with a note of doubt.

"Well, not only me," I replied. "A huge number of people work to protect our historical monuments. We restore them, defend them from destruction, devastation, theft."

"Mrs. Zosha told me that you were something of a detective," he said.

There you go, I thought to myself. This is how the Department's greatest secrets are protected.

"Not at all," I denied zealously. I am going to Frombork to write a new guidebook to the city."

I got the impression that he did not believe me. Again, our conversation broke off. After a while, he fell asleep, and the snake peered out of his pocket. This time, however, it slithered between the boxes in the back seat. The mice, on the other hand, found my sandwiches in the travel bag and set about them. I did not protest.

I felt sorry for the bunny. I stopped the vehicle before we reached Paslenk and reaped some grass in a roadside ditch.

Cagliostro woke up.

"What are you doing?" He asked, seeing that I was returning to the car with a bunch of roadside herbs.

"It's for the bunny," I declared.

"Yuck!" he squirmed with distaste. "Aloysius doesn't touch such trash. This morning, I bought some young carrots for him. And we, where are we going to have lunch?"

"I am about to invite you to a restaurant in Paslenk," I said." But on condition that you leave all your menagerie in the car."

He agreed.

The menagerie was locked in the vehicle, and we headed to the restaurant. And everything would have been fine if not for a silly incident that happened to us at the end of our meal. When I tried to pay the waitress and reached for the money, I pulled a white mouse out of my pocket.

The waitress made a squeak—a pretty loud squeak, one for the whole restaurant. Quite a few guests came running and gathered about us. Then, the manager arrived and made a ruckus.

"Can't you read? Haven't you seen the sign: 'No dogs allowed'?" he shouted menacingly.

"It's not a dog," I explained.

"Of course, I can see that it's not a dog!" exclaimed the manager. "But the sign 'No dogs allowed' clearly means that no other animals are allowed, either! Oh-ho! If a sanitary inspector were to see this, I would have an *administrative procedure* on my head! How would I be able to explain that I don't have a mice infestation here but a customer with mice?"

Cagliostro placed his hand on the manager's shoulder with a

reassuring gesture. He then patted him on the back in a friendly manner and stroked the lapels of his white smock.

"How do you know it is this gentleman's mouse?" he pointed to me. "Maybe it's your restaurant mouse that got into his pocket during lunch?"

"It's a white mouse!" exclaimed the manager.

"Oh, so it is! And it looks like you are breeding them!" said Cagliostro, and taking all the guests as witnesses, he asked: "Would you kindly check the contents of your apron?"

The manager put his hands in the pockets of his white smock.

"I don't have anything in my pockets. They are empty!" he exclaimed triumphantly.

"Is that so?" asked Cagliostro, astonished. "I think I will check myself."

He stuck his hand in the protruding pocket of the manager's smock and, in front of everyone, he pulled out of it by the tail—a white mouse.

"Oh, Jesus!" exclaimed the manager.

"Well, well, look here," nodded Cagliostro with regret.

"Mouse! Mouse! Get the cat in here!" shouted the manager.

But the mouse disappeared somewhere.

Cagliostro placed a hand on the manager's shoulder with a calming gesture again.

"Don't get carried away. All sorts of things happen in catering establishments. Once, instead of a pork chop, I was served a fried rat."

"What are you saying!" yelled the manager. "You, sir, disgust my customers while they are eating. This is punishable by law, sir!"

"...and instead of an eel, I was served a smoked snake," Cagliostro concluded.

And in front of all the guests, he pulled out Peter from the manager's other pocket.

The manager was struck speechless. I looked at the faces of the guests. They looked grim. They looked at the manager as if he were a criminal who should be arrested and sentenced to long-term hard labor.

We escaped from the restaurant. Opening the door of the vehicle, I said reproachfully to Cagliostro:

"Your menagerie was supposed to stay in the car."

"Well, you locked them in your vehicle yourself," he remarked, "But, as you know, everything is an illusion."

"This is no illusion! You took your pests to the restaurant!" I got angry.

"Actually, replied Cagliostro, it seems to me that these "pests" as you say, like you very much because *you* took them to the restaurant. You found that mouse in *your* pocket."

Something moved in my breast pocket. I looked suspiciously at Cagliostro.

"Where is Peter?" I asked with a sharp edge to my voice.

"I don't know. Probably in your pocket."

"Yes," I nodded. "In the inside pocket of my jacket. Take it out of there immediately because I am too disgusted to touch it."

He took Peter out and, from my other pocket, pulled the mice. Offended, I got behind the wheel, and we drove out of Paslenk.

"How fortunate that we will soon part," I muttered. "In the confusion, I paid for your lunch."

"Thank you, sir," he nodded. "But you would have had to do it anyway because I have no money. Not for lunch, not for dinner. I am, as they say, generally washed up."

"I don't care," I growled like an angry dog. "Wait a minute. Didn't you just say 'dinner'?" I asked suspiciously.

"I was deluding myself that you would invite me to dinner, too," he sighed insolently. "In return, I could teach you some arcane arts."

"No dice."

"I will sell you Peter."

"Never!" I shouted.

"What about the mice?"

"No!"

"Oh, don't tell me you want Aloysius! Aloysius and I go back a long way."

"I am a detective, not an animal tamer," I snapped.

"And yet," he rejoined." Don't you think I could be of some use to you? Protecting monuments?

"No."

"Think about it. I could gather information for you, follow people, spy with my second sight. It would not even cross anyone's mind that an illusionist was at your service."

And that hit a note. It was a thought. A fellow like him could indeed come in handy. Valdemar Batura would surely do everything to stay out of my sight—but he did not know Cagliostro. Then again, what did I know about Cagliostro, and did I have the right to initiate him into my affairs?

"I told you that I am going to Frombork to prepare a new guidebook. I am primarily interested in Copernicus," I replied.

"Nay, you are not going to spy on him, are you?"

"Something like that. I'm going to look into some of his mysteries."

"What does he look like?"

"Beautiful, thinking face, very long hair, and in his hand, he holds a lily of the valley."

"He's not some kind of hippie, is he?" he asked.

"Have you lost your mind?"

"Well, I mean, he has long hair and a flower in his hand. Like flower children."

"But, dear sir! Have you never heard of the astronomer Nicolaus Copernicus? You? A graduate of the Sorbonne?"

"Oh, I'm sorry. It's a misunderstanding. I thought you meant someone who uses the pseudonym *Copernicus*. After all, I am called Joseph Balsamo, aka Cagliostro. I know some crazy guys, by the way. They use the strangest nicknames, such as: 'Prophet,' 'Judas,' 'Christ,' and 'Solomon.'"

"Well, all right. I'll buy you dinner," I decided graciously.

Nicolaus Copernicus (1473-1543)

*Copernicus was born and died in Royal Prussia, a semiautonomous and
multilingual region created within the Crown of the Kingdom of Poland
from the lands taken from the Teutonic Order in 1466. The lily of the valley
he holds in his hand in this portrait is a flower with seven florets and is
meant to symbolize the sun, the moon, and the five planets known to man at
the time.*

"Thank you. And one last thing: could you arrange some
accommodation for me? Because, you know, where will I stay in
Frombork? I will earn a little money from my performances, and I will
be able to manage somehow afterward. But first, I will need your help
and patronage. You are, after all, in a very important department. You
open doors everywhere."

"I plan to sleep in a tent or in my vehicle," I explained.

"And there will be room for me in your tent?"

Oh, misery, I thought sadly.

And he said, sadly:

"You're not going to make me sleep on a park bench, are you?
And these poor animals..."

"I will lend you my tent for one night," I decided.

"You have a good heart," he said and handed me a wallet.

"What is that?" I wondered.

"Your wallet."

"How come you have it?"

"I have taken it from you."

"When?"

"When I took the snake from your pocket. You turned your head away so as not to look at the foul reptile, and in that instant, I swiped your wallet."

"You're a pickpocket!"

"No. An illusionist. I did not have the slightest intention to rob you. It's just that—well, out of professional habit, I have to do tricks all the time."

"I don't get it."

"Look, a pianist constantly practices to keep his fingers nimble. I, too, must constantly pick on people, swap, take out, or put in—so that my fingers do not lose dexterity."

How could I argue with that?

"Besides penetrating other people's pockets, can you also penetrate their minds?" I asked mischievously.

"In a way," he replied enigmatically.

"So, you probably know what they think of you."

"Yes. They think Cagliostro is a scoundrel and a dangerous man. But he can be useful to me."

"Ah, yes. That is what I think. But that was not hard for you to guess."

For I thought, or rather imagined—the moment when Cagliostro met Batura, approached him, took his top-secret plans out of his pocket, and penetrated Batura's thoughts, of which I was later informed.

"I also have a dousing wand to discover underground water sources and buried treasures," he said.

"Great! Great!" I exclaimed.

After a while, however, my doubts returned.

"You have a dousing rod to discover buried treasures, but you do not have a penny for lunch?"

"Yeah. You might say, I am unlucky," Cagliostro replied insolently.

CHAPTER 5: IN THE LAND OF THE TERRIBLE ACE

How Warsaw folk should behave in Varmia and Masuria. A few riddles of history. Who is trailing Copernicus? I ignore the No Entry sign and what comes of it. Do I believe in aliens? A meeting with the Terrible ACE. The threatening lady and her iron hands. The vow of silence.

The city of Frombork lies on the water, at the northern end of the Elblong Upland. To the north stretches the dark and placid Vistula Lagoon, with the dak streak of the Vistula Spit visible on the horizon with its charming resort of Krinitsa. To the south, Frombork leans into the Elblong Upland, a rolling moraine plain cut by picturesque ravines and still largely covered with mixed forest.

Varmia Upland on the map of Poland
It corresponds to the historical boundaries of the Bishopric of Varmia, with its capital in Frombork.

After Paslenk, we left Highway E 81—the good road leading from Warsaw to Gdansk—and turned onto the narrow road to Mwinari. This road passed over the Elblong-Kaliningrad highway and, making a huge curve, led to Yendrihovo and then to Frombork. After Paslenk you enter the Elblong Upland, and the closer you get to Frombork, the more ravines you pass, beautiful features carved by erosion into the plain and then uplifted as the glacier retreated. These ravines are forested and very picturesque. Driving on that calm and balmy August day, I had no idea that I was about to face an unusual adventure in one of these ravines—my first great adventure in Frombork.

Historically, this region was known as Varmia. But what is Varmia? Most Polish people, when they hear the word Varmia, associate it with Masuria. "Varmia and Masuria" is a common expression meaning the North-Eastern corner of Poland, with its dense forests and thousands of lakes. But if you ask where Varmia ends and Masuria begins, not many know the answer.

Yet, Varmia and Masuria are geographically different and have very different histories. Masuria is low-lying and has almost three thousand lakes. But Varmia is an upland and has hardly any lakes at all.

Anyone traveling in these regions of Poland for the first time begins to notice something puzzling in the landscape by the time he reaches Nijitsa and Chitno. The architecture is different—houses here are made of exposed red brick and covered with red tile, while in central Poland, houses are plastered and whitewashed. And something else strikes and puzzles, too: the general absence of the roadside crosses, chapels, shrines, saints, and madonnas that you see at almost every crossroads in central Poland. Why is that? Well, here begins the former East Prussia, and what you see is the imprint left on the land by the prevailing Lutheran faith.

But then you drive on a little further north, and suddenly, it's as if you were in central Poland again. The houses are whitewashed, and the window frames are colored. And there are old, leaning crosses at crossroads, and chapels, and madonnas. You are now in Varmia, whose population is mostly Catholic.

And does the religion make a difference?

Yes, it does make a difference. It's important, first and foremost, for you, the traveler. For the way you perceive the land and its people. If you visit a church in a Masurian village and find that you have found yourself in a Protestant church, you should not jump to the conclusion that you are in a German village. These people are Poles, just like you. But they simply follow a different religion. And if you visit a Masurian cemetery and see tombstones with inscriptions carved in Gothic script, don't assume these are German graves. Try to read this Gothic, and you will see that the words and names are Polish. You will be surprised to hear that the Gothic script was originally known as the Cracow script—because it was developed not in Germany but in Cracow. You will be surprised to hear that the oldest Polish books were printed in this script and that the land around you—from Varmia north and as far as Königsberg, became the most important center of the Polish publishing industry.

Walbaum-Fraktur: Victor
jagt zwölf Boxkämpfer
quer über den Sylter
Deich. 1234567890

An example of "Gothic" script
Nazi propagandists imposed it in Germany as supposedly the one and only True German script.

In the period called the Renaissance, in Königsberg, the capital of Ducal Prussia (Russian Kaliningrad today), at the court of Prince Albert, lived, worked, and published the greatest Polish writers of the time.

Why were they there? To a large extent—because of religion. Reformation greatly stimulated intellectual and literary life in Poland and contributed to the birth of literature written in the Polish language rather than in traditional Latin. The writers of the reformed church tried to appeal to the simple folk by writing and publishing in Polish. And since Protestantism prevailed at the court of Prince Albert, these writers found employment opportunities here. But they were not alone. The rich intellectual life at Prince Albert's court attracted other prominent intellectuals of that era, including Catholics. In the sixteenth century, a great many Polish books written in Polish were first published by the printers of Königsberg.

Therefore, when you set your foot in the land of Masuria and Varmia, be careful in assessing its people and traditions. Be tactful and considerate. You will be facing something that seems like a riddle to you but which really you should have learned in school, had you been paying attention.

I thought about these things as we drove on, but as we approached Frombork, Cagliostro started to snooze again. Peter the Snake emerged from his pocket, and a white mouse climbed into my lap.

"Cagliostro! Hey, Cagliostro" I nudged the illusionist on the shoulder.

"What happened?"

He woke up, startled.

"We are approaching the city of Copernicus," I declared.

He looked around, but just at that moment, we were driving through the forest. There were still seven miles to Frombork.

The illusionist yawned, then stroked his black beard. He snatched the mouse off my knee and put it in his pocket.

"Are you really going to Frombork on this clown's business?" he asked.

"Couldn't you speak with more respect about one of the greatest figures of modern times?"

"I thought the greatest figure of modern times was Napoleon," he stated.

"That little corporal?" I replied contemptuously. "His only merit was to take a few scholars with him on his Egyptian campaign—thanks to which the science of Egyptology was born. But Copernicus was an intellectual giant. He dared to say something that the whole world at the time thought was wrong. He discovered and proved by detailed and reproducible measurements that the Sun was in the center of our planetary system and that the Earth revolved around it. And he made this brilliant discovery not in some famous observatory in some famous university of the time, in some major intellectual center, but in the small city of Frombork, which seemed to lie at the end of the world.”

“I gotta hand this to you,” nodded Cagliostro. “I’ve always believed that the country clowns are the best. I usually operate in some provincial holes rather than in Warsaw, for example.”

“Do me a favor, though. Don’t refer to my personal hero as ‘that clown.’”

“Happy to oblige. But it seems to me that even if we call him ‘that clown’ once in a while, he will not be offended but will somehow feel closer and more familiar to us because of it.”

“Well, if you think so,” I agreed. “Because, you see, I think it is possible to imagine a world without Napoleon. But what would the world be like without Copernicus? How would we live our lives if we still thought that the Earth was in the center of the universe and we had no idea about the movements of the heavenly bodies? No space travel, no satellites, no satellite telecommunications, probably even no flight.”

Cagliostro stroked his beard again.

“Speaking of space flight, what do you think about other planets? Do people live on them? I love science fiction books.”

I did not answer. The Frombork skyline appeared before us. Just above the green wall of trees, the Gothic spires of the Frombork Cathedral shot into the sky.

I spotted a road to the right and turned onto it.

“Wait, aren’t we going to Frombork?” said Cagliostro, astonished.

“First, I will take a look at an archaeological dig where my friend works,” I explained. “It’s not far from here, near the Bogdany State farm. They’re excavating one of the best-preserved pre-historical fortified settlements in Varmia. Archaeologists are hospitable people, and you probably have no objections to some dinner?”

“Oh yes, it is about dinner time, is it not,” Cagliostro said, glancing at his watch.

The Frombork skyline

The town skyline is dominated by its Cathedral.
In the back, the Vistula Lagoon, and on the horizon, the Spit.
Copernicus served as one of the sixteen canons of the Cathedral between 1529
and 1543. Canons--clerics appointed by the bishop—formed the governing
body of the bishopric ("the chapter"), and elected the new bishop whenever
the seat became vacant.

The dig was conducted by my old acquaintance. She was nicknamed "Gossamer" because her hair was as light and fluffy as the stuff that floats about in the air in the summer.[8]

Director Marchak had instructed me to contact all research missions operating in Frombork and, naturally, I had to carry out his orders immediately. And besides, might the good Lady Gossamer, I thought, not be able to glean some information about Parsley's work? Perhaps, while searching for Koenig's treasures, he had sought some advice from the archaeologists digging up Frombork?[9]

---

[8] Gossamer: the seeds of the poplar tree are easily dispersed by the wind due to the fine hairs surrounding them. Tufts of this gossamer are seen flying in the air in early summer in Poland.

[9] "Lady Gossamer" is an old heart-break of Mr. Wheels. For which see *Mr. Wheels on the Hallowed Ground* (upcoming)

We drove a mile and found ourselves at a bridge over a small river called Bauda.

I stopped the vehicle and spread the map on my lap. Somewhere near this river, there should be a relatively high hill with the remains of a fortified settlement.

Where we stopped, the Bauda split into several branches, forming a small delta. The delta was a stretch of wetlands overgrown with reed and low bushes and continuing all the way to the shore of the Lagoon. The area looked harsh, bleak, and deserted. Not a living soul anywhere—no one to ask for directions. I looked around and saw several high hills behind the far branch of the river. At their foot, I could see the entrance to a deep ravine. I guessed that we should look for the archaeologists' encampment somewhere in that direction.

I started driving.

"What was that sign?" Cagliostro asked when we passed a red and white plaque nailed to a tree.

"It's a road sign. It means *No Entry*."
"So why are you driving in?"

"I believe it was put up by the archaeologists so that no one would drive in here and disturb them in their work. But, as you know, I am here on official business, on behalf of the Department of Museums and Historic Preservation. I am not obliged by this sign," I piped up proudly.

And how wrong I proved to be!

"As for other planets," Cagliostro resumed our interrupted conversation, "I am of the opinion that Mars is inhabited by some sentient beings. Apparently, we will soon send research probes to Mars. But who knows if the beings from Mars haven't been sending their probes for a long time to photograph us here, study our lives, and draw scientific conclusions."

"We have not seen any extraterrestrial probes," I observed, looking around for someone who could guide us in the right direction.

"What about all those flying saucers?"

"That's nonsense. There are no flying saucers," I declared firmly.

"Oh, I believe in the existence of flying saucers," insisted Cagliostro.

"Because you believe in magic."

Cagliostro nodded with great dignity.

"There are things in heaven and on earth that your philosophers have never dreamed of. I am of the opinion that sooner or later, we will face a Martian invasion."

It was only four o'clock in the afternoon, but inside the deep gorge we drove into, it was very dark. The crowns of trees intertwined above our heads, and the steep walls of the ravine rose steeply on both sides.

"I wonder what they look like?" said the maestro.

"Who?"

"The Martians," he said as if he really had no other worries.

And just at that moment, as if in answer to his question, we were blinded by a harsh light shining from the depths of the ravine. For a brief moment, I became dazed and automatically pressed the brake. The glare was sharp, almost painful.

I stopped the vehicle. The glow turned from white to yellow, and then red, until it finally turned blue, mild, pleasing to the eye, but at the same time perfectly diffusing the darkness of the ravine.

About a few meters in front of my vehicle stood a bizarre creature blocking our path. At first, I got the impression that I had a space creature in front of me, looking at me with five great round eyes. Only one of them flashed with a bluish light, while the others, as if taking advantage of its glow, watched us with great attention.

The bizarre creature had tracks like a bulldozer. It was square, covered with heavy armor so that it resembled a small tank, and had a small rotating dome on top. Five headlight-like eyes glowered in this dome.

It stood motionless in front of us, although I'm convinced that at the moment we encountered it, it had been moving in our direction. It warned me with a sharp glare, forced me to stop, but it also stopped to avoid collision. In the narrow gorge of the ravine, we could not pass each other.

Then, four long feelers, or maybe antennae, emerged out of the vehicle's armor. Then, a second eye lit up. A beam of yellow light groped carefully about my vehicle and even looked inside, illuminating our faces.

"Martians!" whispered Cagliostro and pressed himself tighter into the back of the chair.

For a second, fear gripped my throat. Martians? Could it be that Cagliostro had really sensed an impending Martian invasion?

My thoughts were feverishly churning in my head. I had read many books about the adventures of astronauts in distant galaxies. I watched many movies about the invasions of various extraterrestrial creatures on our beautiful, though imperfect, globe. But none of these books or movies told me how an ordinary person should behave in case of an encounter with Martians.

The yellowish beam of light kept gliding over our faces. It irritated me a little because I had to squint. I turned on my high beams and my fog lights. These fog lights were LED lamps, devilishly powerful. I had equipped my vehicle with them while in France. The two beams of light crossed in the air and collided.

Then the Martian, who must have been blinded by my lights, flashed his third eye. Again, I was struck by a very sharp white light, but its strength was diffused somewhat by my LED lamps. Both of our vehicles were now standing in a blazing torrent of light. It was so bright you could find a needle at the bottom of the ravine.

The Martian was the first to tire of this battle of headlights. He dipped his lights, leaving only a faint, bluish warning light on the dome.

In response, I, too, extinguished my lights and left only the positional lights on.

"And what do we do now?" I asked Cagliostro.

"I think we scram," mumbled the terrified illusionist.

"What? On foot? And what about my vehicle?"

"The hell with your vehicle. Let's blow this joint," he suggested but was too afraid to poke his nose out of the car. He didn't even touch the door handle.

"I am not abandoning my vehicle," I declared.

"Then just put it in reverse and run. Then we will go to Frombork and report to the militia," said the maestro frantically.

"But will this thing let us back out?" I wondered. "Maybe it does not want us to notify anyone of its presence? It'll catch up with us and squash us like a zit. I think we need to parlay. The best way to settle the matter—amicably. I will go up there for a soft chat."

I took the door handle, but Cagliostro stopped me.

"No, no," he groaned pleadingly. "Don't do it. They could be radioactive."

Suddenly, something in the mysterious vehicle whirred, coughed, and choked like a station megaphone. It seemed to me that someone hidden inside wanted to say something to us but didn't quite know in what language. Or maybe those coughs were the language of Martians?

"You should try to make a good impression, too," I suggested to Cagliostro.

"In what way?"

"I don't know. You studied at the Sorbonne. Use telepathy or something," I said.

"Oh, they haven't taught us that," confessed the maestro.

Just at that moment, we were stunned by a loud, booming voice. A seemingly huge speaker roared with all its power:

"Are you going to get out of my way or not?"

"Sweet Jesus! It speaks Polish," groaned the illusionist gleefully.

The voice boomed again:

"Well, get a move on! Reverse and scoot!"

The monster seemed to want to say something else but reconsidered and whimpered, chuckling. Probably, its talking apparatus did not work too well.

And maybe that's why I immediately felt somehow more confident. My old courage returned, the ancient blood of hussars spoke up.

The Polish Hussars

The Hussars were a heavy cavalry formation active in Poland and in the Polish–Lithuanian Commonwealth from 1503 to 1702. Their name is derived from large rear wings, which were intended to demoralize the enemy during a charge.

I climbed out of the vehicle and walked up, then stood in front of the beast.

"And why, good sir, should I back out? I was here first. How about you reverse," I declared in what I hoped was a thunderous voice.

Something buzzed and coughed again in the strange vehicle. And then, the mysterious SOMETHING said in a slightly quieter tone:

"Get out of the way, or I'll run you over."

"What's that? Are you threatening us? Us? Citizens of the Republic of Poland?" I objected. "You get out."

My goodness, how familiar it sounded. It felt as if I were at a gas station and heard the daily interaction between the gentlemen who pulled up to fill up. Martians? What kind of Martians were these? They seemed very Polish.

Even Cagliostro grasped that we were dealing with some compatriot of ours. He leaned out of the vehicle and shouted in my direction:

"Get out of the way. We were here first!"

"You get out of the way, or I will crush you," hooted the mysterious vehicle.

And strangely, somehow, it shook its antennae. And then it began to advance upon us.

Like Raytan, I spread my arms, blocking its path.

Raytan (Rejtan), a member of the Polish Diet, rent his clothes and threw himself on the ground blocking an exit during the proceedings of the 1773 Parliament in an effort to prevent the ratification of the First Partition of Poland. He has become a symbol of dramatic and futile last-ditch resistance. Every child in Poland knows this 1866 painting by Yan Mateyko (Jan Matejko)

"Hey, Mr. Museum-man! Easy on the heroics!" cried Cagliostro, leaning his head out of the window of my vehicle.

The monster came to a stop a few inches in front of my face.

"Why don't you back up?" it asked snarkily.

"Because to do so would dishonor us!" replied Cagliostro.

And then something giggled inside the monster and its voice turned sweet and coquettish:

"I thought gentlemen gave way to ladies."

Cagliostro immediately jumped out of the vehicle.

"It's a lady!" he called out cheerfully. "I bet she's beautiful and wise."

He ran up to the mysterious vehicle. He circled around it but could find neither a door nor a window through which to look inside.

"Oh boy," he marveled. "How did you get inside?"

Indeed, I had also noticed that the mysterious vehicle had neither doors nor windows. The lady who sat in it must have been looking at us through one of the eyes in the moving dome. But how did she get inside it?

"Ma'am! Hello, ma'am," Cagliostro knocked on the iron armor of the vehicle with his finger.

And then a terrible thing happened. A tiny door in the side of the vehicle sprang open, and an iron hand slid out of it. Steel fingers grabbed Cagliostro by the neck and pushed him a few steps away from the vehicle.

"Jesus, Mary, Joseph! She is murdering me!" screamed Cagliostro, held in the grip of the steel fingers.

But the iron hand let go of him and retreated inside the vehicle. The tiny door slammed silently shut.

"What a brutal woman," muttered Cagliostro, robbing his neck.

Suddenly, the vehicle vibrated slightly. The voice now beeped strangely:

"Oh God. A mouse! Two mice came out of his pocket!"

And indeed, two white mice had emerged from Cagliostro's pocket and marched over the lapels of his frock coat.

"Take those hideous mice of yours away immediately!" the female voice demanded.

Cagliostro, who had already acquired a proper respect for the capabilities of this woman, obediently grabbed the mice and stuffed them back in his pocket.

Meanwhile, I got the impression that a somewhat hushed conversation was taking place inside the mysterious vehicle.

A male voice asked:

"What's going on there?"

"Two people have blocked *ACE*'s way," replied the woman's voice.

Ha! This vehicle was named *ACE*!

Well, yes, it was! Only now did I notice the sign stenciled on its side:

ACE

"What the...? Isn't there a 'no-entry' sign at the entrance to the ravine?" asked a male voice.

"See for yourself. These two can't read road signs, Professor," the female voice said.

And suddenly, two iron hands sprang out from both sides of the vehicle. They grabbed me and Cagliostro by the sleeves of our jackets. At the same time, a spotlight turned on, and a murderous beam of light was directed at our persons so that—I assumed—some professor inside the mysterious vehicle would be able to take a close look at us.

"And that car of theirs!" the woman said. "I think they built it themselves. It looks like something from Mars."

"Did you hear that?" whispered Cagliostro in my direction. "They think your car comes from Mars. And they? Where do they come from, then? From Venus?

"Quiet!" the female voice admonished us sharply.

Then we heard the "professor":

"What do we do with the two clowns?"

Out of the corner of my eye, I saw Cagliostro wince.

"We will lock them up in our barracks for a few days," the woman firmly declared. "Otherwise, they'll go blabber all over town about what they've seen, and we will be in a sea of trouble. Crowds of curious people will come, and we can kiss goodbye further experiments."

"What's that?" I shouted, jerking and trying to free my sleeve from the steel grip. "This is an outrage against our personal freedom. I protest! I am an operative of the Department of Museums and Monument Protection. I have serious tasks to perform in Frombork!"

"And what kind of tasks are these?" asked the woman doubtfully.

"I am here on the business of Nicolaus Copernicus," I replied, trying to put on my most grave expression.

"So why are you here and not in Frombork?" the woman asked.

"I was given to understand that an archaeological expedition was working here. I wanted to visit the archaeologists' camp. I swear I won't tell anyone about your *ACE*."

"The dig team has already moved to Frombork," the woman said.

And the professor added:

"I think we can trust this fellow. He will keep quiet about what he has seen. But the other fellow looks iffy to me."

"Who's your friend, Mr. Operative?" the woman asked.

"My companion is an illusionist. He is a maestro of magic. His name is Cagliostro," I introduced the bearded man, who was still firmly held in place by a steel hand.

"Let's detain him," decided the professor.

"What's that? No! I protest!" Cagliostro tried to pull the sleeve of his jacket from the grip of the steel hand.

But the woman came to Cagliostro's rescue.

"I object," she squealed. "He has mice in his pockets, professor. I could not bear mice in our barracks."

"I swear I will keep my mouth shut!" shouted Cagliostro

desperately. "Besides, I have not only mice with me but also a hideous snake."

He reached into his pocket and pulled out Peter and began to brandish him like a baton.

"Wow, it really is a snake," the professor marveled.

I heard a heavy sigh from the woman in the vehicle:

"It seems to me, Professor, that these fellows are harmless lunatics. We should let them go, but let's have them swear an oath of secrecy."

"We swear!" we roared in chorus.

"Very well, now get out of here," the woman threateningly declared.

The iron hands released us from their grip. The headlights on the dome of the mysterious vehicle dimmed. And then, almost silently, it made a turn. Before our eyes, it turned 90 degrees and climbed up the steep wall of the ravine. With its tracks and powerful body, it broke through bushes and thin trees like a knife going through butter.

It climbed quickly, reached the top of the gorge, and disappeared into the forest overgrowing the hill.

And we, a little stunned by what we had experienced, remained standing stupefied in the dark ravine. Another moment elapsed, and our encounter with *ACE* suddenly seemed like a dream. But no. It was not a dream. The trail left by the vehicle was clearly visible on the ravine wall, and there were the broken bushes.

"Shall we... go to Frombork?" I whispered.

Cagliostro did not need to hear this suggestion twice. He was in my vehicle in a split second. So was I. We hurriedly reversed out of the ravine. We dashed to Frombork at a frantic pace, as if fleeing from deadly danger.

Only when we were five miles past the unfortunate No-Entry sign did I slow down, breathe a sigh of relief, and say:

"Dog-gone *ACE*. He nearly ripped out my sleeve. Infernal beast."

"Pssssst! Quiet!" Cagliostor hushed me. "Do not pronounce that name in vain," he muttered.

"That's right. We are bound by an oath of silence," I remembered. "All the more so because you never know with that monster. Maybe he can hear and see at a distance?"

CHAPTER 6: WHO IS CAGLIOSTRO?

What happened at Potsdam. A night conversation about Herder, the Bishop of Warsaw. Cagliostro's strange question. What I know about the Koenig affair. A mysterious note. Bashka. Has Parsley found the second cache? Who is Cagliostro? Night in the Frombork harbor. A mysterious delivery.

"Tell me the honest truth: do we really have the right to rule this part of the country?" asked Cagliostro out of the blue.

I made a puzzled face.

I would never have guessed that such problems preoccupied the maestro.

He sadly nodded his head.

"You see, we illusionists form a kind of international society or, as the malicious say—a cabal. I have performed in Hungarian, Czech, Greek, French, and German circuses. And because we come into contact with people from so many different countries, we sometimes have doubts about our own homeland. Some very beautiful tricks were taught to me in West Berlin by an old German illusionist, a German. He had been born somewhere near Rastemborg, in Masuria, which is today's Kentshin."[10]

"And, of course, he had a grudge that East Prussia was now part of Poland," I guessed.

"In a way. One day, he took me to a very learned professor, who explained to me at length and in detail about the rights the Germans had to these lands. And he was not a stupid man, mind you. I no longer remember the arguments, but they sounded convincing. And he spoke of them very sincerely. And I didn't know how to answer him."

---

[10] Kentshin (Kętrzyn): formerly Rastemborg, a town once in East Prussia, now in the Polish Northeast, was renamed in 1945 after its most famous Polish son.

I shrugged my shoulders.

"You didn't have to answer him like a learned historian, archaeologist, or ethnographer because that is not how the decision was made. The decision to liquidate Prussia was made by the victorious Allies at the Treaty of Potsdam in 1945. Prussia, which had been the most powerful among the German federal states and the breeding ground for German nationalism and militarism, got blamed for causing two world wars and was disestablished. Its territory was divided into three parts: one part remained in Germany and today makes up the federal states of Mecklemburg, Brandenburg, and Berlin; one part was ceded to Poland to receive Polish refugees from the East; and one was given to Russia and makes up the Kaliningrad enclave. And the German population of this territory was ordered out. The decision was made by the victorious allies and no one has asked either Germans or Poles."

I fell silent and took a sip of my tea.

We were sitting on the shore of the Vistula Lagoon, near the town beach of Frombork. I had decided to set up my camp here.

Cagliostro pitched the tent, inflated the mattress he borrowed from me, and made himself a bed with two of my blankets. His pets, fed and tired from the journey, slept in the tent in their boxes.

The evening had fallen. We had cooked dinner on the gas stove, and now, sitting on the beach gently stroked by the waves of the lagoon, we looked out over its black depths toward the Vistula Spit.

Behind our backs, a little to the left, on a steep hill, stood the town of Frombork, lit up with night lights. From somewhere far away came the singing of young voices—it was probably some evening party organized by scouts taking part in "Operation Frombork."
But here, on the shore of the lagoon, it was quiet and empty, with only the waves lapping the shore monotonously.

A light breeze blew off the water and brought the smell of the sea. The moon appeared in the sky, round like like a necklace medallion.

"I don't know," I said to Cagliostro, "what arguments your German professor used when he spoke to you. But the German arguments are usually the same. They say that Germans once lived here for centuries, that the land was ruled by the Teutonic Knights who called themselves The German Order and built many castles that still stand here and, presumably, look German, and that many famous Germans were born here. And that's all very good, but so what?

The "West-shifting" of Poland at Potsdam (1945)

Betrayed by its Western allies and left to the Soviets, Poland was the only member of the original anti-Hitler alliance to lose territory as a result of the Potsdam Peace Treaty. The Soviet Union seized former eastern Poland and expelled the Polish population from the territory. As a sop, Poland was compensated with German territory to its West, from which ethnic Germans were expelled in turn.

"Take the city of Mrongovo. The town square has a museum named after Herder, the German poet and philosopher. We don't hide the fact that Herder was born here. In fact, Mrongovo seems proud of her German son. But what does that have to do with anything? Many important Polish cultural figures came from this area, too, for the land was mostly bilingual—the towns were mostly German-speaking, but the countryside spoke mostly Polish. And we had Dutch and

Lithuanian settlers living here, too.

"And as always happens where different nations live together, people intermarry and change their sense of identity; some Poles decided to become German, and some Germans decided to become Polish. Consider Voytcheh Kentshinski. He was born in a German-speaking family with Polish roots. As a child, he did not speak Polish at all. One day, he found documents showing that he was of Polish descent. A tremendous sense of connection to Poland was awakened in him. His poems, written in German, are permeated with a spirit of ardent Polish patriotism. Today, the town of Kentshin—formerly Rastemborg—bears his name. So, as I say, these lands formed a bizarre conglomerate of nationalities.

"And just because its absolute ruler, Frederick I, crowned himself king in 1701 and declared that his state was a German state, it did not make it so. And just because his state then followed policies designed to force German identity and German language on all its subjects did not mean those policies worked.

"And, at any rate, the argument that 'we were here first' is a little silly. Because, in fact, neither the Germans nor the Poles had been here first. The first people here, the Old Prussians, have been murdered by the Teutonic Knights. Everyone else here has been an immigrant."

Suddenly, something strange happened. I noticed that a small pebble flew out of the coastal bushes behind my back and hit Cagliostro on the knee. The pebble bounced off, rolled, and disappeared into the grass, but I noticed that it had a piece of paper wrapped around it.

I did not let on that I noticed the paper. I continued talking as if nothing had happened. It seemed to me, however, that Cagliostro was not listening to me and that his thoughts were somewhere very far away, or rather very close—that is, with that pebble wrapped in paper that lay in the grass within his reach. But he did not reach for it, probably in fear that I would notice.

A suspicion arose in me. I continued my lecture on the history of East Prussia, and at the same time, I thought that his questions about the history of the land were not at all the result of the curiosity of a man who had once spoken to some German scholar but rather had been aimed at some matter more important to him. But, think as hard as I tried, I could not guess what he was driving at.

For a moment, I felt like putting down my tea, rising from the grass, and grabbing that pebble. I resisted the temptation because I figured that Cagliostro would guess what I was up to, lunge forward, and grab the pebble before I could. I would learn nothing but betray that I harbored suspicions. Wasn't it better, then, to pretend not to have noticed anything and keep an eye on Cagliostro?

When I fell silent, Cagliostro said:

"And yet, despite the fact that so many Poles lived here, we lost the plebiscite after the First World War. The majority voted for the Germans."

"That's right," I nodded, wondering whether this was the question I had expected. "But the plebiscite was not held on terms that would be recognized as a valid vote today. Nor did everyone vote on ethnic lines. Some Lutheran Poles voted to remain in Germany because they feared the power of the Polish Catholic church.

"They probably would not have faired too badly in the new German Republic that was formed after World War One. They were allowed elementary education and church service in their own language, even if Germany insisted on calling it Masurian, not Polish. But then, of course, Hitler came to power, and all that 'liberal nonsense' ended."

"And the robber Koenig?" asked Cagliostro suddenly out of the blue. "Was he local, or did he come to Frombork during the war?"

"Oh, are you interested in Colonel Koenig's treasure?" I said, surprised. I realized instantly that this was the question Cagliostro had been leading up to.

"Oh, yeah, I read about it in the newspaper. It's too bad that you are not looking for his treasure. I could have been helpful in that project. I have my wonderful dousing wand with me."

I almost burst out laughing imagining what Director Marchak would say when he found out that I began searching for treasure with the help of a magic wand.

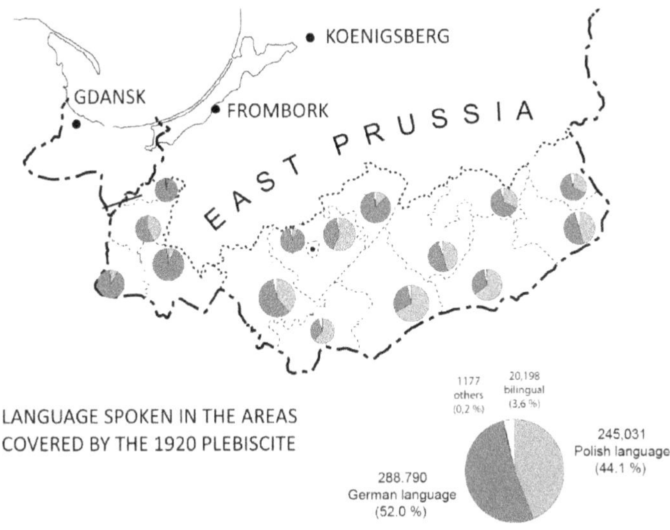

LANGUAGE SPOKEN IN THE AREAS
COVERED BY THE 1920 PLEBISCITE

The 1920 plebiscite

*The Versailles peace treaty ending World War I restored Polish statehood
and ordered plebiscites to be held in the border areas of Poland and
Germany to determine which would join Poland and which would remain
with Germany. Though Polish was the majority language in several districts
subject to the plebiscite, Germans won all of them, in part because the vote
was not fairly held and in part because Poland, engaged in a war with the
Soviets, was unable to contest the plebiscites properly. Cagliostro is wrong
about one thing: the district of Frombork was not subject to a border
plebiscite.*

"Koenig," Cagliostro added, "is German for King—Polish *Krool.*
Maybe he used to be called Krool and then Germanized his name to
Koenig?"

"And why does it matter whether Koenig was someone local
or if he found himself in Frombork only during the war?"

"Ah, but you see, to me, it seems very relevant. For if he was a
local clown, for example, a resident of Frombork; and his family lived
here, then he probably would have known some really good hiding
places. But if, on the other hand, he and his loot ended up in Frombork

accidentally while trying to escape to the West by way of the sea, then he probably hid his treasures in a hurry, just any old place, because he didn't have time to make a proper study. And this would probably be an important clue in the search."

"My goodness, Cagliostro, you are a genius!" I exclaimed. And I looked at Cagliostro with more respect.

Of course, this was an important clue—and *I* hadn't thought of it! Cagliostro, the maestro of magic, proved to be smarter than me in this matter.

"So you don't know anything about this Koenig?" Cagliostro asked.

"Unfortunately, no," I sighed. "I must disappoint you, but I do not have any information."

Suddenly, Cagliostro hunkered down and looked around suspiciously.

"I think someone is creeping around here," he whispered, looking toward the bushes behind my back.

Reflexively, I looked over. Only then did it occur to me that he was probably trying to avert my attention in order to grab the piece of paper. When I turned to face Cagliostro again, he was sitting quietly, relaxed, and motionless, but I felt sure that his deft fingers had already managed to retrieve the note.

"There is no one here," I said. "You fooled me, maestro."

And yet perhaps he had not tried to fool me, for just at that instant, I did hear rustling behind my back, and when I looked around again, I saw a figure emerging from the bushes. I recognized it immediately. It was my friend Bashka, my sixteen-year-old friend in a Boy Scout uniform.

"Ha! My scouting sense did not fail me," he laughed, shaking my hand in greeting. "I guessed that you would come the moment you got my letter. And when, a couple of hours ago, one of our guys told me that he saw a funny car on the street in Frombork, I knew that you were here. Knowing you, I deduced you would be camping by the Lagoon: you like fresh air and nice views and this is the best camping site for that," he stated.

I introduced Cagliostro to the boy.

"I love magic tricks!" exclaimed the delighted Bashka. "We will invite you to our bonfire, agreed? And maybe you can teach us some tricks?"

"Well, sure—"

I laughed:

"Boy Scouts love black magic!"

Cagliostro was very pleased with the boy's reaction:

"And you're a Boy Scout, right?"

"Why, I am a squad leader!" Bashka said.

"So you don't drink alcohol?"

"No," replied the boy.

"And you don't smoke cigarettes either, do you?"

"I don't smoke," he replied.

"So why do you carry cigarettes around?"

His tone suddenly became accusatory.

"Me?" Bashka was astonished. "Never."

Hearing this, Cagliostro reached out to the boy, unbuttoned the pocket of his scout shirt, and, before our eyes, pulled out a cigarette from it.

"Oh, and here you have one more," he declared.

He then reached into the other pocket of Bashka's shirt and took out two more cigarettes.

Our Cagliostro was a true maestro. How did he do it? Bewildered, Bashka looked at me as if looking for an explanation for the mystery. But I had no clue about how magic worked.

"Do not worry," smiled the maestro to the boy. "I know that you did not have cigarettes with you. It was the power of magic that conjured them up. And look, it will make them disappear now. These cigarettes will melt into the thin air."

He put one cigarette on his open palm, then curled his hand into a fist, raised it high up, and blew into his sleeve. He withdrew his hand, his palm opened. It was empty, the cigarette had disappeared, gone without a trace.

I clapped my hands, expressing my appreciation for the illusionist and his skill.

Cagliostro bowed to us as if after a performance.

"Thank you," he said. "And as for performing in front of a Boy Scout audience, I will be honored and delighted to do it. Of course, for some modest fee," he added. "And if, by any chance, you want to learn a trick or two, the fee will have to be a little higher. But I am very happy to teach my audience the secrets of magic."

"And are there any tricks that can be learned quickly?" asked the boy.

"Of course. Unfortunately, you then have to practice it for years."

Then, the maestro yawned ostentatiously.

"Well, I will go to bed now. Gentlemen, let me bid you good night."

He bowed to us again. He crawled into the tent and laced up the entrance behind him. I rose from the grass.

"I'll walk you back, Bashka," I suggested.

The boy understood that I wanted to talk to him in private. We walked along the shore of the Lagoon toward the Frombork harbor.

"Our camp is located on the shore of the Lagoon, but on the other side of the marina, behind the railroad track," explained Bashka. "You will be able to find us easily."

"As for me," I said, "I do not yet know where I will stay. I would prefer to rent a room. After all, I will have to meet with various scientists and spend a lot of time around the city, and I'm a little afraid to leave the camp at the mercy of Cagliostro."

"Maybe they have a room at the PTTK hostel?" wondered the boy.

It seemed like an idea worth trying.

"It will be a good thing to be rid of Cagliostro," I observed aloud.

I told Bashka how I met Cagliostro, about our journey and our conversations. I only omitted the adventure in the ravine when we met the mysterious *ACE*, for I felt bound by an oath of silence in that matter. But I did not conceal the incident with the pebble with a piece of paper.

"And you are sharing your campsite with that guy?" wondered the boy.

"He does not know that I have noticed the pebble—or, at any rate, he cannot be sure that I do, so he will probably continue as he was. In this way, maybe I will learn some things."

Then I told the boy about the coins, about Batura, about the rich man's cross, and about my interview with Director Marchak.

"So you understand," I said, "that my mission in Frombork is extremely delicate. The riddle of the priceless coins is somehow intertwined with the riddle of Koenig's caches, I feel, but that case is handled by Dr. Parsley, a very ambitious and very touchy man. How to solve the riddle of the coins and not get in the way of Dr. Parsley?"

"And what tasks do you have for me?" asked the boy.

What tasks could I give to a boy busy in Frombork with scouting matters? I gave him a description of Valdemar Batura.

"Pay attention," I said. "If this man appears in Frombork, you follow him."

Bashka sighed.

"I can't handle it all by myself. And I can't involve anyone from my unit in this matter either because I have very young boys under my care. But you know," he suddenly lowered his voice and said as if somewhat embarrassed: "I met a Girl Scout troop from Katovitse here. Nice girls. And the coolest among them is their chronicler, Zosha. She is very intelligent, Mr. Thomas. She took first prize in the math Olympics last year."

"Fine," I smiled to myself. "You can involve her in our business."

We passed the Frombork harbor, walked past the train station, and turned again towards the shore of the Lagoon.

"And what's up with Dr. Parsley?" I asked. "Are you in contact with him?"

"He's staying at the PTTK hostel. But we have very little contact. He couldn't say to me: *don't stick your nose into the Koenig case,* because we had found the plan of the caches. On the other hand, he is reluctant to give us any information. He treats me like an intrusive fly. Also, I noticed that he has been very sad and irritated lately. I sensed this was because he was not making progress on the remaining two caches. But then, yesterday, he suddenly became very cheerful. He is not so much walking around Frombork as wafting about on the air. I saw him in the company of a beautiful lady, who I know is an archaeologist and whom they call "Lady Gossamer." And yesterday, the two were seen walking towards the Bauda. They did not return for a long time."

"And?" I asked curiously.

"They returned after several hours, arguing fiercely, though I have no idea about what. And then the lady left for Warsaw. Dr. Parsley escorted her to the train station, and as he was returning to the hostel, he whistled cheerfully. He met me and said: *How are you, Old Boy? I know you're interested in the Koenig treasure, so I'll just tell you: I'll soon have the second cache.* So that means, Mr. Thomas, that he is suddenly on the trail."

"That's very good," I was pleased. But then something puzzled me. "And you say they went towards the Bauda?"

"Yes," he nodded.

So they went to the land of *ACE* with Iron Hands. Could it be that Dr. Parsley had something to do with the mysterious *ACE*? Or did Lady Gossamer lead Parsley to the site of her dig? I had never known Dr. Parsley to be interested in archaeology. And just why did they return arguing with each other?

The boy stopped.

"Here is our camp," he said, pointing to a dozen tents set up in a vast meadow near the shore of the Lagoon. "I'll say goodbye to you, and we'll meet again tomorrow, right?"

"I will try to get a room at the PTTK hostel and find out something there," I replied, shaking Bashka's hand in farewell.

We parted ways. I walked back along the shore of the Lagoon

again, and as I approached the buildings surrounding the waterfront marina, I crossed the railroad tracks and found myself on the edge of town.

It was already night. I was walking in a narrow and winding alley that was sparsely lit by street lights, and the huge massif of the hill and of the Frombork Cathedral was completely lost in darkness somewhere behind my back. The houses there were small, funny things, like matchboxes, and were all dark inside.

The street led out into the fields. I found a path that led to the seashore and... I abruptly stopped, then crouched behind a tall bush: someone was coming from the direction of my camp. Against the starry sky, I made out Cagliostro's silhouette. The maestro was heading toward the harbor. He had one of his packages in his hand. As he walked, he looked around in all directions, occasionally stopping and looking around again. He seemed worried that he might be followed— or perhaps worried about running into me—after all, he had done his best to convince me that he was settling down to sleep in the tent.

I waited until he passed me and then carefully followed in his footsteps.

Yes, he was heading to the harbor. But he did not pass it by, as Bashka and I had done. Instead, he entered the concrete breakwater through a wicket in the fence.

Frombork's harbor is not large. It consists of a wide, walled-in pool, where maybe two dozen motorboats, yachts, and fishing boats sway on barely a wave. From the harbor, a rather long spur of concrete breakwater shielding the pool runs out into the lagoon. At the end of the breakwater, there is a tiny lighthouse. This is where the yachts and ships of the Gdansk shipping industry come in.

I hid behind the small tollbooth and saw that Cagliostro had climbed the concrete spur of the breakwater. He stopped under the lighthouse, lit a cigarette, and seemed to settle to wait for someone because he put the packet on the ground at his feet.

It was very quiet. All we could hear was the steady murmur of the waves hitting the breakwater. It wasn't until ten minutes later that we heard the growl of an engine coming in from the sea. Then, I saw the lights of a fishing boat bobbing on the waves as it approached the harbor.

Another moment and the fishing boat approached the concrete landing, and I saw that someone jumped out and cast a mooring on a wooden pile. Someone else also jumped out of the boat, approached Cagliostro, greeted him, and then took the package in his hands.

So the mystery of the note was now explained. It was probably a message for Cagliostro where and at what time he should wait for the arrival of the fishing boat.

And now I had a little revelation: Cagliostro was in collusion with Batura. Who knew the weaknesses of Director Marchak's secretary better than Valdemar? Batura had worked for the department in the past.

After our conversation in *Honoratka,* he must have come to the conclusion that I would eventually follow his trail to Frombork. He called the secretary of Director Marchak and, learning that they were preparing a business trip to Frombork for me, he became sure of it. Then, a second phone call and a box of chocolates and, boom, there was Cagliostro waiting for me in the corridor of the Ministry of Culture.

I understood perfectly why he had put Cagliostro on to me. It really was a job for a maestro of magic to worm his way into my confidence and report to Batura on my whereabouts.

Of course, I could now come out from behind the booth, appear in front of the two of them, and end Cagliostro's double game. But wouldn't I lose more by doing so?

Now that I discovered his role, Cagliostro was harmless to me. But he could be of great use to me if I wanted to feed disinformation to Batura.

I'll give him such information he'll choke on it, I thought cheerfully.

But then a worry arose. What was in the package that Cagliostro had brought to the harbor?

I thought about these things as I watched the two people

talking at the end of the breakwater and the fishing motorboat rocked beside them. They talked for a long time, too long for my reserve of patience.

CHAPTER 7: A WEEKLY MAGAZINE DRINKS WATER

Scholars and riddles. What is in Dr. Parsley's head. Cagliostro's new tricks. In Fortress Frombork. Who laughs at his own jokes? Miss Ala. Where did Copernicus live? Do weekly magazines drink water and the cat that was afraid of mice.

I did not manage to get rid of Cagliostro. The PTTK hostel, located on a high escarpment near the cathedral, was very crowded, but my service card from the Ministry of Culture made a suitable impression on the lady at the front desk, and I managed to get a room with two beds. In this situation, I felt that I could not tell Cagliostro to get lost and sleep in the street.

The lady at the front desk, who took me for some great scholar from the Department of Museums and Historic Preservation, said:

"You will find good company here and probably many acquaintances. Eminent astronomers, historians, and archaeologists are staying with us this summer. It's the five-hundredth anniversary of the birth of Copernicus: the whole scientific world is looking at Frombork."

She was right. Frombork is a tiny town with a population of just two thousand. It owes its fame entirely to the person of Nicolaus Copernicus, who made his discoveries and wrote his masterpiece "On the Revolutions of the Heavenly Bodies" here.

In the dining room of the hostel, where Cagliostro and I went for breakfast, I saw many prominent scholars. These were people completely consumed by their research—and no wonder, for how wrong are those who imagine science as something boring and devoid of romance! One finds the most dramatic adventures not only on the remote *pampas* of Argentina, or in the jungles of Africa, or in the Rocky Mountains, but also in the vast thicket of human knowledge. Scholars remind me of detectives; only their playing field is often the shelves of libraries and archives.

How many puzzles did Frombork pose—and the figure of Nicolaus Copernicus! For example, we know a lot about his life and work, but where is Copernicus buried? We know a lot about Copernicus' life and work, but where did he make his measurements? Where was his observatory?

Arriving in Frombork, I had known that I would face these puzzles. I was not a scholar, and it was not my job to solve them. But I now observed these professors with respect and admiration, thinking of the many pleasures that my conversations with them would give me.

The only fly in this otherwise promising ointment was the appearance of Dr. Parsley in the dining room. He walked in, saw me, and for a moment—he froze. In the warmest manner I could muster, I invited him to our table and introduced him to Cagliostro, who was having breakfast with me.

Dr. Parsley, Ph.D.—to give him his full name as he always signed it—was a short, skinny young man with long fair hair and an aquiline nose. He looked like Chopin and wore glasses with thick lenses, which did very little to obscure the intense stare of his buggy eyes.

He was an art historian by training like me, and a great expert on Flemish painting. Alas, ever since he had discovered in the attic of a church a painting from the Rubens studio, he fancied himself a detective.

"Do not be concerned," I said to him right off the bat. "I have not come here to take the Koenig case away from you. I am here to write a new guidebook to Frombork."

"I know," he mumbled rudely. "Director Marchak has informed me about it over the phone. I started the Koenig treasure case, and I will finish it."

Dr. Parsley seemed rather suspicious of Cagliostro as well.

"Excuse me, but who are you? I somehow did not catch your profession when we were introduced."

"I am Cagliostro, maestro of black magic," Cagliostro announced proudly.

Dr. Parsley thought we were mocking him.

"You're a juggler?" he growled with visible irritation.

"Yes," nodded Cagliostro.

"Magic tricks? Hocus-pocus?" Dr. Parsley made sure.

"Yes," nodded Cagliostro again. And he added: "I am also a douser. You do know that it is possible to discover hidden treasures with the help of a dousing wand, don't you?"

Dr. Parsley's suspicion reached a crescendo.

"A wand?" he made sure. "A wand for detecting treasure? So, Thomas, if you are with this gentleman and his wand, it means you came here with dishonest intentions."

I shrugged.

"Mr. Cagliostro deigns to make fun of us," I declared with some embarrassment. "Do you really believe that I would look for treasure with the help of a dousing wand?"

Dr. Parsley pondered—as was evident from the deep wrinkle that furrowed his balding forehead.

"A wand?" he wondered aloud. "*Hm,* who knows if a wand might not prove useful."

"In which case, sir, I am at your service," Cagliostro eagerly declared, but Dr. Parsley only waved his hand.

"No, no. I don't need help. Besides, I don't believe you. I don't believe anybody. I don't even believe that you are a maestro of magic."

"What's that?" Cagliostro raised his voice in irritation, thus drawing the attention of all the researchers assembled in the dining room. "I feel insulted and demand satisfaction! Besides, do you know who I think you are? I think you are a flippant man, a man who thinks only of parties and dancing, of balls and cotillion dances. That, sir, is what I think you think about."

And as all the scholars assembled in the room watched, Cagliostro sprang from his seat, took hold of Parsley's nose with his left hand, and with his right, began to pull a long paper streamer out of it. He pulled it out and pulled it out, and the streamer seemed endless—good six or eight feet long in the end. Everyone watched the proceeding with breathless amazement.

The streamer finally fell to the floor and twisted like a snake.

Before Dr. Parsley could catch his breath, Cagliostro grabbed him by the ear. And—before our eyes—colorful confetti burst out of it in a veritable shower.

"The good doctor has mice in his head, too!" shouted Cagliostro as he pulled out a white mouse from Parsley's other ear. The scholars roared with laughter. And I thought with horror: *If Cagliostro pulls a snake out of Parsley's mouth, they will throw us out of the hostel.*

But Cagliostro seemed to understand the limits. Holding the mouse by the tail, he carried it out of the dining room into the garden and, in front of everyone, pretended to release it there.

And all the while, Dr. Parsley, PhD, sat in his chair paralyzed.

"This... this... this is awful," he finally stammered.

He had a bewildered, terrified look on his face. Another roar of laughter rolled over the room.

Eventually, Dr. Parsley's momentary paralysis passed. He jumped up from the table and ran out of the dining room just as the maestro returned from the garden. The illusionist entered the hall with triumphant air and sat stiffly at my table.

I won't say that I felt good: all eyes were on us.

There goes my reputation, I thought. But I consoled myself with the thought that these serious men and women of science were looking at us with sympathy: indeed, scholars are not without a sense of humor.

I quickly settled our bill and gave the waitress a hefty tip, apologizing for the confetti and streamers scattered on the floor.

In the corridor, I said to Cagliostro:

"If you try your tricks with mice and snakes one more time, we're through. I've had enough of this. This is getting really annoying."

"Ah, yes?" said the maestro, embarrassed. "Very well then, I will try to mend my ways."

I left him at the hostel and went to the cathedral hill.

According to an old tradition, there had once been a modest fort on the hill where the monumental complex now stood. Then, the owner of the hill, a widow, gave it as a donation to the bishop of

Varmia, Anselm, and he moved his seat here because his former seat, Branievo, was too close to the Old Prussian territory and often suffered border raids. At first, Anselm built only a small wooden church here, but in 1329, the construction of the current brick cathedral began. The site was ideal for a defensive installation: the hill had steep slopes and was surrounded by deep ravines. And once the mighty defensive wall went up, the builders dug a deep moat, threw a drawbridge over it, and the cathedral complex became a formidable fortress.

At the time, the diocese of Varmia was a state within the Teutonic state, the bishop having both spiritual and temporal power—he ruled like any feudal prince: he owned the land; the peasants owed rent and labor to him; he approved city councilmen across his province, was Varmia's highest judge, and, in the event of war, he owed a contingent of troops to the Teutonic Order. In the early years, his diocese was often threatened by the Old Prussian tribes, who, although they had by now been conquered by the Teutonic Order, rose time and again in bloody uprisings. The bishop's independence was under constant threat from the Teutonic Order itself, for whom the existence of a practically independent principality in the geographic center of their state felt like an insult. The powerful defenses of the stronghold of Frombork were particularly important in this calculus.

When, after a series of wars, Poland finally defeated the Teutonic Order in 1466, the bishopric of Varmia became part of Poland, but the Teutonic Knights never really accepted the fact and constantly plotted to regain the territory. This is why Canon Nicolaus Copernicus, appointed by the bishop as the administrator of the church property, also had to test his mettle as a military commander. The list of his military accomplishments includes fortifying the city of Olshtin and then defending it against the Teutonic Knights in 1521.

Thinking about all this, I arrived at a steep promontory. Before me was a steep ravine and on the other side—the Frombork cathedral complex. A red-brick barbican with massive defensive towers and gates with portcullises surrounded it.

I descended the steep steps leading into the defensive moat—which now was a paved street—and climbed up the steps on the opposite side of the ravine, passed by the western gate of the Keep, and entered the cathedral courtyard from the south, through its main gate flanked by beautiful semicircular defensive towers. The courtyard in front of the church is vast, with many ancient trees, mostly oaks. Along the inside of the defensive wall, there used to stand the *curiae*—the Latin name for the houses of the canons. According to regulations, every canon of Frombork—and there were sixteen of them—had to maintain one dwelling inside the fortress and another outside its walls. The former were called in Latin *curiae intra muros* and the latter—*curiae extra muros*. Of course, these outside *curiae* were much more spacious, surrounded by gardens and outbuildings, for according to the regulations, each canon had to maintain three riding horses for himself and his servants.

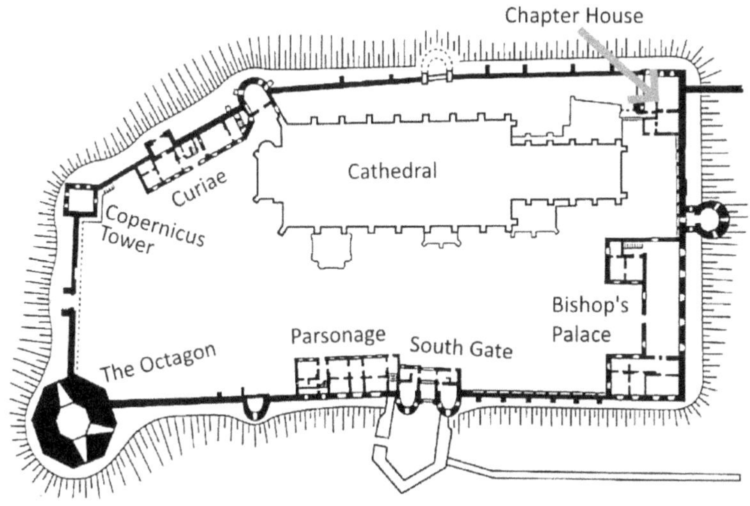

The Frombork Cathedral Keep

Why do I mention this? Because these *curiae* became quite a contentious subject among scholars and a lot of ink has been spilled on the controversy: where exactly did Copernicus live? Did he live in the inner curia, that is, in a house attached to the inside of the defensive walls of the Keep? Or did he live in the outside curia? And if outside, then—where exactly was that outside curia of Copernicus? It's not a trivial matter because if we knew the answer, we would perhaps be able to guess where he made his observations.

Only two intramural *curiae* survive today, and one of them preserves beautiful late-Gothic wooden ceilings still covered with polychrome and a Gothic portal, both of which probably remember Copernicus. The Copernican museum was located here for a while before it was moved to the bishop's palace in the eastern part of the fortress.

The bishop's palace, in a mixed Gothic-Baroque style and built on a horseshoe plan, had been destroyed during World War Two but has now been restored. The museum has also absorbed the Gothic corner tower and the chapter house. The old chapter house remains intact, and a picturesque arched passageway leads from it to the cathedral.

The Chapter House at Frombork

A chapter house (also: chapterhouse) is a building or room that is part of a cathedral, monastery, or collegiate church where meetings are held. The Cathedral Chapter (or the Council of Canons) meets there. In this photo: the Frombork Chapterhouse is in the center, the Cathedral to the left, and the Barbican (defensive wall) to the right.

But anyone who arrives in the Frombork cathedral courtyard first notices two massive towers. The first of these, in the southwest corner, is the bell tower. Its lower floors are really a late-Gothic octagonal bastion. Its walls are thirty feet thick. The tower is called the "Octagon" on account of the eight-cornered shape of the bastion, which had originally been erected as casemates—a nest for artillery guns. Much later, in the second half of the seventeenth century, Bishop Rajeyovski erected a quadrangular Baroque tower on top of the octagon—to house the cathedral bells.

Aerial view of the Frombork Cathedral Keep
Top right, the Octagon with the octagonal bastion at its bottom.
Bottom right, the Copernicus Tower.

In the northwest corner of the Keep stands another tower of a completely different character. Short and squat, topped with a pointed roof, it is probably known to every person in Poland from the reproductions of a famous painting by Yan Mateyko. This is the famous "Copernicus Tower." According to tradition, this is where Copernicus lived, where he had his observatory, and where he made his observations and measurements.

The "Copernicus Tower" inside the Frombork Fortress

As I admired the two towers, from behind me, from the cathedral, came the deep, rumbling sound of the Frombork organ. Someone began practicing a Bach fugue. It seemed to me that I could not find a better theme music for visiting the interior so I went inside.

The cathedral had been erected between 1329 and 1388: the construction took more than half a century. It is a huge building with three naves and a star vault ceiling.

One enters the cathedral through two richly carved stone portals. The interior of the cathedral is enormous: it is three hundred feet long! The first thing that strikes you as you enter is the huge number of altars, mostly baroque and rococo—running up and down both sides of the interior—and their extraordinary woodcarving work. Each canon—and there were sixteen—was in charge of one and was usually buried there.

The Frombork Cathedral
The Curiae to the left, Shembek's Chapel on the right.

The interior of the Frombork Cathedral.
Note the "star vault" ceiling.

In the left nave stands the former main altar. It features a wooden polyptych—that is, a painting painted on several independently moving wooden panels. It is dated to 1504 and is one of the most valuable examples of late Gothic sculpture in Varmia. In the central nave stands the newer altar which replaced it, executed in the Baroque style and intentionally modeled on the main altar of the Royal

Cathedral in Cracow. It was made by Cracow stone masons with stone quarried near Cracow and brought down the Vistula for the construction. This was as much an artistic decision as a political one: a symbolic unification of Varmia to the Polish Crown.[11]

Among all the side chapels, the most prominent is a Gothic chapel built in the fifteenth century and known as the "Polish" chapel. At a time when most services in the cathedral took place in Latin and occasionally in German, this chapel was reserved exclusively for services in Polish—including sermons and confessions. Rather unusually for Poland, whose favorite saints tend to be champions of charity, like Saint Anthony of Padua, the patron of the Polish chapel at Frombork is Saint George, the patron of soldiers and knights. His cloak is red and white—reflecting the heraldic colors of the Polish Crown.

One other chapel, much later, is also very striking. This is the beautiful Chapel of Bishop Shembek, built in the typically Polish, flowery Baroque. Its interior walls and dome are decorated with polychromes by a painter from a nearby town, Mayer, and it has an elaborate iron grill—the work of an artist from nearby Reshel.

All along the inner walls of the Cathedral, as well as on the floors, are numerous epitaphs of deceased bishops and canons of Varmia. Most bear Polish names and Polish coats of arms. And, on a pillar not far from the main pulpit, you can see the epitaph of Nicolaus Copernicus, placed there by the Chapter in 1745.

Nicolaus Copernicus died in Frombork. Is he buried here, near

---

[11] *Corona Regnis Poloniae.* A legal theory dating back to the 12th century proposed that an entity called The Polish Crown (*Corona Regnis Poloniae*) came into existence in AD 1025 when Pope John XIX allowed Duke Boleslav the Brave to crown himself "King of Poland" in a church ceremony. This amounted to a recognition by the Pope—and therefore the Church—of the existence of such a political entity; that this entity comprised certain inalienable geographical bounds; that it was separate from the Roman Empire of the German Nation and not subject to it; and that its rulers were in all respects equal in precedence to the rulers of all other kings of Christendom: France, England, Bohemia, Denmark, Sweden, Norway, Germany, and Hungary.

the epitaph? Perhaps inside the pillar or at its foot?

I left the cathedral lost in thought, the Bach fugue still in my ears. There is something very special about the sound of the organ playing inside the vast space of a stone church—and for a reason: the instrument was invented for the acoustics of such spaces. It was designed to sound all-powerful, to reverberate in the very fiber of your being. When you listen to a church organ in a vast Gothic cathedral and raise your hands, you can feel the vibration of the air in your fingertips.

But there was no time to devote to the experience of organ music: several daunting challenges lay before me. I had my marching order from Director Marchak; I had to track down and interview all the researchers working in Frombork; and... I had to take the fight to Batura, who, I guessed, had already found Koenig's second cache. Cagliostro had brought him a package, and I could guess what it contained: five silver cups, which Batura was going to swap for the golden chalices of the treasure.

I sat down on a bench under an oak tree, facing the Copernicus tower, and I drafted a plan of action in my notebook:

1) Interview historians to find out where Copernicus' observatory was.

2) Interview archivists to learn the status of the search for Copernicus's grave.

3) Interview archaeologists: the guide should feature their latest findings.

4) Learn something about the recent appearance of the three rare coins on the market.

When I wrote the last point, I laughed. It seemed ridiculously easy to write it. As we say in Polish, paper is patient: it never objects to the nonsense we write.

My laughter drew the attention of a tall girl in long bell-bottom pants and glasses with a camera slung over her shoulder. Over her other shoulder, she had a tourist backpack. She was young, maybe twenty-three or five. Her dark-rimmed glasses harmonized perfectly with her fair complexion and the lush locks of her auburn hair.

She looked like a tourist—in the summer, there were always many of them in the courtyard of the Frombork Cathedral.

"Were you drawing a cartoon?" she asked me. "Laughing at your own jokes in this sacred place?"

I closed the notebook and put it in my pocket.

"That's right. I was drawing a cartoon," I said." And you came here to chat up strangers?"

"Actually, no," she laughed. "But it has occurred to me to ask you to take my photo against the background of the Copernicus Tower. I'm all alone, and I'd like to have that picture."

She wore a red turtleneck, and, well, I like the color red. And she was pretty in general and had a happy, smiling face, and I am fond of such faces.

So I jumped off my bench and took her camera. She set the light and the exposure time. She planted herself under the Copernicus Tower, and I snapped her photo.

"Thank you kindly," she nodded to me as she collected her camera. "There. Now I have a picture against the tower where Copernicus lived and worked."

"Actually, we don't know that," I said.

"No?" she asked. "You think the photo did not work?"

"Ah, no. I am sure you set everything just right, and all I had to do was press the button to take a perfect shot. And I am rather good at that last bit, if I may say so. But what I wanted to say was that we do not know that Nicolaus Copernicus lived in that tower or that he had his observatory there."

"What do you mean? We all know the Mateyko painting. It shows Copernicus at the top of this tower, looking at the stars."

Copernicus making measurements

This 1873 painting by Yan Mateyko (Jan Matejko) imagines Copernicus in the Copernicus Tower in Frombork.

"Oh, but Mateyko based his painting on oral tradition. And, really, what else could he do? How could he imagine an astronomer, if not sitting at the top of a tower and looking at the stars? But in following Mateyko, we forget that an astronomer needs instruments in order to make measurements. And the instruments of the time were enormous. Do you know what a quadrant looked like? It was a huge thing, maybe six feet across. Where would it fit in that tower?"

"Maybe there once was a terrace on top of the tower?"

"If there was, there are no traces of it. A terrace would have needed support, and we have found no traces of such support. In fact, I've recently read a paper by a historian at the Masurian Institute, who argued convincingly that the tower had never been used by the canons. You see, the tower had been designed for defense, and the military commanders of the Keep felt that the presence of the canons would compromise its military function. And in any case, when the 1521 Teutonic invasion destroyed the chancery, the canons were *forced* to look for rooms in the keep, meaning that they usually lived outside.

Still, the tower had a connection with Copernicus. He owned it. He paid thirty pounds for it."

The Quadrant of Hevelius (1644)
A quadrant is an instrument used to measure angles up to 90°. Different versions of this instrument were used to calculate various readings, such as longitude, latitude, and time of day.

The young woman seemed somewhat deflated by my story.

"That's too bad," she sighed. "It just seems so romantic to look at this tower and imagine that this is where Copernicus lived and worked. And how come you know all this?"

"I'm from the Department of Museums in Warsaw," I explained. "I've come here to write a Frombork guidebook."

As we talked, we walked away from the Copernicus Tower and made our way out of the fortress.

"Well, thank you for the guided tour," she said. "I'd be happy to buy you a coffee in return. Is there a coffee shop in town?"

She was very pretty—and I could not shake the feeling that, in some vague way, she seemed familiar.

"I am honored to accept your invitation, " I said. "But I have to ask you: haven't I seen you somewhere before?"

She stopped and looked me over.

"This is rather old."

"What is?"

"When guys want to make acquaintance with me, they usually start by saying: *Excuse me, do I know you from somewhere?*"

"I see. But I really do seem to remember you from somewhere."

"I think you're imagining things," she stated firmly. "Now tell me, is there a cafe near here?"

I knew only one cafe in the entire town of Frombork—near the harbor. We strolled through the town towards it.

It was a sunny day and would have been hot had it not been for the cold breeze from the Lagoon. The breeze carried the pungent smell of the sea.

The town of Frombork really is charming. The houses that survived the war are painted in many colors, and some of them look like dollhouses. That summer was the summer of "Operation Frombork," and at every step, we saw Boy Scouts or Girl Scouts in their uniforms, and from time to time, we passed a whole troop tidying up flowerbeds and lawns.

Near the historic water tower (late fifteenth century), we came across Cagliostro. He was beaming.

"I have secured two performances for the Boy Scouts! And both will involve teaching tricks! I even received an advance. And I have decided to reimburse you for my expenses."

He handed me the money.

"This fine gentleman is an illusionist," I introduced Cagliostro to my companion, who, hearing about magic, made a puzzled expression.

Cagliostro looked at the young woman with obvious delight.

"You've made quick work of it, mister, there's no question," he said. "I've barely let you out of my sight, and you've already met a lady."

And instead of going his own merry way—I don't know—take care of his bunny cruelly abandoned in his cage in our room or the snake and mice (didn't he have some kind of mouse in his pocket?), he hung around. He seemed determined to keep us company.

"Will you stay in Frombork for a while?" he asked the young lady.

"A few days," she replied.

"And you came here all by yourself?" he kept drilling.

"No. I'm here with my colleagues."

Cagliostro kept up the interrogation and did not let me get a word in edgewise. He was sweet on her, I guessed. We entered the cafe, which was located in a rickety, low-slung barracks. We ordered two large coffees for me and the young lady. But Cagliostro only asked for a glass of water, which, as it turned out, was all part of a plan.

"What is your name?" he kept up the barrage.

"Ala."

"Ala? That's a very nice name," enthused Cagliostro. "Makes me think of my carefree school years, of my first school primer, in which the very first word we learned to read was Ala. *Ala ma kota,* was its first sentence." ("Alice has a cat.")

And this rang a bell.

"Ah, yes! Just a little further on, there was the second sentence: *This is ACE.* And further on: *This is Ala's ACE.*"

Cagliostro looked at me sharply. I saw a clear warning in his eyes as if he were saying: *Do not use that name in vain.* He did not want to expose himself to ACE and his iron paws.

But I repeated:

"It's Ala's ACE."

And then it came to me. Some realization, some memory, a reminiscence of some experience. Why did this girl seem familiar to me? I had never seen her in my life, never met her. And yet, it was as if I had already known her... perhaps... perhaps... perhaps heard her voice? Her voice coming out of the bowels of an iron monster? *ACE?*

Oh my, could it be *her*? The mysterious lady inside the mysterious vehicle?

Ala noticed my confusion. She smiled flirtatiously at Cagliostro and said:

"And are you really an illusionist? Can you do magic tricks? Let's see one!"

"Ah, but the magical arts require great concentration," declared the maestro. "Allow me to focus a little on today's paper."

He pulled the illustrated weekly *Mirror* from his pocket.

Or somewhere, because it seemed like he pulled it out of thin air.

He leafed through it for a while, turning page after page. But his gaze did not linger anywhere. A waitress approached us, carrying two cups of coffee and a glass of water on a tray.

"Who's having coffee?" she asked.

"The lady and I are having coffee," I said.

"And a glass of water for my newspaper," said Cagliostro, rolling up the newspaper into a tube.

The waitress looked at him crossly, thinking that Cagliostro was making a joke. But he took the glass of water from the tray and poured its contents into the rolled-up *Mirror*. He poured the water slowly. We could see clearly how the contents of the glass disappeared into the newspaper tube, and not a drop leaked onto the floor.

"Well, well, I guess my newspaper was really thirsty," said Cagliostro to the waitress. And he unrolled the newspaper and began leafing through it again. The waitress stood staring at him, petrified like Lot's wife, when she saw the destruction of Sodom and Gomorrha.

"What have you just done?" she stammered.

"What do you mean, what have I just done?" the maestro feigned surprise. "I should be asking you: why have you not brought me water, but only an empty glass?"

"You've just poured the water I brought you into the magazine," the waitress said.

"Into the magazine? Look, you can see that there is nothing in the magazine," said Cagliostro, opening the weekly and leafing through it as if looking for the missing water.

"Well, you poured the water into the newspaper. I saw it," said the waitress uncertainly.

"I have poured something into the newspaper?" Cagliostro made a puzzled expression again. "Let's see what you have brought me then."

He rolled the newspaper up again, shook it, and a stream of colored confetti jutted out of the tube.

"Here's what you've given me," he declared, handing the waitress his glass filled with confetti.

The waitress looked at Cagliostro as if he were an apparition. Then she suddenly laughed strangely and left for the buffet, presumably to tell the buffet girl about the strange guest and his water-and-confetti trick.

Cagliostro calmly folded the magazine and put it in his pocket. He looked proudly at Ala, looking for an acknowledgment of his skills.

But Ala only shrugged her shoulders.

"Kids' stuff," she said. "I can do better."

"Oh? What can you do?" asked Cagliostro, indignant.

"A trick with a mouse," she replied. "With a trained mouse."

"What?" I roared in a terrible voice. "Cagliostro, I forbid games with mice. We have agreed on this."

"I haven't brought my mice," sighed Cagliostro regretfully. "You've forbidden mice."

"Ah, so, maestro! So you do have a trained mouse?" Ala asked, suddenly interested.

"Well, I have two white mice. But mice cannot be trained," said Cagliostro. "They are un-trainable."

"You're wrong there," Ala replied scornfully. "Maybe *white* mice are too stupid to be trained. But mine is a grey mouse. It does everything I want it to do."

"You're kidding," said Cagliostro with cold indifference, still upset that his trick had failed to impress Ala.

"Well, let's have a look," declared Ala. And from the pocket of her pants, she pulled out by the tail—a gray mouse!

"Jesus!" I groaned. "Not mice again!"

Ala put it on the floor, and the mouse began to scurry between the legs of chairs and tables.

There were only a few guests at the cafe, but they immediately started yelling:

"A mouse, a mouse! Look, a mouse!"

The buffet girl jumped onto the buffet counter. The waitress jumped onto a chair. And the mouse ran all over the room. Ala began to call to it:

"Come here, darling! Come here, dearest!"

The mouse, as if hearing Ala's voice, stopped and then slowly headed in our direction. Ala called her like a dog, smacking her lips and whistling softly.

Suddenly, a huge cat jumped out of the corner of the cafe.

"Oh-oh. Say goodbye to Miss Mouse," Cagliostro said with venom.

"Oh, the cat! The cat is about to catch it!" cried the guests from their tables.

"Get the mouse! Get the mouse!" shouted the buffet girl from the height of the counter.

Fast as lightning, the cat descended upon the mouse. It slapped the mouse with his paw, trying to pin it down, but then drew the paw back sharply as if hurt. It then tried to grab the mouse with its teeth and immediately pulled back again.

And then the most incredible thing happened—the mouse didn't run away at all. On the contrary, as if angered by the cat's attack, it turned to face him and... advanced. And then, as if it was the most natural thing on earth, it... attacked! No one in that room has ever seen such a thing before.

The cat tried to pin the mouse with its paw again. And once again, it pulled its paw back sharply as if scalded. It took a few steps backward, meowing with rage or fear. And the gray mouse advanced against slowly, menacingly. It pulled up and... bit the cat on the paw! The cat gave another meow and... ran, and the mouse followed. It chased the cat right across the room until the poor feline jumped onto a table. Only then did the mouse leave him alone and return to us.

Ala grabbed it from the floor and put it in her pocket.

"Whoa," said Cagliostro with true professional appreciation. "That was incredible. Could I see your mouse?"

"Oh? Did I ask to see your newspaper?" Ala answered, clearly enjoying her victory. "You showed us a trick, I showed you a trick. That's all. Let's let others judge whose trick was better."

CHAPTER 8: I AM NOT CLAIRVOYANT

Toys these days. I have a revelation. The devil, the mountain, and what followed. The grievances of Dr. Parsley. How to dig up a hill. I'm not clairvoyant. The story of the widow Gertrude and bishop Anselm. The snake. Ambitions and archaeological bans. Is Dr. Parsley beautiful?

Interest in our table continued for a while. The waitress, in particular, watched us with apprehension. But Miss Ala's mouse did not arouse horror or revulsion: everyone had realized quite quickly that the mouse was an automaton, a kind of toy. And, as closely as I had watched the mouse's movements, I had noticed that, as Ala released it on the floor, she simultaneously took a small, black apparatus out of her purse and manipulated it as the mouse scurried around. The animal's legs did not move: the "animal" "ran" on wheels, which gave a little rustling sound, unlike a real-life mouse.

We had all heard of these modern toys, of course—all kinds of tiny vehicles, turtles, frogs, and other beasts operated by radio waves from a small transmitter. Only two years earlier, *Modern Toys* by Yanush Voychehovsky had sold out in a flash, testifying to the great interest in such matters. And Ala presented us with just such a remote-controlled toy. The cafe guests soon got over the initial excitement and returned to their conversations.

We also got back to our coffee, and this time, Cagliostro actually drank the second glass of water the waitress brought him.

I was very tempted to ask Ala about *ACE*, but Cagliostro's presence stopped me. I didn't think he had connected Ala with the voice that had spoken to us from inside the terrible vehicle, and it seemed unnecessary to clue him in. Besides, I was obliged by my vow of silence: had Ala chatted me up in the cathedral courtyard only to check if I was talking to people about *ACE*? What other secret powers did this pretty maiden have? What if, upon finding out that I dared to mention *ACE* to anyone at all, she were to summon some other sinister mechanism and kidnap me and put me away for a few days in that ominous barracks of hers?

Meanwhile, Miss Ala dwelt on the charms of Frombork and talked about the impressions she had formed while visiting the area.

"It's so pleasant around here," she said. "Three days ago, I took a boat trip from Frombork to Tolkmitsko. Then, I visited Krinitsa. Then I went to the Devil's Mountain, and now I am getting acquainted with the town of Frombork."

Suddenly, something squeezed my throat. I could no longer hear her words; they became a kind of meaningless blur to me. For a moment, I found myself unable to speak. Finally, a sort of squawk broke out of my mouth:

"Waitress? Could we pay?"

Ala and Cagliostro looked at me, surprised by the sound of my voice.

"Sorry," I muttered, coughing. "I seem to have a sore throat."

I sensed that Ala took notice of my panicky stare and the strange trembling of my hands as I took out the money. We left the cafe. I rushed forward as if I were in a hurry somewhere, but Ala walked slowly, with a strolling step, and I had to turn back to rejoin her.

Oh, if they only knew what was going on inside me! What a terrible storm of thoughts barged through my brain! I had the feeling that I had sprouted wings, that in a moment, I would take off and fly into the skies. It was the wonderful feeling of a man who had hit upon a long sought-after clue.

Oblivious to my state of mind, Cagliostro noticed a vegetable stand.

"Excuse me, lady, sir," he said, bowing to Miss Ala. "I have to buy vegetables for my bunny. Say, will I have the pleasure of your company to dinner?" he turned to me.

I nodded. Ala spoke up:

"Shall we drop by the harbor? Will you take pictures of me against the backdrop of the Lagoon?"

"Naturally, naturally," I replied absentmindedly. But as soon as Cagliostro disappeared into the vegetable store, I grabbed Ala's hand.

"Let's go! There is no time to lose!"

"What? Where? What happened to you?"

She tried to jerk her hand free.

"You must take me to the Devil's Mountain! Immediately. Right away. Do you understand what it means? The Devil's Mountain? Ha, ha, ha," I burst out in an insane cackle. "Devil's Mountain is *Teufelsberg*!"

And saying this, I dragged Ala towards the hostel, where my vehicle was parked.

Strangely, she did not resist. She did not understand what happened to me, but she was curious and allowed herself to be led to the vehicle.

"Devil's Mountain is on the left bank of the Bauda River," she explained to me on the way. "You must take the road that ends in the *No Entry* sign."

Ha! Only yesterday, Cagliostro and I had passed by the Devil's Mountain! But how could I have known that it was the Devil's Mountain?

I opened the door of the vehicle.

"Are we going to ride in this contraption?" Ala hesitated. "Won't it fall apart on the way? God, we'd better go on foot. It's only a kilometer and a half from here."

"We do not have a minute to lose," I growled. Clearly, it was a waste of time to explain to Ala the birds and bees concerning my vehicle. Let her think whatever she likes: that it is pathetic, ridiculous, and resembles a dugout crossed with a tent, a vehicle from Venus or Mars, something I found in a scrap yard!

We dashed down the Frombork Hill and jumped onto the road leading to the Bogdany State Farm.

I braked so abruptly that my passenger almost knocked her head against the window. I stopped the vehicle and opened the back door.

"Get in," I said to a Boy Scout walking along the roadside.

It was Bashka. He'd been walking in the direction of Devil's Mountain.

"I'm tailing Dr. Parsley," the youth explained. "He said he knew where Colonel Koenig's second cache was, and just now, I saw him leave in the direction of the Devil's Mountain."

"Was he heading for the Devil's Mountain?" I cursed under my breath.

"Yes. He was with this archaeologist lady and another woman, a dark-haired lady. I have seen him with her several times before."

"This is bad," I frowned. "We are sure to run into him, and there is bound to be a huge stink about me interfering in Parsley's treasure hunt."

Then I remembered Miss Ala.

"I am sorry, Miss Ala. This is my friend. We call him Bashka," I introduced the Boy Scout.

"Is he a private eye?" Ala became interested.

"Something like that," the boy nodded modestly.

Ala nodded with a smile.

"And I almost believed you when you said that you came to Frombork to write a guidebook. Meanwhile, as it turns out, you are after Koenig's treasure."

"Well, yes, I am also interested in the treasure," I admitted. "But the truth is that I did come here to write a guidebook to Frombork. The treasure hunt has been assigned to my colleague from the same Department."

"Dr. Parsley?"

"Dr. Parsley."

The bridge over the Bauda River appeared before us. Ala pointed to a hillock on our left rising among the riverside wetlands: it was quite high and steep and as flat at the top as a pancake. Its regular shape and its flat top clearly indicated that it had been raised by the hand of man.

Three people were sitting on the grass on the top of the hill: Dr. Parsley and two women. One of them I knew well—she was Lady

Gossamer.

I pulled over to the edge of the road and stopped. We got out of the car and headed across the meadow towards the hill.

So this is where Colonel Koenig buried his second cache? I asked myself.

If so, then the location had been well chosen. The surrounding area seemed deserted and wild. The Bauda flowed to the sea in several branches here, scrubby bushes grew everywhere, and the land was marshy and treacherous. On the far bank of the Bauda rose a tall mountain, overgrown with trees—we had met *ACE* in its deep ravine the preceding day.

As I had feared, Dr. Parsley was upset to see me.

"Were you brought here by the affairs of the Frombork guidebook?" he asked with irony.

I decided to lay it all out.

"Look, Parsley. I have told you this morning that no one is going to take away your assignment. I have another assignment."

"Yes, the Frombork guide, of course," he repeated with deep sarcasm.

"Well, yes, that, too, but not only that," I replied with seriousness. "During your absence, a new and rather suspicious business came up. I was not supposed to tell you about it but I will because it is just possible that this new case is somehow connected to Koenig's treasure. And if so, our investigations may intertwine. For all this, I swear to you that if I come across the slightest clue leading to Koenig's treasure, I will tell you about it immediately."

"Thank you," he nodded, but a note of sarcasm remained in his voice.

"You have a difficult task before you," I added, looking around the hill. "It seems to me that *Teufelb* from Koenig's sketch is the Devil's Mountain. But then what?"

"Trouble, huh?" said Dr. Parsley cautiously. "Oh, yes, you're right. Pure trouble. I have deciphered the clue to Koenig's second cache: the Devil's Mountain. So what? How do I look for the cache on this hill? It is full of holes and ditches, old bricks, and abandoned roof tiles. The whole hill would have to be dug up."

"Yes," I nodded. "This does seem rather hopeless to me. So, you see, I repeat: I do not envy you your task. I really prefer to work on my stuff."

These words seemed to put to sleep the snake of ambition devouring Dr. Parsley. He declared proudly:

"Well, the situation may seem hopeless to you. But I am different. I have taken on the task and will carry it through."

I said hello to Lady Gossamer. Ten years ago, when she was still a budding archaeologist, we explored the mysteries of an old 12th-century collegiate church together and discovered an ancient reliquary.

And, briefly, something else connected us, too.

But, as I say, this was ancient history. She had a husband now, two lovely children, and led archeological digs of her own. But she remained as girlishly charming as ever and her hair was still like gossamer.

The other woman—Dr. Parsley introduced her as Miss Anielka—had an hourglass figure and a wasp's waist, and accentuated both with the cut of her pants. Her black hair was trimmed in a bob. She was in her early twenties, twenty-three or maybe twenty-four. It was difficult for me to understand what attracted her to Dr. Parsley, who, his eye wild and his long hair tousled, his nose hooked like an eagle's beak—did not offend with excessive beauty. But perhaps he had charmed her with his stories of the Flemish masters, about whom he spoke with such passion and fire that he almost became beautiful.

Alas, he also considered himself a detective.

"Dr. Parsley," said Lady Gossamer, "became so passionate about his clue that he wanted to hire workers and dig up this hill. Unfortunately, I had to object. By the look of it, there has once been some kind of a fort here, and the place should be properly excavated by professionals. I even went to Warsaw to get the funding for it, but it got turned down—for the moment, all resources are dedicated to the excavation on the Cathedral Hill in Frombork. And this means that while Dr. Parsley is allowed to walk about this hill looking for his treasure, if I as much as see him with a spade here, I will call the militia, and he will be arrested on charges of destroying material cultural property."

Dr. Parsley interrupted her mid-sentence. He started waving his arms like the wings of a windmill and shouted:

"How am I supposed to find Koenig's treasure then? We know that he buried his second cache here and I am not allowed to sink a shovel here! So maybe I should search with a wand? By the way," he remembered something and turned to me, "what happened to that magician of yours?"

"He's at the PTTK hostel," I said. "I imagine he is feeding his animals now."

And turning around, I left Dr. Parsley shouting something and began to survey the top of the Devil's Mountain. Bashka and Ala followed me. They watched me with such intense concentration as if they were expecting me to stop at any moment, point my finger, and shout: "Here is Koenig's cache!"

Alas, I was not clairvoyant. The hillside was overgrown with bushes and tall grass, and there were ditches everywhere. If Koenig had indeed buried his loot here twenty-six years ago, it would not be found without the help of a team of archaeologists and a whole regiment of workers. But to excavate the entire hill would take two archaeological seasons at the very least. In a word, the situation really did seem hopeless.

I backtracked to where Lady Gossamer was sitting.

"Does this hill really represent such value for science?" I asked.

"The whole area does, Thomas," she replied. "This whole area is one huge archaeological reserve. In 1911, a famous treasure hoard was discovered only fifteen hundred feet from here. It consisted of silver and gold coins and dozens of pieces of bronze jewelry and was buried here in the sixth century—a full four hundred years before the first mention of the place in the written record. Legend has it that there had been a stronghold in this area—over there, on the other side of the Bauda, on that hill overgrown with trees—and that it was the seat of the Prussian tribe of Nartsen. The widow of the last chieftain of that tribe was named Gertrude and was converted to Christianity by

Bishop Anselm. In thanks, she donated her domains to the bishopric.

"Anselm then began to erect a bishop's fortress on one of the hills she had donated. His German clerics called it Frauenburg, or "lady's castle"—today's Frombork—in memory of the donor. But this hill, called the Devil's Mountain, also has its place in this legend. An ancient Prussian temple may have once stood here."

"And has anyone dug here?"

"No, not here. But we have made several digs on the Bogdany hill and discovered the remains of a ninth-century stronghold. I should add," Lady Gossamer looked at Bashka with a smile, "that your Boy Scouts helped in that excavation. We discovered a very old tomb with various grave goods, like spurs and half-finished amber jewelry. Of course, the dig is not complete, and it will be some time before we have a complete picture of the site. Once we finish, the fortified settlement will be opened to tourists, and there will be much to see. There are wonderfully preserved ramparts, moats, and traces of ancient gates. But we don't know whether there was any connection between that site and the Devil's Mountain. So, you can understand why no one will be permitted to dig here for treasure."

That certainly sounded reasonable, even if Koenig's treasure was buried here. Still, did we really have to wait for an archaeologist's shovel? And would Dr. Parsley accept this? He stood at the top of the hill with his hair blowing in the wind and exclaimed:

"I have to find the cache, even if I have to go to that crazy wand-wielder of yours for help. And I will dig up this treasure, even if I am arrested by the militia afterward!"

We looked at him with compassion. A gigantic, hungry anaconda of ambition lived inside that frail little man.

I suggested that we all ride in my vehicle, for it was already lunchtime. But only Lady Gossamer and Bashka got in with us. Dr. Parsley and Miss Anielka decided to remain on the Devil's Mountain. Parsley seemed convinced that he might discover the second cache at any moment.

And the young lady? Maybe she fancied Dr. Parsley?

Ala bid us goodbye, too. She walked across the bridge over the

Bauda River, then turned into the forest and disappeared from our sight in the Land of the Terrible ACE.

CHAPTER 9: THE DEVIL'S TREE

Waltzing Zosha. A war council. A new lead. Who eavesdropped on us. Out and about. How Branievo was captured. The tragedy on the Lagoon. The arrest of a criminal. The Devil's Tree. A new difficulty. Valdemar Batura again. The treasure-finding wand. The wrath of Dr. Parsley.

I ate lunch alone in the dining room of the PTTK hostel. Cagliostro—the waitress informed me—had eaten in a hurry and left. I did not find him in our room either. The bunny was munching fresh lettuce leaves in its cage, but the other cages were missing, as were the snake and the two white mice. I assumed that the maestro had gone to demonstrate his tricks.

Immediately after lunch, Bashka and a girl named Zosha came to my room. She was a resolute and outspoken young lady despite her fourteen years. She was nicknamed "Waltzing Zosha" because she seemed to walk on tiptoe and, at times, to fly through the air. She had fluid, dancing movements and could not sit still for a moment—she constantly had to sway, or walk, or spin, or dance. She had an awful lot of freckles on her nose and cheeks, very light hair, and blue eyes. I liked her at first sight. When she was introduced to me by Bashka, she winked at me mischievously, did a pirouette, and said:

"I like adventures. And Bashka assured me that adventures follow you."

"Oh, we will not lack adventures, it seems," I replied, sincerely worried.

Worried? Yes, worried. Because though it is pleasant to read about adventures in books or watch them on the screen; and it is also nice to recall your adventures once they are over; but when you experience them, they are not always pleasant. You sometimes have the feeling that you're caught up in some huge maze from which you cannot find the exit. It seems to you that you are wandering in the dark, and time and again, you knock your head against a wall. And these knocks are sometimes very painful. They even leave bumps.

Bashka said that he was able to devote a lot of time to me that day because his team had been dismissed: several boys were involved in preparations for the evening event—which was to include some magic tricks. And the few who could neither sing nor recite were given the afternoon off. As for Waltzing Zosha, the chronicler of the girls' team, she managed to get a release from camp for the afternoon.

I sat down with my two friends in my room for a briefing on Colonel Koenig's treasures. Of course, by age and office, the honor of making the keynote speech fell to me.

"The situation is very serious," I began, "and requires an immediate decision, for we have reached a dead-end. None of you has seen an individual matching the description of Valdemar Batura thus far and yet Batura must be here, somewhere, I am sure of it. He cannot possibly have given up on Koenig's treasure. Of course, I didn't come here to look for the treasure because that is Dr. Parsley's job. My business is to explain the mystery of the priceless coins. But since I suspect that Batura stole those coins from the first cache; and since I am sure that he intends to rob the second and third caches, too; it is inevitable that I must also track down Koenig's treasure to prevent the robbery."

Bashka interrupted me:

"You've seen the Devil's Mountain. One would have to dig up the entire hill to find the cache. If Dr. Parsley is not allowed to dig there, how will Batura do it? You said yourself that the situation is hopeless: the second Koenig cache cannot be discovered without a major dig."

"And that is the dead end I had in mind," I explained. "And now I am thinking of Cagliostro's question again. You see, I believe it was really Batura's question: did Colonel Koenig find himself in Frombork in 1945 by accident, or was he a local boy? in other words, did he hide his loot in a hurry, in any old way, in the first place that came to mind, or whether he had the local knowledge to know good hiding places. I think Batura sent Cagliostro to learn what I knew about Koenig. But I also wonder whether he wanted to know if I could be misdirected—perhaps to the Devil's Mountain. I am a suspicious man. The Devil's Mountain seems wrong."

"So you think the second cache isn't there?" asked Bashka.

I made a movement with my hand as if I were pushing this idea onto the back burner.

"First of all," I said, "why did Koenig make his sketch? That is, did he draw a plan with someone else in mind, someone who would search for these treasures on his behalf; or did he draw it for himself as a simple memory aid? In other words, did Koenig make a plan of the hidden treasure, or was he simply taking notes?"

"It seems he made a note for himself," replied Waltzing Zosha. "His plan is not detailed enough for a stranger to decipher."

"I agree," I nodded. "I think it was a note to himself. I think Koenig was not expecting death. Perhaps he even thought that the Soviet offensive might be repelled, that the Nazis would retake Frombork, and he would return here and reclaim the loot. Still, the key to the whole affair remains this: did Koenig find himself in Frombork by accident, or was he a resident of the town? We would need to find some old resident of Frombork, a person who had lived here before the war and was here during the war. Koenig had the rank of colonel, and Frombork is a tiny town. If he came from here, he would have been well known among the locals."

"I think I know just such a person!" cried Bashka joyfully, and Waltzing Zosha nodded eagerly. "A week ago, an old man named Stefan Dombrovski came to one of our campfire evenings. He comes from Frombork. He talked about the old Frombork before the war, about the war years, about the terrible tragedy on the Lagoon after the defeat of the Nazis."

"Where does he live?"

"In Stara Street," said Bashka. "I don't remember the house number, but I can take you to his apartment because we escorted him all the way home."

I took out a notebook and, writing it down, repeated out loud:

"Stefan Dombrovski, Stara Street…"

And as I did that, I accidentally glanced toward the door. I noticed a barely perceptible vibration of the handle. Someone had put his ear to the keyhole and bumped the handle with his head. Instantly, I sprang from my chair and opened the door. We saw Cagliostro straightening himself up.

"You were eavesdropping," I said with indignation.

He was embarrassed, perhaps even ashamed.

"But only for a very short time," he said apologetically.

Then, in a more confident tone, he explained:

"I heard voices from our room and wondered whether to enter. I was afraid that I might disturb you because I thought you were talking to one of the professors here. But I now see that you are here in the company of young people."

He lied brazenly, but what could I do? I pretended to accept his explanation. He, in turn, as if nothing had happened, entered the room, greeted Bashka and Zosha, rummaged for something in his belongings, and left, saying:

"I won't be disturbing you again."

"I wonder how much he has heard?" I muttered. "I am pretty sure he heard the name Dombrovski and will inform Batura immediately. We must act quickly."

With these words, I ended our war council. We left the room and the hostel. Bashka led us to Stara Street, which was near the old monastery.

We found Mr. Dombrovski sitting on a bench next to a flower bed in front of his tiny house. He was an old man, hunched over, with a furrowed face and a sumptuous mustache. I understood immediately that I could not lay out our case too quickly, or he might grow suspicious and not give us any information at all. So, I started our conversation with other matters, then broached the subject of the war, which had so painfully affected the residents of the city and the surrounding area. I hoped that among the many questions about the war days, I would be able to smuggle in this one: had Koenig come from Frombork.

Few people realize that even after the sounds of cannons in central Poland had long fallen silent and children in Warsaw, Lublin, Wooj, and Kyeltse began to go to school, fierce fighting still continued here. The resort town of Krinitsa on the Vistula Spit was captured by the Red Army only on May 3, 1945—five days before the fall of Berlin; and in the vicinity of Shtutovo, separated from the world by a huge expanse of a plain flooded by blown-up dykes, Germans surrendered only after the news of the fall of Berlin. The Nazis had turned East Prussia into one big fortress, and it took a lot of time, men, and resources to capture it.

Frombork was captured on February 11, 1945, after fourteen days of fighting. But the nearby city of Branievo seemed outright unattainable, as it was protected by naval artillery. Rounds from the 200-millimeter guns wreaked terrible destruction among the Soviet infantry and tanks attacking Branievo.

The battle lasted seven weeks, day and night. Every homestead, every foot of land had to be captured and sometimes recaptured. The final five-kilometer stretch separating the Soviet soldiers from the city took a week to traverse. And when the city finally fell, it looked like a zombie. All districts were laid completely flat, and whoever saw it in those days could not imagine that the city would one day be rebuilt, that life would return, and that people might live there like everywhere else.

But that was not the end of the drama of the "holy city of Varmia," as Branievo was called. A senseless order from the Prussian commander, Gauleiter Erich Koch, commanded the civilian population of Varmia and Mazury to evacuate. It was a very cold winter, snow lay about in drifts. Columns of peasant carts dragged along on the icy roads like ghosts, carrying people's belongings, small children, women wrapped in scarves. Thousands upon thousands of such carts arrived on the Lagoon, where, the Nazis had said, ships would be waiting to take them out of the range of Soviet guns. We do not know how many people driven from their homes died of hunger and cold along the way, but those who reached the ice-bound Lagoon found no ships awaiting them. They were told that ships were waiting beyond the spit and that they had to get there over the ice. And again, thousands of carts pulled across the Lagoon, getting stuck in the wet snow and falling into crevices in the ice. They were whipped by sleet and freezing rain from which, out on the Lagoon, there was nowhere to hide. Some froze in the wind, some fell through the ice and drowned. Nearly half a million people died during this tragic trek to nowhere—to nowhere, as it turned out, because no ships were waiting for them on the other side of the spit.

All of this is worth remembering today when you look at the peaceful waters of the Vistula Lagoon, when you walk in the streets of rebuilt Branievo, and when you admire the colorful Frombork.

"And do you know what happened to Koch in the end?" I asked the old man.

"Oh, yes," he said. "As the battle for Branievo raged, he sat in the safety of his villa on the Vistula Spit, a villa surrounded by a minefield and barbed wire and guarded by the SS. Later, when the inevitability of defeat became apparent, he escaped to Germany by ship. And then, in the summer of 1945, an elderly gentleman with turtle shell glasses appeared in the small town of Hasenmoor near Hamburg. He was short, stocky, and elegant. He rented a small house, claiming to be Rolf Berger, a former major of Wehrmacht. Soon, his wife came to stay with Mr. Berger, and Mr. Berger, who until then had been a bit of a recluse, began to regain his humor and even to frequent the local pub, sipping beer and playing billiards. Five years passed. By now, Mr. Berger had become so close to the local people that he even appeared at the gathering of the Germans expelled from East Prussia. He told them about the farm his family had owned there. And then, one day, someone shouted: *This is Erich Koch! Damned Erich Koch!*"

"This time, he did not manage to escape. He was arrested, and on March 9, 1950, he was deported to Poland. A Polish court sentenced him to death," nodded the old man.

I asked:

"And Colonel Koenig? Have you heard of a Nazi by that name?"

The old man gave me a sly look. And then he chuckled.

"Ah, is that what you're after? Will you ask me about *Teufelsbaum*, too?"

I shuddered. We exchanged glances with Bashka and Zosha. *Teufelsbaum? Teufelsbaum*, meaning the Devil's Tree? Was *Teufelb.* not *Teufelsberg*, but *Teufelsbaum*?

"Yes, I did mean to ask you about that, too," I stated frankly. The old man giggled again.

"I do know where the Devil's Tree grew. Near the Koenig house. In fact, it grew in their yard. No one else knows about it except me. And no one else will point it out to you because there is no trace of the Devil's Tree or the Koenig house—both were wiped away by artillery shells."

"Where were this house and this tree?" I asked.

The old man shook his head.

"I'm not going to tell you. I mean, I will not tell you today. Not today, nor tomorrow. Maybe next week…"

"Why?"

"Because I may only reveal the location to a person looking for Koenig's treasure on behalf of the state," he said, making a very important face.

I wanted to say: *You are talking to him. I am looking for Koenig's treasure on behalf of the state*, but I bit my tongue. I had no right to say that. Officially, the search belonged to Dr. Parsley.

"And how will you know that he is searching for Koenig's treasure on behalf of the state?" I asked.

"I spoke to someone who also asked about the *Teufelsbaum* and the Koenig house. He informed me that someone from the government would soon arrive in Frombork to search for Koenig's caches and that he would bring this man to me. The treasures must not be allowed to fall into the wrong hands."

"I agree," I nodded. "But did you reveal the location of the house and the tree to the person who promised to bring this man to you?"

"Oh, I only mentioned it vaguely," said the old man.

I had no more questions. The whole thing was blindingly

obvious. Valdemar Batura had beaten me to the punch and had learned about the location of the Devil's Tree. Once he discovered the second cache and replaced the gold goblets with silver ones, he would bring Dr. Parsley to the old man and Dr. Parsley would then "make the discovery." Until such time, Batura forbade the old man to provide any information about the Devil's Tree to anyone.

"The man who had spoken to you is a common crook," I said, pulling out my service card. "I am from the Department of Museums and Historic Preservation."

The old man carefully studied my ID.

"A crook?" he quipped. "He didn't look like a crook. You don't think he will bring this government man to me to look for Koenig's treasure?"

"Oh, he will bring him," I said.

"Then why are you calling him a crook?" he became indignant.

I tried to explain the matter to the old man, but he just waved me off.

"When this gentleman about whom you say that he is a crook returns here, I will question him," he promised. "But for now, the secret of the Devil's Tree remains with me."

I realized that the old man would not be persuaded and would not reveal anything until he saw Batura again.

There was nothing left for me to do but say goodbye to him.

"I will come here to see you later this evening," I said. "And I will bring this government man, this man who is searching for the Koenig treasure on behalf of the state. His name is Dr. Parsley."

I said this because I felt it was necessary to act as soon as possible. Maybe Batura hadn't yet had time to swap the goblets yet? It seemed to me that, for the sake of the common good, Dr. Parsley should be told about the Devil's Tree. Dr. Parsley would then understand what role Batura played in the case and would rush to ask the old man about the Devil's Tree. He would then find the cache and—perhaps, just perhaps—beat Batura to the goblets.

We left the old man's garden. Around the corner of Stara Street, I stopped.

"Listen up, friends," I said to Bashka and Waltzing Zosha. "Things are piling up. I will now run to Dr. Parsley, and you stay here and keep an eye on the old man. We may have managed to rile our elderly friend. Perhaps he will try to contact Batura or go to him. If so, this is our chance to find out where Batura is. So keep an eye on the old man, and I'll rush to get Dr. Parsley."

But on that day, all evil powers conspired against us. The lady at the reception of the PTTK hostel pointed to the key to Dr. Parsley's room hanging on a hook.

"Unfortunately, he is not here," she said. And seeing my distraught face, she added: "Maybe he is at the beach?"

I didn't think that Dr. Parsley was lounging at the beach—unless the hour-glassed beauty named Miss Anielka had turned his head and he forgot about the treasure.

And, in any case, searching for Dr. Parsley at the city beach, among hundreds of mostly naked people, seemed like a pointless endeavor. I was rather inclined to think that Parsley, along with the Hourglass Lady, was still on the Devil's Mountain, snooping around in search of the treasure.

I jumped into my vehicle and rushed toward the Devil's Mountain. And my prediction turned out to be mostly correct, although not completely. The Hourglass Lady was not on the Devil's Mountain. But Dr. Parsley was—strolling slowly up the hill in the company of... Cagliostro.

I burst out laughing. They presented such a funny sight. Cagliostro had his eyes closed and an inspired expression on his face. In his extended hand, he held a thin rod. He strode forward carefully like a blind man, supported by Parsley, who watched to make sure that Cagliostro did not fall into some ditch. Both men strode with dignity, uphill, as if carrying the Holy Host during a Corpus Cristi procession. Every now and then, Cagliostro would stop and say:

"The twig twitched. There is something here."

"But what? But what?" queried Dr. Parsley impatiently.

"Probably an ordinary piece of iron," replied Cagliostro. "Had it been gold, the rod would have vibrated quite differently in my hand."

And they kept walking: one with an inspired face, the other with an expression of utmost concentration.

"Parsleeeeeeeeeeeeey!" I shouted, standing at the foot of the hill. "I need to speak to you in private!"

Dr. Parsley abandoned Cagliostro's arm reluctantly and walked downhill towards me.

"What do you want now, Thomas?" he growled. "Why are you disturbing my work?"

"Do you really believe in Maestro Cagliostro's magic wand?" I asked.

"Perhaps," he replied, offended. "Yes, I admit it does look like clutching at straws, but what am I to do when I am not allowed to use an ordinary shovel? Besides, I read in an academic journal about a douser who was able to detect underground water. Until recently, people derided the practice, but a new, fresh look is emerging, and perhaps there is something to dousing after all."

"Dear colleague," I began softly. "Don't you realize that you are in the hands of charlatans and crooks? Don't you understand that you are in the clutches of Valdemar Batura?"

"Batura is here? Have you seen him in Frombork?"

"I have not seen him, but I can smell him," I replied honestly. "He is acting through deputies. I think Cagliostro is one. Who knows, maybe the Hourglass Lady is, too."

"What? Miss Anielka? Are you trying to make me believe that that lovely lady is a member of Batura's gang? I don't believe it. And as for Cagliostro, deat Thomas! Isn't he *your* companion? You two even room together! So maybe you are Batura's accomplice, too?"

"Oh, come on, this is serious business."

"Yes, indeed, this is serious business," he confirmed. "Perhaps you should consult a doctor. It seems to me that you suffer from excessive suspicion, a kind of persecution mania."

"Listen to me carefully, Parsley," I said, holding back my anger. "Batura intends to do the following: he wants to find the caches before you, swap a few precious items in each for worthless pieces, keep the valuable pieces to himself, and then lead you to discover the rest."

"Do you mean to say that this is what happened to the first cache?" asked Parsley quietly.

"Yes," I replied.

It turned out that I had chosen the worst possible way to break this to Parsley. I offended his ambition. I goaded the gigantic anaconda of his pride. Parsley turned pale.

"Do you mean to say, Thomas, that the first cache was discovered not by me but by Batura, who then *fed* the solution of the puzzle to me? I know what you are getting at. You wish to diminish my merits!" he shouted and made a dramatic gesture with his hand, indicating my vehicle parked on the side of the road. In other words, he told me to leave.

"Parsley!" I cried out. "Listen, you've got to understand what's going on here. There are no treasure here. That *Teufelb.* from Koenig's plan is not *Teufelsberg*. It is *Teufelsbaum*. I know a certain old man who can give you information about it."

But Dr. Parsley covered his ears with his hands and, without listening to me, turned around and began to climb the hill.

What was left for me to do? I sadly hung my head and marched back to my vehicle. Driving away, I looked back and saw Dr. Parsley take Cagliostro's by the arm. The two walked down the hill again, slowly as if in a procession.

In his outstretched hand, the maestro held a thin dousing rod.

CHAPTER 10: KIDNAPPED!

I'm a pirate. The blue Opel. Master engineer Christopher Zegadlo. Concerning the love of cars. The Red Mustang. The mock vehicle. The old man kidnapped. The incident at the petrol station. The chase. Ala's amazement. The Temptation of Valdemar Batura. I lose the second round.

I was so shocked by the behavior of Dr. Parsley that I nearly collided with a blue Opel in front of the *People's Inn* in Frombork. We met at an intersection of two roads of the same priority, and the "right-hand rule" was in effect, meaning that a car coming from the right had the right of way. And since the blue Opel was on my right, and I should have yielded. But I was thinking about Parsley, about Batura, and about the impossible situation I was in. Plunged into these unhappy reflections, I barrelled down the street, and only at the last moment did I notice the blue Opel.[12]

My brakes squealed. The brakes of the Opel squealed. We both came to a sudden stop only a few inches from each other. What followed? What usually happens at such times: the angry driver of the Opel jumped out of the car and started yelling at me:

"Don't you know the rules of the road? Maybe you should go back to a driving school because, clearly, you do not know how to drive! You are a pirate! You have just tried to force the right of way!"

He was a young, handsome man of about thirty. Tall, athletic, tanned dark brown, wearing a plaid shirt. In his car, in the shotgun seat, I saw—Ala. Yes, that Ala, the Ala of the dreaded *ACE*.

"You are absolutely right," I said with deep remorse. "I became lost in thought and nearly caused an accident."

"Well, people who are in love should stroll in the park, not

---

[12] Opel Kadett was a four door sedan manufactured by General Motors in Bochum, West Germany, 1962-1965.

drive on the roads!" the man yelled.

Miss Ala got out of the car and put her hand on the arm of the angry young man.

"Come on, Christopher," she said. "Don't get all worked up. This gentleman is a friend of mine."

And she smiled at me.

The driver continued to fret for a while:

"You pick nice friends! We barely escaped alive! Just think what may have happened!"

It was clear that his car would have had a dent in the door—a terrible fate indeed for a car acquired with such a vast financial investment.

"Never mind him, Mr. Thomas," Ala explained. "Chris is crazy about his car. He washes and waxes it constantly. And when he has a nightmare that someone has scratched his car, he wakes up drenched in sweat."

"Oh, don't exaggerate," replied the Opel-man. "It is no crime to take care of one's car. I've worked for it, I've paid a lot of money for it. Is it a surprise that I don't want anyone to smash it? Even if he is a friend of yours."

"Yes, he is a friend of mine," nodded Ala. "He is the museum man I have told you about."

The Opel man measured me from head to toe with an ironic gaze.

"Ah, so this is you..." he said, and he extended his hand to me.

"I am Master Engineer Christopher Zegadlo," he introduced himself.

"And I am Thomas," I replied.

We shook hands.

What do two drivers do when they reconcile after a near collision? If they are in a hurry, they each go their way. And if they have time—and we both had time—they pull over to the curb and start a friendly chat.

I won't say that this chat was exactly thrilling. Master Engineer

Zegadlo worshipped technology. His worship of it resembled a religious cult. Anything that did not constitute technology seemed to Engineer Zegadlo of little interest, indeed, contemptible. Had I represented the Museum of Technology, perhaps Master Engineer Zegadlo would have seen some value in me. However, since I did not have an engineering degree but a degree in art history, Mr. Zegadlo treated me like a harmless lunatic who devotes his time to useless and unimportant matters.

A special object of Master Engineer Zegadlo's worship was cars. The smallest spot on the body of his car was a stain on his honor, and every scratch on the paint hurt him as if his own body had been scratched. Such was the man whose beautiful blue Opel I had almost smashed. Now, do you understand the nature of my predicament?

Master Engineer Zegadlo was very eager to talk about cars. Both his own and those of others, about their shortcomings and advantages, their features and specific needs. It seemed to me that if someone showed him a van Gogh painting and a beautiful Taunus,[13] only the Taunus would manage to interest him, although a van Gogh painting is worth a thousand Taunuses on the world market.

Master engineer Zegadlo was a sufficiently handsome man to justify Miss Ala's presence in his Opel. I also guessed that Miss Ala had something to do with technology since she had sat in the dreaded *ACE*. But I also saw her looking with interest at the sights of Frombork, which made me think that her interests were a little broader than those of the Master Engineer. Personally, I hate narrow-mindedness in any field. I don't like humanists who don't find it worthwhile to know the difference between a four-stroke engine and a two-stroke engine and auto engineers with whom you can't discuss existentialism. Despite the fact that the modern world requires great specialization, I do not believe that a man who narrowly sticks to just one particular field can experience great success in it. Success in the world requires broad knowledge since we never know which fact will come in handy. I have been to the villa of a great Soviet physicist at the

---

[13] Ford Taunus 17/20M IV was produced in Cologne 1964-1967.

research facility in Dubna, near Moscow, and seen in his home a magnificent collection of contemporary art. He talked about his paintings lovingly and knowledgeably. And I know a writer who can make beautiful furniture: he wields a planer as well as he holds the pen.

Mr. Zegadlo represented the narrow-minded technocrat type, but Miss Ala was different. Maybe that's why, when he started talking about cars, there was an expression of slight boredom or even embarrassment on her face.

And it just so happened that right next to where we parked our cars, right in front of the *People's Inn* in Frombork, there stood a magnificent, red... Ford Mustang.

A convertible Ford Mustang.

The body had clearly been designed by a very talented artist because even though the car stood motionless, it seemed to be flying in the air. At the same time, it seemed extremely light and agile and probably developed dizzying speeds on the highway and took turns perfectly. The heavy silhouette of an Opel was no comparison, let alone my vehicle, which, truth be told, did look less like a car and more like a frog.

"Now, this is a car!" declared master engineer Zegadlo, looking at the red Mustang with worshipful admiration.

And his words were spoken in the kind of tone in which, I imagine, Pontius Pilate uttered the famous *Ecce homo* at the sight of the whipped and thorn-crowned Christ. It seems to me that master engineer Zegadlo admired the red Mustang with an admiration he would have been wiser to reserve for Miss Ala's beauty. I got the impression that she noticed this as well because she now spoke up with a bit of derision in her voice:

"The car was made by mortals, and therefore, there is no need to fall on one's knees in front of it. I think people are more interesting than cars."

Engineer Zegadlo waved his hand dismissively.

"Ah, Ala, you can't even imagine what a wonderful feeling it must be to drive such a beautiful car."

"Yes," I agreed with what I hoped was a carefully disguised

irony. "It is probably more satisfying than taking a pretty girl by the hand."

Master Engineer Zegadlo turned a suspicious eye on me. Perhaps my irony had gotten through to him. He replied accusingly:

"You find it difficult to understand me since you are content to drive that awful thing of yours," he pointed to my larva-like beast.

"It's a perfectly good car," I said, straightening up my back with pride.

"You call this a car?"

"It drives on the highway just like any other car," I said. "It is not beautiful, that is true, but that is another matter altogether. The body was made by my uncle, a home-grown inventor. My car, however, is very useful."

"Useful?" picked up the master engineer. "Useful in what way? As a circus carriage to drive jugglers around at the fairground?"

"Why, I even went abroad with my vehicle!" I said.

"What?" Zegadlo was outraged. "And maybe you had the letters *PL* attached to this monstrosity so that everyone would know that you are from Poland? Sir, you bring shame upon our country and our technology. What will strangers think of us?"

"Not all that glitters is gold," I stated philosophically. "Someone in France wanted to buy my vehicle and was willing to pay a good sum."

"I think I know why. He probably he wanted to donate your vehicle to a museum of oddities. I have heard that there are such museums abroad."

"My vehicle has a lot of special features... although I do not deny that it also has some shortcomings, too," I began to explain.

"Why it has nothing but shortcomings. It is the quintessence of a shortcoming! No looks, no speed, no grace, no..." Here, the Master Engineer broke off because he discovered that he had a shortcoming himself: he lacked the vocabulary required to express fully his contempt for my vehicle.

Miss Ala, who must have been made uncomfortable by this attack on my car, said:

"Our *ACE* is not beautiful either."

"*ACE*?" burst out the outraged master engineer. "*ACE* is the pinnacle of modern technology! In him, beauty would be superfluous. This vehicle, on the other hand, is... it is..." he searched his head for a moment and finally exclaimed joyfully: "This is junk!"

And just at that moment, the Hourglass Lady, a.k.a. Miss Anielka, emerged from the *People's Inn* like the goddess Aphrodite from sea foam. She approached the red Mustang, opened the door, and sat behind the wheel. Engineer Zegadlo followed her every move with stunned admiration. And when the beautiful lady put the key in the ignition, and the engine purred almost imperceptibly, it seemed that master engineer Zegadlo's heart also began to beat in a new and joyful rhythm.

"Now, this is a car!" he whispered as if in a trance.

The red Mustang pulled out from its parking spot with a magnificent and almost soundless lunge. It turned around at Frombork's market square and then sped off in the direction of Branievo. After a few seconds, it disappeared from sight.

And when it was gone, it seemed that the sun stopped shining for master engineer Zegadlo. His face grew sad. He hung his head in melancholy and said:

"I wish I had a car like that..."

And he fell silent. Miss Ala took advantage of this moment to direct our conversation to another topic.

"Has Dr. Parsley found his treasure yet?" she asked.

I started to tell the story of the dousing wand but did not have the time to finish because a boy in a Boy Scout uniform ran up and, saluting me, asked:

"Are you Mr. Thomas?"

"Yes."

"Commander Bashka has ordered us to find you and report that a red Mustang had kidnapped the old man."

"What?" I gasped.

"I actually do not know what this means," replied the boy. "But Bashka told us to find you and give you this report."

Master engineer Zegadlo heard the boy's words as well. He didn't know what they meant, either, but he understood that someone had kidnapped someone else, and that meant that he had to go to the rescue. Or maybe he also wanted to show off his gung-ho spirit and the road qualities of his Opel?

He shouted in a thundering voice:

"Someone kidnapped someone else? Mount up, ladies and gentlemen! We will catch the red Mustang! Jump into my car, and I'll catch the bandit."

I shook my head.

"If you don't mind, I'll drive mine. Anyway, we don't even know what direction the red Mustang took. We must first talk to my friends who've been watching over the old man."

Our engines roared. I moved first, and Master Engineer Zegadlo and Ala followed. I led the way to the old man's house.

As soon as I entered Stara Street, Waltzing Zosha and Bashka jumped out onto the curbside. I braked. Their report was short. They realized that every second was precious.

"Two men came to visit the old man, and then a red Mustang pulled up, driven by Miss Anielka, that sexy acquaintance of Dr. Parsley. Later, one of the men led the old man out of the house and packed him into the Mustang. And Miss Anielka got behind the wheel, and they drove off."

"Er? Why do you think the old man was kidnapped?" I asked.

"There were what you would call *big clues*, I suppose," said Bashka. "His hands were tied, and he seemed to resist. The man had to push him into the car. It seems rather clear that Batura does not want us to learn the location of the Devil's Tree."

"Which way did they go?"

"They took the road for Branievo. I heard Miss Anielka say: 'We have to fill up,' so I think they first went to the gas station on the road to Branievo."

I shrugged my shoulders.

"Who sets out to kidnap a man with an empty tank?"

Zegadlo was of a different opinion.

"What are you saying, Mr. Thomas? Even criminals forget to tank sometimes. Mount up, ladies and gentlemen! Mount up! I'm sure we'll catch up with the Mustang at the station. Leave that old hearse of yours because it's only going to slow us down. We will have to fly."

I shook my head.

"Your Opel will never catch up with the Mustang. Would you like to ride with me?" I turned to Ala.

My voice must have sounded very insistent because Ala got into my vehicle. Waltzing Zosha and Bashka also jumped in.

I started the engine and stepped on the gas. My vehicle jumped forward like a spurred racehorse. We took off in the direction of the gas station, and the Master Engineer's blue Opel followed us some distance behind.

At least a quarter of an hour must have passed since the kidnapping of Dombrovski, and yet, when we arrived at the gas station, the Mustang was still there. Miss Anielka had filled up, raised the hood, and was adding engine oil. Something gave me the odd impression that she was... waiting for us.

I saw immediately that there were no passengers in the Mustang. There was only a large bundle on the back seat, covered with a blanket.

I jumped out of my vehicle and approached Miss Hourglass. As I approached, I looked inside her car. And then something unexpected happened. The blanket stirred as if someone underneath were trying to break free. For a moment I saw a flash of someone's face. I thought I recognized the thick moustache of Mr. Dombrovski. It seemed clear: the man who had pushed Dombrovski into the car got off somewhere along the way, and the bound old man was pushed into the back seat and covered with a blanket. He was now trying to break free.

"Just a moment, ma'am," I said to Anielka. "Can we have a word with you?"

Miss Anielka seemed to have realized that I had spotted the old man. She closed the oil cap, slammed the hood shut, and jumped behind the wheel.

I grabbed the door of her car, and Master Engineer Zegadlo, who had just arrived at the station, grabbed the other. But the Mustang had already started rolling, and we had to let go of the door handles.

The Mustang's tires squealed. The car swung out of the station and took off down the road toward Frombork, and then, tires squealing again, turned onto the highway for Elblong. I jumped into my vehicle and sped after the Mustang. Behind came Master Engineer Zegadlo in his blue Opel.

In Frombork, I slowed down because we were in a built-up area with a 30-mile speed limit. Zegadlo seized the opportunity to pass me and to forge ahead.

"Ah, this wreck of yours!" growled Ala. "We should have gone in the Opel!"

I muttered through clenched teeth:

"We'll see about that, ma'am. My vehicle can sometimes be a *very good car*."

She pretended to chuckle, but I think she found my joke very silly.

The road to Vezhno is narrow, winding, and tree-lined. None of us could go too fast, and it would have been sheer madness to try to overtake. So we drove one behind the other: the Mustang, the Opel, and me, waiting for an opportunity to take off: the Mustang to pull away, the Opel to overtake the Mustang and block its way, and I—to overtake the Opel and the Mustang.

"You said," I called back to Waltzing Zosha and Bashka, "that two men entered Dombrovski's house, but only one man led him out. What happened to the other man?

"Perhaps he stayed in the house?" Waltzing Zosha offered.

"That's odd. Very odd," I muttered. "And even that man disappeared. This kidnapping looks very suspicious to me."

"Any kidnapping is suspicious," said Ala. "Maybe they figured Anielka would be able to carry the bound old man away all on her own. Perhaps the two men had other business to attend to? They are looking for Koenig's treasure, aren't they? They bundled off the old man so that neither you nor Parsley could interview him and extract information. To achieve this, Anielka alone was enough. They stayed in Frombork."

"Maybe," I nodded but sensed a nagging doubt. Still, there was no more time to talk: we got on the Elblong highway, and, to my surprise, the Mustang took off in the direction of the Soviet Border.

A few words of explanation are necessary here. In the years leading up to World War II, the Germans had begun the construction of a huge, four-lane highway to connect Elblong and Königsberg—now Kaliningrad in the USSR.[14] They managed to complete only one section of this project, however: the highway has only two lanes, and the construction of the second has been abandoned.

Like any highway, this one has no intersections; all crossroads go either under it or over it via specially built tunnels or bridges. The exits have their own lanes so as not to slow the traffic, which means that one can really step on the gas here.

But the Elblong-Königsberg highway is empty today because, since the liquidation of Prussia and its division between Poland and the Soviet Union in 1945, it no longer serves any purpose. Polish-Soviet border crossings are elsewhere, and the locals use other roads—roads that actually go places they want to go.

Nevertheless, this was the road on which our race now took place. There were still several miles of empty highway between us and the border. I do not know what the maximum speed of a Ford Mustang is, but after just a few minutes of driving on the highway, I noticed that my speedometer went over a hundred miles per hour. But even this was not the end. The Mustang kept on accelerating, and the blue Opel began to fall behind.

And then an event took place that elicited a sigh of contentment from Ala's lips and cast Master Engineer Zegadlo into such astonishment that he nearly ditched his car.

Of course, by the time she saw my speedometer touch a hundred miles per hour, Miss Ala began to blink her eyes in

---

[14] In the Kaliningrad enclave, part of Russia today.

astonishment because, in her head, she could not imagine that the *hearse* could reach such a speed. But then I pressed the accelerator even harder.

The three hundred and fifty mechanical horses of my vehicle's Ferrari 410 Superamerica engine howled and took off with a kick. We were squeezed into our seats. The car's yellow blood gushed into the car's twelve cylinders. Its two carburetors pumped the rich oxygen-gasoline breath into their vast and hungry mouths.

One hundred and ten. One hundred twenty. One hundred and thirty. One hundred and forty.

I overtook the Opel with as much ease as a downhill cyclist overtakes a walking man. I overtook the red Mustang with as much ease as a cyclist overtakes a peasant wagon.

"This... *vehicle* of yours," exclaimed Miss Ala, "I think it's... enchanted."

Overtaking the Mustang, I glanced at Miss Anielka. Surprisingly, she was neither astonished nor horrified. I could almost swear that something like a triumphant smile appeared on her face.

"Could it be that she has somehow won?" the idea flashed through my mind.

But barely did my vehicle find itself in front of the Mustang, I saw a huge red sign before me:

BORDER ZONE

and a minute later—we were really flying by now—I saw far ahead of us the row of red-and-white border posts. Closer to us, there was a barrier across the road and a uniformed and armed border guard.

At the sight of the two cars flying towards him, the sentry snatched his automatic pistol from his shoulder and placed his hand on its butt with a very transparent gesture. The two speeding cars had given him the impression that their owners intended to ignore the border and ram the Soviet Union.

I slammed the brakes, and the Hourglass Lady in the Mustang

did the same. All eight of our tires squealed, and my vehicle rocked a little, but I managed to stop at least two hundred feet before the barrier. When I looked in the rearview mirror, I saw the hood of the Mustang just ten feet behind me. I jumped out of the vehicle and ran up to the red car. I didn't care to speak to the driver—I wanted to free the old man, kidnapped and kept under a blanket in the back seat.

But what I saw instead—was beyond all my imagination.

I felt as if someone had suddenly poured a bucket of cold water over me. Or as if I had suddenly, in broad daylight, seen a ghost.

Lo and behold, behind the wheel of the red Mustang sat Miss Anielka, smiling at me with her most endearing smile. And in the back seat, comfortably stretched out and smoking a cigarette, sat... Valdemar Batura. The blanket lay neatly folded beside him.

Yet, back at the gas station, we had all seen the old man tied up; we saw his mustache; we saw how he struggled to get out from under the blanket. And from that moment on, we never lost sight of the red Mustang: we stayed on its tail the whole way. And for all this, somehow, along the way from Frombork, Mr. Dombrovski disappeared, and Valdemar Batura appeared in his place.

How could we not feel stunned?

And while we stood there next to the red Mustang, looking at Valdemar Batura in mute silence, the blue Opel caught up with us and out of it jumped out Zegadlo, Master Engineer. He no longer cared about the red Mustang, much less its passengers. He was only interested in my vehicle.

"Good Lord!" he called out pleadingly. "Good Lord! I have to see under your hood! What have you got in there? Witches' brooms? I've never seen anything like it. What speed! What speed! What a magnificent machine!" he half-moaned with delight, for he loved cars more than anything else in life.

I returned to my vehicle and lifted its hood. The Master Engineer counted the cylinders with the utmost devotion and stroked the carburetors, the cables that supplied electricity to the plugs, the alternator, the V-belts on the alternator, and the blazing-hot radiator. He stroked them with the shy tenderness of a youthful lover.

And in the meantime, Batura put on a show of complete indifference. With a cigarette in the corner of his mouth, he got out of the Mustang, took a few steps toward me, and said:

"Thomas, Thomas. I had known, of course, that you have an excellent car. But I didn't expect it to be this fast. It is indeed a wonderful machine. I will never risk racing against you again."

"Where is Mr Dombrovski?" I growled. "You kidnapped him! What did you do with him?"

Valdemar Batura curled his lips in an expression of distaste.

"Mr. Dombrovski? The old man from Stara Street? Kidnap him? Me? Why would I ever do such a thing? Do you see him anywhere here?"

And he opened his arms in a sweeping gesture as if inviting me to search.

I felt giddy.

The world is an illusion, I thought, recalling Cagliostro's words. And Batura continued:

"Kidnapping! Tisk, tisk! Thomas! You forgot that I, like you, abhor brute force! I value brains, intelligence, creativity. It is not my custom to kidnap anyone or force anyone to do something they do not want to do."

"Where is he then?" I shouted threateningly. Valdemar Batura smiled patiently.

"I know how you value honesty, dear Thomas. Therefore, I will tell you the truth. I did not kidnap Mr. Dombrovski. Instead, I gave him a reward for informing me about the location of the Devil's Tree. I offered him a two-week vacation in one of our beautiful Polish resorts. I paid for his stay and gave him the tickets for the journey."

Batura glanced at his watch and said:

"Now, just as we speak, the Krinitsa ferry is leaving from the Frombork harbor. Though, mind you, I do not say that Mr. Dombrovski is on board. Because you see, ten minutes ago, a train left the Frombork train station for Gdansk, from where there are connections to Zakopane, Lower Silesia, and Kolobzheg. Still, I do not say that Mr. Dombrovski has departed on that train, either, for in five minutes, another train will leave for Olshtin, from where it is easy to catch a connecting train for Bialystok. From Olshtin, one can also catch a bus to any of our great lake resorts. And what about Byeshchady? That area has been quite popular of late. One way or another, I swear to you, Thomas, you will find our Mr. Dombrovski in one of our beautiful holiday resorts.

"But if searching for him seems pointless to you, have patience and wait. I swear that in two weeks, Mr. Dombrovski, healthy and hale, will appear in Frombork and will probably be happy to tell you where the tree called *Teufelsbaum* had once stood. Unfortunately, there is nothing more I can do for you."

I lost. I lost the second round against Valdemar Batura. Once again, he outsmarted me and now he stood before me, smiling his most charming smile and *mocking* me.

"I'm sorry, dear Thomas," Batura said, "that you ended up here, in this back of beyond. But I think you'll admit that I didn't *tell* you to drive out here; in fact, I did nothing to make you do so: I just put on a mustache and went for a drive, all perfectly innocent activities. All the same, please understand my situation: you set up sentries around the old man's house. How could he catch his ferry or his train unobserved? So, you see, I had to play the role of a kidnapped old man. I lay down under this blanket in the back seat of this car. I could have led you all the way to Elblong or Malbork. I could have meandered and backtracked. But I know that you live on a modest salary, and Director Marchak will never reimburse you for the high-octane gasoline you just burnt. Taking into account the state of your finances, I decided to head for the border. And now we will all return to Frombork in the greatest harmony. What do you say, Thomas?"

Having said this, Valdemar Batura bowed to Miss Ala, to Waltzing Zosha, to me, and to Bashka. He got into the red Mustang, which turned and took off in the direction of Frombork.

"You were right," whispered Bashka. "Batura is brilliant."

How bitter is the taste of defeat! I hung my head and did not perk up even though Zegadlo continued to *ooh* and *aah* over my engine. My triumph over Zegadlo was nothing compared to the triumph that Batura had achieved over me.

Bashka and Zosha tried to cheer me up:

"Don't worry, Mr. Thomas. After all, Mr. Dombrovski is probably not the only old resident of Frombork from before the war. Maybe someone else here who knows the place where the Koenig house once stood?"

Miss Ala touched my shoulder and said in a warm voice:

"If you ever need my help, look for me in the ravine near the Devil's Mountain, and then follow the path along the edge of the forest. That path will lead you to a long barracks fenced off with chicken wire. You will find me there. And now I would very much like you to explain to me what it was that I have just seen. Who is this Batura? Why did he pretend to kidnap the old man? And how is it that you are not looking for Colonel Koenig's treasure, but at the same time, you are looking for it?"

Explanations were due. The master engineer was still busy studying my engine, so I had time to tell Ala about the case of the priceless coins and my suspicions about Batura.

I did not think that her help would ever be of much use to me.

But I was wrong this time, too.

CHAPTER 11: A TREE OF BAD INFORMATION

After my defeat. The Thirteen Years' War. How the Masurian people became Lutheran. The curse. Can I count to twenty? The world is an illusion. A tree of bad information. Attempting to drown in the bathroom sink.

Ala and Zegadlo departed for the Land of the Terrible ACE. Bashka and Waltzing Zosha returned to their camps, and I ate dinner alone in the PTTK hostel. I didn't even look in my room for fear of running into Cagliostro and throwing in his face: "You Judas!"

Clearly, having overheard my conversation with the Scouts, he relayed its contents to Batura, who then immediately set about making the old man disappear.

I was exhausted by the overwhelming feeling of defeat. I wanted to rethink what I was doing, and instead of going back to my room, I went for a walk through Frombork. Solitary walks stimulate positive thinking.

It was evening. As if in despair, seagulls were screaming on the shore of the Lagoon. A passenger ferry arrived at the quay from Tolkmitsko, and for a moment, the small port became crowded. Then, sailboats from the local yacht club began to return from a day on the water, and I could hear the loud conversations of the sailors on the still evening air.

Darkness seeped into the streets of the town, spilling over the empty lots where houses, destroyed in the war, had once stood and in whose place beautiful flowerbeds now wafted their scents.

Strolling from the port towards the Cathedral Hill, I gradually succumbed to the charm of the evening. And although I tried to concentrate on the topic of Koenig's second cache, my thoughts drifted to completely different and distant matters.

I was in Frombork, the old capital of the region of Varmia; and Varmia had once been a region at the heart of the Teutonic State. The Teutonic Order, founded in Palestine during the Crusades, had come to this country in the thirteenth century to make war on the local pagan people known as Old Prussians. It made a quick job of ethnically cleansing them—murdering some and driving away others—and bringing in new settlers from Germany and Poland to take their place. It then began to make war on its Christian neighbors—Poland and Lithuania and, with the support of the Pope and of the German emperor, it soon grew into a dominant power in Eastern Europe.

A hundred-year war for survival followed between the Teutonic Order on the one hand and the united nations of Poland and Lithuania on the other. After initial successes, the order was dealt a devastating defeat in 1410 at the battle of Grunwald, the greatest battle of the European Middle Ages.

Yaghello (Polish: Jagiełło, Lithuanian: Jogaila) (1352–1434)
Grand Duke of Lithuania and King of Poland dealt a devastating defeat to the Teutonic Order at the battle of Grunwald in 1410, the biggest battle of the European Middle Ages.

Then, forty years later, Yaghello's son, King Casimir, fought another war with the Teutonic Knights, a war known in history as the Thriteen

Years' War (1454-1466). That war had started as a rebellion of the ordinary citizens of the Teutonic Order—its landowners, peasants, and city burghers—who formed an association and invited the king of Poland to depose their masters. Why did they do it? To put it simply, they had grown tired of the arbitrary and autocratic rule of the Order and its heavy taxation, and they looked to the liberties and low tax burden enjoyed by Polish subjects as an attractive alternative.

In the course of the Thirteen Years' War, King Casimir summarily defeated the order, and the Treaty of Thorn in 1466 returned Gdansk and Pomerania to Poland and handed to it the Vistula Delta, the cities of Malbork and Elblong, and the entire bishopric of Varmia, leaving only Masuria in the hands of the Order. And the Order was obliged to recognize the King of Poland as its feudal master.

But why was Varmia handed over to Poland? If you look at the map, you will see that Varmia lay at the heart of the Teutonic State and was not even contiguous with Poland; nor had it ever belonged to the Polish Crown before, so why was it handed over to Poland now instead of some other province? The reason was simple: Varmia had been the center of the opposition to the Teutonic State, and the rebellion of 1454 started with a congress in one of its principal cities—Branievo. If any part of the Teutonic state was going to be transferred to Poland, it had to be Varmia first and foremost.

The Order continued to exist as a legal and political entity for another sixty years, and in 1525, it ceased to exist in a rather peculiar manner. In 1510, the Order elected its last Grand Master—Albert Hohenzollern, Duke of Brandenburg, a man who also happened to be the half-German/half-Polish nephew of the King of Poland. After trying for some time to win independence from Poland, in which efforts he received some support from the Pope and the German Emperor, and fighting a short and disastrous war against his uncle 1519-1522, Duke Albert decided to change tack. He turned his back on the Pope and the Emperor, made up with his uncle, King of Poland, converted to Lutheranism, and dissolved the order, seizing most of its assets for himself but making sure to share some of the loot with his top generals who also left the Catholic church and took wives. Albert now declared himself Duke of Prussia and took an oath of loyalty to the King of Poland, thereby becoming the first great oligarch in the history of Eastern Europe—a man to acquire vast state assets by questionable means.

Albert of Prussia (1490-1568), the First East-European Oligarch
The last grand master of the Teutonic Order effectively "privatized" (stole) its assets. Here: in a portrait by Lucas Cranach the Elder.

Now, it so happened that during that last Polish-Teutonic War of 1519-1521, Albert had invaded Varmia, and the local population, both German and Polish—the people who had rebelled against his Order sixty years earlier—now fought him tooth and nail, including our half-German/half-Polish hero, Nicolaus Copernicus, then residing in Olshtin. Copernicus led the defense of the Olshtin castle, and, as it turned out, the great astronomer proved a capable general, and the Teutonic Knights, after a series of fruitless assaults, had to abandon the siege.

The Teutonic Knights now shed their habits, converted to Lutheranism, took wives, and soon the bishops of Sambia and

Pomezania did the same, with parish priests following their example. In this way, one fine day, the Masurian people, from being Catholic, became Lutheran. But the people of Varmia, who had seceded from the Teutonic Order sixty years earlier, remained with the old faith. And so it remains today: for all the changes of borders which unfolded here over the centuries, Varmia remains a Catholic island in the sea of North-Eastern Poland, still to a large extent Lutheran.

Thus, pondering, I started heading back to the hostel. I was tired after a day full of frustrating adventures.

A light was on in my room. Cagliostro was sitting at the table with an innocent expression and playing a card solitaire. The snake, curled up in a circle, was sleeping on a pillow on my bed, and the white mice were running about on Cagliostro's bed. The bunny was noisily munching its carrots in its cage.

The innocent face of Cagliostro, whom I considered a traitor and a Judas, awoke a terrible anger in me. I reflected that he'd been playing all sorts of pranks on me with total impunity, and I had pretended not to know about them.

He probably thinks I am a fool, I thought to myself as my anger built up.

"Maestro," I said, looking around. "Do you not get the impression that in our absence, someone has been through our room?"

"I don't. Do you?"

"I do, as a matter of fact. As far as I remember, you had ten boxes. And now I only see nine. What happened to the tenth one?"

This momentarily surprised the maestro. I had meant the box that he had given to Batura at the harbor the night before. But he quickly regained his usual self-assurance.

"The world is an illusion," he yawned, pretending to disregard my words. "Are you sure you can count to ten?"

"Well, I do have an advanced college degree," I replied. "Admittedly, it was not the Sorbonne, but nevertheless, I think I acquired the ability to count to ten."

"Ah," he sighed, "if I am not mistaken, you are a student of the humanities. Mathematics is probably not your strongest suit?"

"All the same, I think I can count to ten."

"And up to twenty?"

"I think I can count to twenty, too, believe it or not."

"Up to twenty?" he feigned amazement. "I never suspected you of that. Counting to twenty is an extremely difficult art, and even I, who, after all, studied at the Sorbonne (and also studied with Tibetan monks), sometimes get confused when it comes to counting all the way up to twenty."

"Do you want to examine me?" I asked, feeling the hair at the nape of my neck bristling with rage.

"I will be happy to test your math skills," he stated. He got up from the table, reached into one of his nine boxes, and took out a small bag and a tray. First, he handed me a bag and asked me to untie it and look inside.

"There are coins in the pouch," I said.

"You know how to count, don't you?" Cagliostro reassured himself. "So please count the coins, taking them out of the pouch. Please take out five coins first."

I reached into the pouch and took out five coins, placing them on the tray.

"Now, please take out five more coins."

Again, I put five coins on the tray. The bag was already empty.

"So... let us see. How many coins were there in the pouch? Huh?" asked Cagliostro.

"First, I took out five coins, and then I took out another five, meaning there had been ten coins in the pouch. And here they are: one, two, three, four, five, six, seven, eight, nine, ten."

"Please check the bag carefully. Maybe you left some coin in there?" said the maestro.

I looked into the pouch, shook it, felt inside it. There was no doubt that the pouch was empty.

"So you say there were ten coins in the pouch?" said

Cagliostro, taking the pouch away from me.

"Well, yes. Five plus five is ten."

"And this is what they taught you at the university?" giggled Cagliostro.

And in one swift motion, he poured the coins from the tray back into the pouch. A second later, he poured the coins onto the tray again. Only this time, there were a lot more coins.

"Please recalculate," said the maestro.

I counted. There were eighteen coins on the tray.

"So five plus five is not ten, but eighteen," said Cagliostro.

He poured the coins into a pouch, tied the pouch with string, then tucked everything back into one of his boxes.

"Are you still sure that I had ten boxes?" he asked mockingly.

I nodded.

"You see, Mr. Thomas, the world is an illusion. Isn't it?"

After a while, looking coldly into his eyes, I said:

"One day, I will play such a trick on you that you will go back to study with the Tibetan monks. And now, maestro, I propose we go to sleep."

That said, I gently removed the sleeping snake from its pillow and transferred it to Cagliostro's bed.

I undressed and slipped under the covers. I fell asleep almost immediately, heavily and without any dreams.

How fortunate it is that man does not have the gift of predicting the future and does not know what Fate is readying for him. If I knew what fate was readying for me, I would probably not have dared to sleep.

I woke up quite early, washed and shaved. The maestro was asleep, and when I nudged him on the shoulder, he muttered that he intended to sleep until noon and was ready to forego breakfast.

So I went to the dining room alone, and since I am by nature a very sociable person and quickly forget grudges, having noticed Dr. Parsley alone, I sat down at his table.

"Any luck with Cagliostro?" I asked politely.

He swallowed a bite of bread with butter, took a sip of tea, and replied, not sensing the irony in my voice:

"The wand pointed to a number of places where there are metal objects in the ground. But, as you know, the damned archaeologists will not allow me to dig there. Anyway, this matter is no longer relevant at the moment. Koenig's second cache is elsewhere."

"Ah, so it is the Devil's Tree, after all!" I exclaimed in triumph. "You finally allowed yourself to be convinced to look for the Devil's Tree!"

He raised his eyebrows in surprise.

"What are you talking about, Thomas? The Devil's Tree? What is this satanic idea again?"

"I mean the Devil's Tree, which once grew in the front yard of Koenig's house."

He tapped his finger on his forehead.

"I've only heard of one magical tree: the tree of the Knowledge of Good and Evil, or rather, of Good and Bad Information. You, Thomas, have bad information. That's all I can say. And in connection with this Devil's Tree of yours, I advise you frankly: don't try to mislead me again. I warn you: Director Marchak is coming here from Warsaw tonight. He called me about this business. I advise you to get busy with your guide to Frombork because Director Marchak will probably want to check on your progress in that area."

He surprised me with this news. Director Marchak was coming to Frombork? What for? I have wasted the past day on a fruitless search for Koenig's second cache. What will I tell Director Marchak if he asks me about the guide?

I felt that the ground had shifted under my feet. But still, I thought it was appropriate to warn my competitor.

"Yesterday," I said, "I suggested to you that your associate, Miss Anielka, of whom you seem very fond, might be collaborating with Valdemar Batura. You were outraged at the thought and at me for suggesting as much. But today, I know this for a fact. I have seen Miss Anielka drive Valdemar Batura about town in a red Ford Mustang."

I had the story about the kidnapping of the old man at the tip of my tongue, but since there actually had been no kidnapping and since I was made a fool of, I chose to remain silent.

Dr. Parsley nodded his head in regret.

"Oh, Thomas, Thomas, you unfaithful and untrustworthy Thomas. My heart, as you say, does indeed incline towards Miss Anielka, as yours, if I'm not mistaken, gravitates toward Miss Ala. And in this context, it may sadden you to hear this. This morning, before breakfast, I went out to the newsstand to get cigarettes—and do you know what I saw? A red Mustang driven by Valdemar Batura. Next to him sat Miss Ala. I warn you, Thomas. The girl you are sweet on is cooperating with Batura."

I gasped. I was struck speechless. Ala in Batura's red Mustang?

And then I realized that I knew nothing whatsoever about Miss Ala. It was not clear to me why I had placed great trust in that pretty person. Were both Miss Anielka and Miss Ala working with Batura? I felt like Batura had completely ensnared me in a spiderweb of his agents.

I got up from the table and, like a drunk, marched to my room. I ran the water from the tap and put my head under it. For a few minutes, I let the cold water pour over my blazing head until finally, I heard a voice from Cagliostro's bed:

"Excuse me, Mr. Thomas. Are you trying to drown yourself in the sink?"

I did not say a word. I carefully wiped my head with a towel, combed my wet hair, and went out. I knocked on the door of the astronomer, Mr. P., and asked to speak to him in connection with the guidebook I was preparing. Then, until noon, I walked with Mr. P. about Frombork Hill, discussing the problem of the location of Copernicus's observatory.

And after lunch, I roamed around Cathedral Hill in the company of the historian, Mr. S., discussing the question of the location of Copernicus's observatory.

After all these conversations—it was already approaching evening—I had such chaos in my head that, again, I felt the need to go to my room and put my head under the tap. Fortunately, Cagliostro was not in the room, or he would have tried to apply artificial respiration.

CHAPTER 12: THE DEVIL'S IMAGE

The search for the Devil's Tree. What Waltzing Zosha saw. On the villain's trail. Night in the Cathedral. Entrance to the underworld. Teufelsbild, or the Devil's Image. Among coffins and skeletons. Trapped. Koenig's second cache.

An all-day search yielded good results: Bashka and Waltzing Zosha found several people who had lived in Frombork before and during the war. All of these people had known the Koenig family and pointed out the place where their house, later destroyed during hostilities, had once stood. Colonel Koenig's father, according to their accounts, was a bricklayer well-known in the area, while his son made a career in Hitler's notorious SS.

Waltzing Zosha led me to a huge square near the historic water tower. Bashka was already waiting for us there.

"So, where did the Devil's Tree grow?" I asked, looking around the square.

The boy sighed:

"This, unfortunately, no one can say. Apparently, some old trees had once grown here but were then shattered by artillery shells."

Bashka's team had cleared the square of the rubble left by the war and planted a beautiful lawn with pansies. He was proud of their work and now stood before me casting uncertain glances, now at the square, now at me.

"If you think me must," he finally said with a sigh, "we could dig it up to look for the Koenig stash."

"And destroy your work?" I said.

I shook my head.

"We do not know where the Devil's Tree grew. Digging up the whole square makes no sense. Let's leave this to Dr. Parsley. It's his job to find Koenig's loot."

Bashka was clearly relieved. The square looked beautiful, and the thought of digging it up seemed awful.

"Then I'll be off," he said hurriedly. "We have an event at the camp tonight. Scouts from another unit are coming for a visit."

Waltzing Zosha and I remained in the square. She was her unit's chronicler and had more free time.

As usual, she was unable to stand in place. She kept spinning in place as if inviting me to dance. The thought of dancing a waltz with Zosha on the square where the Devil Tree once grew seemed so comical that I laughed out loud. My laughter worried her.

"It's a good thing that you decided to leave this business to Dr. Parsley, but you're not going to sit on your hands, are you?'

"Ha! I believe you are angling for an adventure?" I guessed.

"Of course," she said. "I must have something to write about in my chronicle!"

"Never fear. The adventure will come to us on its own. Let's let Dr. Parsley trouble himself with the treasure, and let us… turn our attention to the person of our friend, Valdemar Batura."

"Your friend?"

"Oh, yes. The thought of this man keeps me awake at night," I said with much exaggeration because, so far, I had slept rather well. "I am sure that he is behind the mystery of the priceless coins. So far, my instincts have been right: I guessed Batura would be here, and lo and behold, here he is. But where? Where is he hiding? If you have some time, Zosha, could you look around Frombork, and if you spot Batura, let me know? I'll be at my hostel."

"Aye, aye, sir," she saluted, shook my hand, and danced off in the direction of her camp by the Lagoon while I entered a bookstore next to the water tower. I decided to look for a German-Polish dictionary, for it occurred to me that by going through its entries one by one, I might be able to discover more instances of that mysterious *Teufelb*. If *Teufelb* did not stand for *Teufuelsberg* or *Teufelsbaum*, then what did it stand for?

The bookstore was tiny and had no German dictionary, but it did have an album of reproductions of paintings. It was expensive, definitely not for my pocket, so I only skimmed through it before leaving for the hostel.

Remembering the imminent arrival of Director Marchak, I sat down to organize the notes I had taken while talking with the astronomer and the historian: the new Frombork guide had to take into account the latest research on Frombork.

I had been working for some time when I heard a knock. The door swung open, and Waltzing Zosha stuck her head into the room.

"I just saw Valdemar Batura," she declared.

"Where?" I jumped up from the table.

"In the old moat by the cathedral. He seemed to be waiting for someone."

I left my notebook on the table, and Waltzing Zosha and I ran out of the hostel, crossed its garden, and descended the steep stone steps leading down to the path at the foot of Cathedral Hill.

It was already late evening. We stopped halfway and looked down at the sparsely lit street. In the glow of a distant streetlight, I saw the slim silhouette of a man. Yes, it was Valdemar Batura. He wore a leather jacket and was smoking a cigarette. He, indeed, did seem to be waiting for someone. Maybe for Cagliostro?

But now, he suddenly looked up and saw us on the stairs. He quickly threw down his cigarette, put it out with his foot, and marched up the alley that, as we knew it, climbed up to Cathedral Hill. He immediately disappeared from our sight, but in the silence of the evening, we heard the sound of his footsteps.

It has long been my objective to find Batura's hideout. So we now moved speedily forward so as not to lose sight of him. But just as we reached the bottom of the moat, he was already up on the hill and disappeared behind the corner of the octagonal tower. Obviously, he had been up to something and was now trying to lose us.

We ran around the tower and saw him disappear through the main gate of the fortress. Why did he flee from us into the courtyard of the Cathedral rather than towards the city? I didn't stop to think about it; I just sped up. Zosha and I reached the gate and found ourselves in the cathedral courtyard.

It was very dark. The moon hung over the Lagoon, but the

mighty Gothic cathedral cast a deep shadow over the yard.

For a moment, we stopped helplessly, trying in vain to see something in the dark. Then, a sound reached our ears from the side of the passage between the chapter house and the cathedral. It seemed to us that someone was walking under its arched roof, heading for the northern part of the courtyard, between the cathedral and the northern wall.

I didn't have a flashlight with me, and it was so dark I could barely see my hand. The great black mass of the cathedral loomed before us, its contour outlined only by the dim light emanating from a window in the museum in the bishop's palace. The glow from the window illuminated an area of just a few feet before it, and the rest of the world was sunk in impenetrable darkness. We wandered through the dark until we found ourselves under the arched passageway.

The northern part of the courtyard was a little brighter for although the high defensive wall obscured the moon, its light reflected off the walls of the cathedral diffused in the air about us.

Tourists rarely visit this part of the fortress. It is like a narrow street between the wall and the church. Tall grass grows here, and through it runs a narrow path. We could see almost to the end of the alley, up to the historic curia buildings backed against the far wall. If our ears hadn't been mistaken and Batura had entered this passage, we should have seen him now: even if he had run, he would not have been able to reach the end of the passage. Yet, Batura was nowhere to be seen. We moved forward, looking around in all directions and paying particular attention to dark niches in the walls of the Cathedral. There were quite a few of these, and a man could easily hide in the shadows of one of them.

In one, we found an iron door leading into the cathedral. It seemed to be locked and gave the impression of not having been used for many years. But since Batura seemed to have vanished into the thin air, it seemed a good idea to try the door. Waltzing Zosha grabbed the door handle. And the door... swung open easily without even a rustle, as if its hinges had been freshly oiled.

I lit a match, and we saw a narrow corridor leading to a side aisle of the cathedral. We entered the aisle, but the match went out in my fingers: we were again surrounded by complete darkness.

And now, imagine the massive hall of the cathedral at night. A little moonlight diffused through the narrow, tall windows overhead, everything else plunged into complete darkness. If Batura had entered here—and it seemed that he might have—looking for him was a waste of time. There were hundreds of places here where he could hide: pillars, altars, niches, chapels, confessionals, stalls, pews, the chancel, the pulpit, side aisles, the choir with the organ. And I did not even have a flashlight. Matches dispelled the darkness for ten feet at most. And when they went out, the darkness became even deeper.

We stood in a side aisle, listening. Perhaps Batura would make some noise? But there was such a complete silence in the church that it seemed to ring in our ears. Our breathing seemed terribly loud to us.

All we could see in the dark was the eternal red light over the altar, which, in Catholic churches, symbolizes the presence of the Holy Spirit. I was already thinking about leaving the cathedral, closing the iron door, standing guard at it myself, and sending Waltzing Zosha to find the sexton or the parish priest to inform him that a thief had snuck into the cathedral. But before this decision matured in me, we both saw a faint glow somewhere to the right of the main altar.

And immediately, without whispering or giving each other any sign, we both began to creep in that direction. We crossed the aisle, and we saw that the light was coming from behind another iron door in the wall—this one opened a crack. Could it be that Batura had gone into some side room? But why did he not close the door behind him?

Waltzing Zosha opened the door wide, and it creaked ominously with a grim sepulchral squeak. We saw a small landing and a narrow winding staircase leading down. I guessed it led to the underground crypt. A candle stub was burning in a small niche on the landing. We had seen its light from far away. It now illuminated the landing and the staircase.

My heart began to beat very fast.

We were on the trail of some unusual mystery. A stairway to the underground... at night. Lost in the dark. With only the light of a candle to go by! Can you imagine a better treat for a professional adventurer?

I did not hesitate for a moment. I stepped onto the platform and took the candle from its niche. I went first, followed by Waltzing Zosha, and we began our descent into the underground.

After a few turns, the stairs reached a level floor, and behold, in the dim light of the candle, we saw a rather large crypt with a vaulted ceiling.

It was filled with coffins.

They stood side by side, tightly crowded together, and in places lay one on top of another.

Most were clearly baroque in style. One of the coffins, crushed by the others standing on top of it, had collapsed and revealed its interior—a human skeleton grinning at us with its yellowed teeth.

In a corner of the crypt, I saw a half-open coffin in which the human remains that had fallen out of other coffins had been collected. In total disarray, there lay tibias, ribs, skulls, and a whole desiccated corpse of some canon, still wearing the tarnished remains of a black cassock.

A little further, against the wall, was a stone tablet; it must have fallen or been removed from some wall, and it now stood there, keeled over forlornly. A carved skeleton looked at us from the tablet and, pointing a finger at us, said in a Latin inscription:

WHAT YOU ARE, I WAS.
WHAT I AM, YOU WILL BE

Our breaths moved the candle flame, and the shadows we cast danced on the walls and the vaulted ceiling of the crypt. It seemed to us that some black figures were creeping out from behind the coffins and beckoning to us.

"Oh, God! Look!" groaned Waltzing Zosha and grabbed my hand.

I followed her gaze. She was looking at a terrible effigy of the devil embedded in the wall of the crypt. It was a bas-relief of a monstrously ugly face, half-man, half-animal with horns. Its mouth was open, and it leered at us, showing sparse, sharp teeth.

Around the bas-relief, I saw a red line, a trace of freshly chipped plaster. Not long ago, someone had tried to remove the bas-relief from the wall. A hammer and chisel were still lying on the ground.

"What is *that*?" asked Zosha, terrified.

"Why, Zosha. This is a *Teufelsbild*," I said with the sinking feeling of realization. "The Devil's Image. Behind this image lies Colonel Koenig's second cache."

"So, you found Koenig's second cache?" whispered Zosha cheerfully.

"Me?" I shrugged and added bitterly:

"No, Zosha. Batura has found Koenig's second cache. And now he brought me here on purpose."

"What do you say? I will immediately run for the boys, for Dr. Parsley. We will recover the treasure!" whispered the girl feverishly.

I sadly nodded my head.

"I think we'd be better off looking for some comfortable place to spend the night while the candle is still on. Once it burns out, it will be completely dark in here."

"Why? Why can't we just go out the way we came?"

"I don't think we can, Zosha. If I understand the situation correctly, the door at the top of the stairs is already locked. We will have to spend the night here."

She did not believe me. She took the candle stub out of my hand and went up the stairs. After a while, she returned to the crypt.

"You are right," she whispered. "Someone locked the door behind us. And what... What will happen now?"

"It seems to me that we will be most comfortable in that corner," I said.

"And no one will free us from here?" she was now getting seriously frightened.

"Oh, no! Someone will free us. Tomorrow morning, I guess. Tomorrow morning, the opera continues," I said in an indifferent voice.

"Who locked us in here?"

"Valdemar Batura, of course."

"But why?"

"You will soon find out, but I think you can guess. It is the same story as with old Mr. Dombrovski. Batura has led me by the nose. He has made a fool of me again."

"I see. But we can now look into that compartment behind the bas-relief. We have a hammer and a chisel."

"Yes, but the candle is about to go out. Besides, Zosha, that would be doing exactly what Batura wants us to do. And I take you for my witness that I did not even touch the chisel or the hammer; and that I did not try to look behind the bas-relief."

"I don't understand."

I sighed.

"See the red crack around the stone panel? Batura has been here before us. He has taken the panel off the wall. I'm sure he has robbed the cache, and I don't want to go near it now, or the suspicion will fall on me."

I took off my coat and headed to a corner of the gloomy crypt to make a bed.

"No, not there. There are coffins and skeletons there," groaned Zosha.

"There are coffins and skeletons everywhere here," I stated reassuringly. "Do not be afraid of the dead. They are truly dead and cannot possibly harm us. They have been lying here quietly for centuries, indifferent to us and the world, sleeping their eternal sleep."

I folded my coat and put it in the corner of the crypt. I sat down on it and made room for Zosha by my side. The girl reached out to hold my hand. She was tall for a thirteen year old but she really was just a child.

"Are you not afraid?" she finally asked, to overcome her own fear.

"No, Zosha. I have already told you that I am not afraid of the dead."

The candle began to die down slowly. Zosha looked around the crypt.

"Do you think Copernicus lies here?" she asked.

"No. These coffins are mostly Baroque in design, and Copernicus lived during the Renaissance. Coffins reflect the style of their era. Gothic coffins are different, Renaissance coffins are different, and Baroque coffins are different. For example, Gothic coffins are angular, trapezoidal boxes. And these, as you can see, have full, rounded, gentle bulges."

"So, are you really not afraid?"

"No. How about you?"

"Me?" she wondered. "I don't think I'm afraid either. Besides, I really wanted to experience an adventure. And this is a real adventure, isn't it? When I tell the girls that I spent a night in a crypt, among coffins and skeletons, no one will want to believe me," she mused aloud.

And knowing that she would soon be telling her friends about her adventure seemed to give her courage. All the same, she never let go of my hand.

And now we sat there in silence for a long time, watching as the burning candle faded, the flame diminished, and the crypt began to darken.

"I shouldn't be afraid of the dark," Zosha suddenly spoke up. "My father is a miner. Coal mines are a real maze of very dark passages. Miners carry special lamps with them, but all the same, they spend half their lives in the dark."

"They are brave, aren't they?"

"Oh yes. And it isn't just the dark. Mines are actually dangerous. There are gases, and sometimes the ground shifts. And sometimes there is a fire. I am a miner's daughter and should be brave."

With these words, she seemed to regain courage.

The candle sizzled and went out. Maybe it was even better that way: we stopped seeing the coffins surrounding us on all sides.

And now there was complete silence. I could hear my own heartbeat. Then, as the chill of the crypt began to penetrate our bodies, I took off my jacket and covered the girl with it.

Zosha put her head on my shoulder and continued to hold my hand. Her grip was strong, but then, gradually, it eased. I guessed that she had fallen asleep.

But I couldn't sleep for a long time.

Maybe because it was so cold.

Or maybe because I suddenly understood all the mistakes I had made.

CHAPTER 13: FIVE SILVER CUPS

We are released. Dr. Parsley accuses me. What he was hiding. Second cache. Five silver cups. Everything turns against me. Cagliostro knows nothing. The Director's shoe and the Snake Spirit. Breakfast with the Director. Where Copernicus made his observations. I confront the traitor.

I don't know how long I slept. I was awakened by the sound of footsteps overhead. Someone, even several someones, were walking on the stone floor above the crypt. I looked at the phosphorescent hands of my watch: it was approaching six in the morning. Here, of course, it was still as dark as the inside of a tomb—which, of course, it was.

Zosha also woke up.

"*Brrr*, how cold I am," she whispered and shuddered, shaken by the chill of the crypt.

We heard the creak of the door, then footsteps on the stairs. A light flashed, and a moment later, three people entered the crypt: Dr. Parsley, Director Marchak, and an older, hunched-over man holding a thick, burning candle.

They saw us sitting against the wall of the crypt.

Dr. Parsley said:

"And what did I say, Director? As soon as I learned from Mr. Sexton here that a key to the crypt had gone missing, I immediately became suspicious.'

I stood up from the ground and straightened my back. After a night spent in an uncomfortable position, I could feel every bone in my body.

The man with a candle approached me.

"Why did you steal the key to the crypt?"

At this, Dr. Parsley erupted in irritation.

"Do you hear, Director? Thomas was supposed to write the Frombork guide, but instead, he is looking for Koenig's treasure. And by what methods? By theft!"

Director Marchak studied me, creasing his eyebrows threateningly.

"It seems you have some explaining to do, Mr. Thomas."

I yawned, gently rubbing my sore bones.

"I have certainly not stolen the key," I declared. "Valdemar Batura and his gang are in town, Director. Our friend here, Zosha, spotted him in town, and I followed him, hoping to discover his hideout. Instead, he led me here, into the underground, and then locked the door behind me. And here I am."

"What are you talking about?" Dr. Parsley was outraged. "You saw it yourself, Mr. Director: the door was unlocked, and the key was in the lock!"

"Oh? Was the door unlocked?" I was surprised. "I see. That can only mean that Batura unlocked the door before you arrived."

Dr. Parsley pointed to the *Teufelsbild* on the wall and the chisel and hammer on the ground.

"I see Thomas has already managed to get to the cache."

"Not at all," I replied. "I haven't gone near it. When we entered, the chisel and hammer were already lying on the ground, and that red crack around the panel was already there. I take our friend Zosha as my witness."

Director Marchak blushed at the sight of the girl shivering from the cold. He stroked her head, then turned on me:

"How are you not ashamed to take a child with you on overnight missions? See how frozen she is."

"Sir," said Zosha quickly, "this wasn't a planned overnight mission. Mr. Thomas did not plan to stay here overnight at all! Someone locked us up in here. Mr. Thomas is telling the truth."

Dr. Parsley started waving his hands angrily again.

"I don't believe it!" he shouted. "I don't believe a word of it. Young ladies know how to lie very well. I know. I lied a lot when I was in school."

Director Marchak did not voice his opinion, for, like any

superior worth his mettle, he was a cautious man and did not make hasty decisions.

"Let's take a look at Koenig's cache," he suggested. "This is why I came here. So this is the *Teufelsbild*," he added, looking at the devil's face.

Dr. Parsley grabbed the chisel and hammer. With great eagerness, he set about removing the stone image from the wall. The work went quickly because someone—Batura, of course—had already done it before. With little effort, Dr. Parsley removed the panel from the wall.

Behind it, in a stone niche, we saw four beautiful miniature paintings: one, at first glance, appeared to come from Holbein's studio. In a large box, wrapped in old, war-time German newspapers, was a table service of Sèvres porcelain. The cache also contained twelve artfully crafted Baroque candlesticks exquisitely worked in silver. Next to them stood five silver mass chalices of what I thought was rather primitive workmanship.

All of these items, with the exception of the chalices, were of great museum value.

"Well, well, fortunately, nothing has been lost. Koenig's inventory checks out down to the last item," said exultant Dr. Parsley. "I hope, Mr. Director, that in the minutes of the opening of the cache, you will spell it out that I am the discoverer of the hoard. After all, I was the person to notify you by phone concerning the discovery and to ask you to come here. Meanwhile, Thomas appeared on the spot uninvited. But it wasn't he, but I, Parsley, who discovered Koenig's second cache."

"I will make a note of this," Director Marchak said as he calligraphed the protocol busily in his notebook.

I offered shyly:

"In my view, the chalices should be gold and set with precious stones. But these are silver and of little value. One can purchase such chalices very cheaply in state antique stores."

"What's that?" objected astonished Dr. Parsley. "How do you know that these chalices should be gold? Were you present when

Koenig cataloged them?"

"Obviously not. But I don't think anyone goes to a great length to hide things of little value. As we know, Mass chalices have sometimes been gold and sometimes set with expensive stones. I think a robber like Koenig would have looked for such chalices, not for ordinary silver cups."

"But you can't be sure!" Parsley declared triumphantly. "You are only trying to diminish my success. And you wish to sow confusion in our Director's mind. Do you know anything about these chalices for a fact, or are you just speculating?"

"No, I do not know anything for a fact," I answered honestly. "And no, I cannot be sure; I *am* only speculating. On the other hand, I do know that someone has been here before us and has opened the cache. And I assume he did not do it for curiosity's sake."

"But you can't be sure," repeated Parsley angrily. "These are just your assumptions."

"Calm down, gentlemen," Director Marchak intervened. "If you have complaints or suspicions, please settle them with me later. For now, sign this protocol."

And he gave the protocol to the sexton, Dr. Parsley, Waltzing Zosha, and me to sign. And then he signed it himself.

"I would very much like to ask, Mr. Director," Dr. Parsley said, "that you indicate in the postscript to the protocol that we found Thomas and the girl at the site of the treasure."

Director Marchak added the amendment. With this little touch, Batura's wily plan was brought to completion. I had been trapped. Any suspicion I put forward regarding the integrity of the find would automatically turn against me. I would never be able to prove that the chisel and hammer were not mine and that I did not touch the Devil's Image at all.

I took Waltzing Zosha by the hand, and we left the underground. Oh, with what joy we welcomed the streaming sunshine that spilled all over the cathedral courtyard.

The day promised to be bright, and the sky was blue, without a single cloud. It was natural to be overwhelmed with joy on such a morning, but I had nothing to be happy about. Waltzing Zosha understood this because she said to me with compassion in her voice:

"This was a major screw-up."

"Yes. I was KO'd in the third round. By all the rules of the sport, I should leave the ring."

"Will you?"

I thought about this for a while.

"No, Zosha, I will not. This is not a boxing ring. I have to recover what Batura stole."

We shook off the dust of the crypt from our clothes. I thanked Zosha for her help in tracking down Batura. I shook her hand and asked her to tell Bashka about our night adventure.

"Do you have any new assignments for us?" she asked.

"We need to find out where Batura is hiding. I have to find out if he really substituted silver goblets for gold ones," I said.

"But how can we do it?"

"I don't know," I said, and then I added:

"I mean, I don't know *yet*."

We parted ways. She went back to the scout camp, and I—to my room in the hostel.

Cagliostro was still in his bed, although no longer asleep.

"Oh God, how I worried about you," he said." You were gone all night."

"Some miscreant locked me up in an underground crypt in the cathedral," I said.

And I told Cagliostro about my adventure, even though I was certain that he knew all about it: he had almost certainly participated in setting me up. But I wanted to make him feel that I still knew nothing about his role.

"I am defeated," I said. "My honor has suffered a grievous blow. Still, when I think about it, I am happy to know that Koenig's second cache will go to a museum."

"And nothing from the cache is missing?" Cagliostro asked.

"Everything seems in order. The items and their number agree with the inventory that Koenig left behind."

"In that case... what was the point of locking you up?"

I played along:

"I presume the idea was to make sure that Dr. Parsley and I quarrel."

I lied because I didn't want Batura to know that I knew about the swap of the cups.

"Very likely," Cagliostro said.

Just as I finished shaving, Director Marchak knocked on our door.

"I invite you to breakfast, Mr. Thomas," he said ominously. "I want to talk to you."

I introduced the Director to Cagliostro, who was still in bed.

"Maestro of black magic?" asked Director Marchak as if to let me know that—in my current situation—only arcane knowledge could save me. "Dr. Parsley has told me that you have joined forces with a sorcerer."

"I owe my acquaintance with Mr. Cagliostro to your secretary," I said.

"Is that so?" Director Marchak seemed genuinely surprised. "You were introduced to Mr. Cagliostro by my secretary? I never thought that my office dealt with magicians. If my memory serves, the circus desk is a floor higher."

And just at that moment, from among the nine boxes under Cagliostro's bed, peeped out the head of Peter the Snake. Director Marchak studied the beast carefully but did not let on that he spotted it. It did not fit his worldview that snakes might slither about the hotel rooms of polite people, and he preferred to think that he had succumbed to an illusion.

"The world is an illusion," Cagliostro said soothingly as if he were reading his mind.

"Is that so?" kindly nodded Director Marchak. "As far as I am concerned, I have fewer and fewer illusions in my life."

But the snake kept on creeping farther and farther out, that is, closer and closer to Director Marchak's foot. It seemed it was profoundly interested in the Director's right shoe.

"*Hm. Hm,*" grunted the director twice. But those famous threatening *hms,* which usually caused panic among his subordinates, made no impression on the snake. It continued slithering towards the Director's shoe. Director Marchak couldn't stand it any longer.

"What animal is this?" he asked, struggling to contain his anxiety.

I said nothing, pretending to be busy putting on a fresh shirt. In any case, I stood with my back turned to the Director.

Cagliostro also did not deign to take any interest in what the director was pointing to. He stretched out more comfortably on the bed and said while studying the ceiling:

"Sometimes people think they see something while, in fact, they see nothing. They think they understand something and yet they understand nothing. As for me, right now, I see a yellow stain on the ceiling that resembles a basilisk. And yet I am a reasonable man and realize that it is not a basilisk but an ordinary yellow stain."

"*Hm,*" grunted Director Marchak again. "It seems to me that something is crawling over me. On my back," he added.

I turned around and looked at the director's back.

"It's just a mouse," I stated.

"You're not going to tell me there are mice walking all over me, are you?" the director barked angrily.

"The world is an illusion," yawned Cagliostro. Meanwhile, the mouse moved from the director's back to the director's shoulder.

"And yet something is definitely crawling over me," the director stated again.

"I told you it was a mouse," I said, buttoning up my shirt.

"I see a snake near my leg," said the director.

"Perhaps you do," I agreed indifferently and began to tie my tie.

Meanwhile, the mouse passed from the shoulder to the sleeve of Director Marchak's jacket.

"You were right. It is indeed a mouse," the director looked at the white mouse marching down his sleeve. "And yet your words seemed unbelievable to me."

"Ha!" I picked up on the director's phrase. "Sometimes my words do seem unbelievable to you, and then they turn out to have been correct all along."

Director Marchak tried to catch the mouse by the tail, but the mouse escaped onto the table. The director rose carefully from his chair, making sure not to trample the snake.

"Let us better go to breakfast, Mr. Thomas. Even as a child, I didn't like the zoo."

Our breakfast—to use the language of diplomats—"passed in a cordial atmosphere." We chatted about this and that, carefully avoiding the subject of Koenig's stash, slippery as snakeskin. Finally, however, Director Marchak asked:

"Do you still think I'm like that rich widower who placed a cross with eleven diamonds on his wife's grave?"

"Absolutely, Mr. Director. Allow me to explain. Each time a Koenig's cache was found, a little *hocus-pocus* took place. First, three extremely valuable coins were lost, and yet—as far as the ledger went—nothing was lost. Then, five chalices disappeared, and yet everything seemed to be in order. In both cases, everything agreed with Koenig's inventory."

"And what evidence do you have for this?"

"Well, you saw the hammer and chisel and the red crack around the Devil's Image."

"Ah, yes, but I also saw not Valdemar Batura but you, dear Thomas."

"I said that I'd been lured there and then locked up."

"The door to the underground was open, Mr. Thomas. And the key was still in the lock."

"When you arrived, yes. Not when Zosha and I tried to leave the underground. Look, is the presence of Batura in Frombork not enough to convince you that we might have a problem?"

"Batura is a free man, just like you and me. He can stay

wherever he wants. I'm not saying, by the way, that he isn't looking for Koenig's caches. He is free to do so, naturally. Everyone and his little brother is free to look for any treasure they like. The point, however, is how he will act when he finds the cache. As long as he is only looking, we can't bring any charges against him. I demand evidence that something is missing."

"And you will have it," I said forcefully.

"And now let us get down to business, Thomas. Let's go for a little walk through Frombork, and let us have you show me what you have done in the hours paid for by our department."

I collected my notebook, and we went to the Cathedral Hill. There, sitting under a great oak tree, I pitched my idea of the new guide to Director Marchak.

"I have collected information concerning both the ancient and recent history of Frombork and Varmia, and it is all very interesting, but I still believe that the central focus of the guide should be Copernicus. It seems to me that—without in any way diminishing the veneration with which both tourists and the general public treat the Copernicus Tower—the guide should present the current state of modern research in this regard. Oral tradition holds that Copernicus tracked the movements of the stars from his tower but modern research suggests that the observatory of Copernicus must have been located elsewhere."

"Please go on. This is very interesting," said the director.

"Let's start with the facts established by modern scholars," I said, unaware that in a moment, I, too, would make a remarkable discovery. I blazed away with swagger, spewing out information obtained from astronomers and historians.

"To test the oral tradition, Polish astronomers tried to make measurements of the sky from the Copernicus Tower. They even added a special porch to the tower for this purpose. And what did they find? Astronomer P.," I consulted my notes, "states irrefutably that, quote, *the notion that any useful observation of heavenly objects could be made from such a balcony is, from an astronomical point of view, completely absurd. Every step of the observation would require an adjustment in the inclination of the instrument, which must be kept vertical as one of the cardinal conditions for successful observation.* Unquote."

"Where, then, did Copernicus make his observations of the sky?"

"The same astronomer suggests that the other tower in this part of the wall was more suitable for making observations—the huge Octagon where the fortress artillery was kept. It had enough space to set up the necessary astronomical instruments. Between the tower and the outer wall of the Octagon, there are thirty-five feet of flat and solid terrace. In addition, there was an easy passage along the top of the Barbican from the Copernicus Tower to the Octagon. Copernicus could easily have walked along the top of the wall to make his observations."

From the bench where we sat, we could clearly see the bulging silhouette of the Octagon. And that was when I experienced a flash of revelation. Ants suddenly began to crawl down my spine. I felt I was on the cusp of solving an extraordinary mystery. Just a moment more, and I would know what had kept me awake for so long.

But Director Marchak interrupted my train of thought:

"Please go on. This is very interesting."

I shook off the strange premonition and continued, looking into my notebook every now and then:

"Testimonies of near-contemporaries of Copernicus are helpful here. Copernicus's book, *On the Revolutions of the Heavenly Bodies*, caused quite a stir when it appeared. In 1584—a relatively short time after Copernicus' death—the Danish astronomer Tycho de Brahe sent his collaborator, a certain Elijah Cimber, to Frombork to repeat Copernicus's measurements using instruments somewhat better than Copernicus's—in order to check the reported results. This Elijah Cimber left a detailed diary of his activities in Frombork. It is natural that someone who wants to check someone else's observations probably makes them in the same place, especially if he is allowed to do so. But this Cimber, Mr. Director, did not climb the Copernicus Tower at all and conducted his astronomical research in the garden of

Canon Eckhard of Kempno, outside of the Keep. He wrote: 'the garden located closest to the west of that tower from which Copernicus allegedly made his observations.'"

De revolutionibus orbium coelestium
(On the Revolutions of the Heavenly Spheres)
is the seminal work on the heliocentric theory by the astronomer Nicolaus Copernicus. The book, first printed in 1543 in Nuremberg, Holy Roman Empire, offered an alternative model of the universe to Ptolemy's geocentric system, which had been widely accepted since ancient times.

"Interesting," muttered the director.

"And, oh, Mr. Director! Why didn't Elijah Cimber climb the tower with his instruments but make his observations from the garden of the curia by Canon Eckhard of Kepno instead? Well, because he thought it was impossible to make observations from the tower. And I am pretty sure that Copernicus himself thought so, too. And if we add to this the fact that Mr. Eckhard's curia formerly belonged to Copernicus, it becomes almost certain that Cimber made his observations from the same place as Copernicus, that is, *from his garden*. Not only that! Copernicus himself, in his *De Revolutionibus*, does not tell anyone to climb any tower but advises them to build a *pavimentum* instead. And what is this Copernican *pavimentum*? Why, it is nothing more than a patio made of lime, gravel, and sand, supported on a foundation of brick-and-lime mortar. As our scholars have calculated, such a Copernican *pavimentum* must have been about twenty square meters, say twenty by twenty feet. It is difficult to suppose that Copernicus advised astronomers to do something that he himself did not do. On the contrary, it is reasonable to think that Copernicus might have built just such an outdoor *pavimentum* in his garden; and that perhaps this Elijah Cimber fellow, who made his observations in the garden of Ekhard of Kempno, used the very same patio. It is also relevant to note that during the Teutonic invasion—when Copernicus conducted the defense of Olshtin—the Teutonic army attacked Frombork and destroyed Copernicus's instrument. Yet we know that the Teutonic Knights failed to capture the Frombork stronghold and only destroyed the outlying buildings. So, Copernicus' instrument was at that time not in the fortress, not in the tower, but in the outer curia. And that is where Copernicus conducted his operations."

"And where is this *curia* located?"

"That's the problem, Mr. Director. There are three candidate *curiae*: Saint Stanislas, Saint Michael, and Saint Peter. If we assume that Copernicus surveyed the sky from somewhere near the Octagon, then the closest would be the *curia* of St. Peter. An excavation was carried out there, but no traces of any *pavimentum* were found. But if one assumes that what Cimber had meant was the curia closest to the Copernicus Tower, then the curia of St. Stanislas seems the right place. And recent research seems to confirm this hypothesis. According to recently found documents, the curia of Copernicus was the St. Stanislas. Currently, the PTTK hostel stands there—it's the place where I cohabit with the Maestro, his snake, his two mice, and a rabbit."

"I have not seen this rabbit," the director shook his head. And then he added with seriousness: "And you want to write about all these things in the guidebook? Won't it bore casual tourists?"

"I don't think so," I replied. "It seems to me that it is worth showing people how interesting research can be, even archival research.

After all, it just might seem that there is nothing more boring than rummaging through old papers. And yet, when one does so, one finds a mystery at every step. If we only knew how much the historian's work resembles that of a detective! How he puts together individual facts and documents of the oddest provenance to reveal the truth: that the Copernican curia was the curia of St. Stanislas. And now, Mr. Director, I will tell you about the state of research on Copernicus' tomb."

I took a deep breath.

But the director interrupted me:

"Maybe we should put this matter on hold for a moment. You may have been too excited to notice that a certain young lady has been hanging about, photographing us and giving you some mysterious signs. You were too busy going through your notes to see her, but I have my eyes wide open, which is why I am your superior, not the other way around."

I looked around the courtyard and spotted Miss Ala in the vicinity of the Shembek Chapel.

You traitor! I thought and angrily gnashed my teeth.

Director Marchak rose from the bench with great dignity.

"I can see you have not been wasting your time," he stated ambiguously. "I am tired. I rode the train all night, then went straight to the crypt from the station. So, I will take a brief lie-down at the St. Stanislas Curia, where a room has been secured for me by our very good Dr. Parsley. You will tell me about Copernicus's grave a little later."

That said, the director bowed and walked away with dignity.

CHAPTER 14: FIVE GOLDEN CUPS

Is Ala a traitor? Her strange proposal. I borrow the five silver chalices. Looking for a hole in the whole. A trip to the land of the Terrible ACE. "Beware, danger." Is it a dog, or is it a monster? What I saw on CCTV. The third villain. The five golden cups. The Terrible ACE performs a trick.

"You traitor!" I said angrily when Miss Ala approached and sat down on the bench next to me.

She made an offended face and began rummaging through her bag. Finally, she took out a black box that looked like yet another tiny radio transmitter.

"Traitor!" I said again. "You don't even try to defend yourself."

She shrugged her shoulders.

"I am considering whether I should summon *ACE* to deal with you."

"*ACE*?!"

I massaged my tender shoulder, still remembering the beast's steel grip.

"And if I do not summon him, it will only be because I do not want to cause unnecessary sensation in Frombork," she stated. "All the same, I won't allow myself to be offended."

"But you're cooperating with Batura! You've been seen in his company! Riding in his red Mustang!"

"Ah, is that what you're referring to?" she laughed. "Do you really think that if I were an associate of Batura, I would allow myself to be seen in his car? I was on my way to Frombork to get groceries. Batura happened to be passing by and offered me a ride. Was I not to take advantage of it? Then, the same thing happened in the afternoon. He drove me back in his red Mustang."

"What a gentleman," I barked scornfully.

"Well, yes, he is a very well-mannered man," she confirmed. "Of course, I am perfectly aware that his interest in me is entirely due to the fact that he saw us together during the car chase. He gave me a ride to figure out why I had been there."

"Wait! Wait! You were *walking* to Frombork? Could it be that the Master Engineer's blue Opel has broken down?" I asked with derision in my voice.

"Alas, no. Rather, the Master Engineer has broken down. He is now forever crossed off the list of my followers. He lives for the sake of appearances. Shallow things impress him. And, good sir, I prefer people who do not pay too much attention to superficial features. What is important to me is not the shiny paint job on a car but what the car hides under the hood. I am not interested in a man just because he is pretty, has beautiful hair, a slender figure, and dances well; or, not only because of that, at any rate. What is more important to me is what he has under the dome. End of story. Period. I will not ride in the blue Opel again."

I nodded my head melancholically. I reflected that I, too, had turned out to be a man easily misled by appearances. And that's why I lost for the third time in my battle against Valdemar Batura.

I told Ala about the preceding day's adventure and my night in the basement of the cathedral.

"I lost again. And, again, I lost entirely because of my own conceit," I said. "I thought I was being extremely clever. The moment I arrived in Frombork, I fell for the Devil's this and the Devil's that. And yet, had I but thought about this entire business more carefully, I would surely have cottoned on to Batura's devious plan to feed me clues and lead me into wild goose chases. For instance, I might have realized that the kidnapping of the old man was way too blatant: that it had to be a trap! And how could I have let myself be lured into the underground crypt? That was *really* stupid. Just stupid."

Miss Ala was thinking about something. She plucked thoughtfully at a strand of her hair.

"You say that the cache had contained five gold missal chalices set with precious stones, but only cheap silver chalices were found by

Parsley?" she ascertained.

"Yes. I am sure this is what's happened. Batura has not come here to take in the sea air."

An expression of determination suddenly appeared on Miss Ala's face.

"I think I can help you," she said. "But for this, I need the five silver cups."

"What?"

"Don't ask too much. I also have my secrets."

"And how will I get you the silver cups? Do you think Director Marchak will just give them to me?"

"Just borrow them from him. Sign a receipt. After all, you said yourself that they do not represent much value."

"OK. But how will I justify the request to borrow the cups?"

"That's your business. But by giving me these cups, you stand a good chance of being able to present Director Marchak with the proof he wants."

"You plan to provide me with proof of Batura's guilt? How?"

"Please don't ask!" she stomped her foot. "Just let me have the five silver chalices."

I got up from the bench.

"In this case, I better speak to Director Marchak."

We walked over to the PTTK hostel. I asked Miss Ala to wait in my room, which Cagliostro had meanwhile left, and I knocked on the door of Director Marchak's room.

He had probably been sleeping because he now opened the door dressed in his pajamas.

"What is this about?" he muttered angrily. "I told you I was tired."

"I would like to borrow those five silver chalices from the cache."

"Why?"

"I suspect that they are contemporary forgeries."

"Nonsense. I believe they were made at the end of the last

century—even if their value does not exceed the sum of ten thousand zlotys."

"Still, I would like to borrow them. You instructed me to give you proof that Batura had compromised the cache, but now, when I want to find the proof, you make my search difficult."

"Ah, so that's what it is? Well, all right. I will lend you those cups."

And he led me to a corner of his room, where the contents of Koenig's second cache lay in a wooden crate, locked with a huge padlock. Director Marchak found the silver chalices and handed them to me.

"Do you need a receipt?"

"That's alright. I trust you."

I left him, carrying the five chalices in my hands. In the corridor, I ran into Dr. Parsley. He cast a suspicious glance at the cups.

"Why are you taking them?" he asked.

"I want to inspect them."

"Why?"

"It seems to me that they are only silver-plated and therefore almost worthless."

"You are wrong. I've looked at them carefully. They are made of solid silver. They do not have a great value, it is true, but it is not my fault that Koenig turned out to be a fool. Anyway, this is hardly surprising. He was not a connoisseur of art. He was just an ordinary Nazi thug, stealing whatever fell into his hand. In his stashes, we find priceless and worthless things all mixed up; magnificent coins and ordinary pfenigs; priceless miniatures and ordinary mass chalices.

"Do you mind if I study them, though?"

"No," he shrugged his shoulders and left. I went into my room and set the cups on the table.

"Here they are," I said to Miss Ala. And I looked around the room. "*Heh*, I was afraid I might find you standing on a table or a chair."

"Why?"

"I live with a snake and two white mice."

"Oh!" she squealed, horrified, and also looked around the room.

"But it seems," I continued, "that Cagliostro has taken his menagerie with him."

Miss Ala calmed down. She sat down and pointed to the cardboard boxes under Cagliostro's bed.

"I will need a box like that."

"They belong to Cagliostro."

"All the better."

"But that's theft," I noted.

"No. It will be a loan. I will soon return the cups to you along with the cardboard box."

I pulled out from under the bed the box in which Peter lived, put the cups in it, and handed it to Miss Ala.

"And now what?" I asked curiously.

"Now I'm going home," she declared.

She took the box under her arm, and with a nod goodbye, she left the room.

I sighed heavily. For a moment I had the feeling that I had gotten myself into some kind of trouble again.

I did not occupy myself with the matter for too long, though. Instead, I saw to something that was a hundred times more important. Armed with an electric torch, I went to the Fort.

I did not return until lunchtime.

In the dining room, I found Director Marchak eating his lunch in the company of Dr. Parsley. I sat at their table and ordered my food.

"And how goes the expertise?" asked Director Marchak.

"What expertise?"

"The chalices. You took them from me this morning, did you not?" the director stated.

"Ah, well, yes. Indeed, I did."

"In that case, please return them to me right away, as I am

sending the whole box back to Warsaw."

I gasped.

"Are you planning to send the treasure back by mail? They may get lost," I worried.

"Oh, relax. I have arranged for a courier to carry the crate."

"*Hm,*" I grunted uncertainly. "I'll need the goblets for a while yet."

"Oh, come on, you have had enough time for your expertise. Anyway, you can finish it in Warsaw. For now, please bring the cups to my room."

Damn, what am I going to do? I was horrified.

Dr. Parsley, having noticed the expression of embarrassment on my face, added with a mischievous grin:

"Thomas seems to be desperately trying to find fault with the cache. You might say he is looking for a hole in the whole. Only he won't find one."

I quickly swallowed my lunch, rose from the table, and almost ran out of the hostel. I was getting into my vehicle when Bashka intercepted me.

"Mr. Thomas! Mr. Thomas!" he called out joyfully. "We have found Batura's campsite! He's in a tent at the mouth of the Bauda, on a small sandy promontory."

"Ah, it doesn't matter now," I replied, starting the engine. "Never mind."

"Never mind?" he repeated, very disappointed. "And do you know what a great book I bought at the bookstore? *Magical Tricks* by Alexander Vadimov, the Soviet illusionist. Be sure to take a look!"

And he handed me a thick book with a bright yellow cover.

"Lend it to me," I said, touched by a sudden thought. "I will look through it today and return it to you tomorrow. Now excuse me, but I'm in a big hurry."

"Won't you take me with you?"

"No," I shook my head. And I added with all seriousness: "I'm going to the Land of the Terrible ACE. If I do not return by tonight..."

I stammered and waved my hand. "Forgive me. I can't tell you more."

"What land? Land of terrible who?" asked the boy.

But I was bound by an oath of silence.

"Look. If I do not return for a long time, report to Cagliostro. Perhaps he will suggest what to do."

This said, I took the book on magical arts from Bashka's hand and drove off as fast as my steed would carry me, that is, with all the speed of my three hundred and fifty mechanical horses.

I was going to find Miss Ala in the Land of the Terrible ACE to reclaim the five silver chalices. Why on earth had I agreed to borrow them from Director Marchak? What was Ala going to do with them?

It wasn't far to the Land of the Terrible ACE—especially at the speed of my vehicle. Here was the first bridge over the Bauda, then the second bridge, the hill, and the ravine where we had met *ACE*. Miss Ala had said to follow the path at the end of the ravine. It was supposed to lead through the forest to the barracks where Ala worked.

I drove through the ravine and parked the vehicle at the edge of a dirt road at the foot of *Teufelsberg*. I found a narrow path, but before I stepped onto it, I looked around carefully.

The day was sunny and serene. I had a blue sky overhead. Snow-white clouds passed over it from time to time. They were moving fast—there seemed to be a strong wind blowing up high. On the ground, however, it was all stillness and a vast, overwhelming silence. The heat of a sizzling August day lay on the land and the forest enticed with its pleasant cool. Birds chirped merrily, but for me, who still had my recent meeting with the terrible *ACE* fresh in my mind, the wood seemed somehow threatening.

I stood at the edge of the forest for a while, not daring to go deeper into the forest. I had the sensation that *ACE*'s iron body was lurking in the forest gloom and that the monster's glass eyes were observing me from behind the trees. I thought of its steel hands, ready to seize me as soon as I entered the path. I would have boldly ventured on if I knew that Ala was sitting inside the beast. But what if someone else was in charge of *ACE* at the moment? Like Christopher Zegadlo,

Master Engineer? There was no doubt in my mind that Ala and Zegadlo worked together. So, it was likely that they took turns in the Iron *ACE*. And Zegadlo was probably angry with me over losing Miss Ala's affection. Oh, no, I did not wish to fall into his hands—or rather, into the hands of the terrible *ACE* when he was driving it.

And yet, I couldn't stay here indefinitely. Director Marchak was waiting for his silver cups.

Once again, I looked at the blue sky. And then, having summoned all my courage, I stepped onto the forest path. I tried to walk as quietly as a Mohican and took cover behind the trunks of the trees at every rustling sound. Then, each time, before I moved on, I made triple sure that the rustling had not been caused by the terrible *ACE*.

The path meandered like Peter the Snake.

There was not a living soul anywhere.

Only twice did I see warning signs:

"Beware, Danger."

Univitingly, they both featured a skull and cross bones.

Despite these warnings, I continued on, but my soul was, as they say, perched but lightly upon my shoulder. What danger did the signs warn me of? Would there be... landmines? Or would another creature—as dangerous as the multi-eyed *ACE*—crawl out of the bushes in a moment?

I had the impression that the deeper I went into the woods, the denser, darker, and gloomier it became. It also seemed to me that the birds had disappeared: I no longer heard any chirping.

Maybe I should turn back? flashed through my head. But I imagined the look on Director Marchak's face when I told him I didn't have his silver chalices. And then I saw the triumphant, mischievously crooked face of Dr. Parsley mocking me. And that drove me on.

I continued for another two hundred feet along the path, and suddenly, a forest clearing opened up in front of me. In the middle of it, I saw a long tin barracks fenced with chicken wire. Above the barracks rose a huge antenna mast.

There was a gate in the fence. An inscription above the gate proclaimed:

THE EXPERIMENTAL CENTER
OF THE ROBOTICS DEPARTMENT
OF THE TECHNICAL UNIVERSITY OF G.
ALL UNAUTHORIZED PERSONS KEEP OUT

The gate in the fence was locked. I looked for a bell button but found none.

How do I get to the barracks? I wondered and walked closer to the gate.

Suddenly, a yellow dog jumped out of a small shed near the door of the building. It ran a dozen steps toward the gate and started barking loudly. The dog was as big as a wolfhound but did not resemble any breed I had seen before. And it ran somehow stiffly, as if on stilts.

I backed away from the gate, and the dog immediately retreated to its kennel. I took a step toward the gate, and it jumped out again. It barked as loudly as all other dogs but did it monotonously, always the same, like—a recording?

I backed away from the gate again and the dog—into its kennel. I approached the gate, and it jumped out of the kennel again and started barking.

"Good dog, good dog…" I tried to calm the beast.

It did not growl or bark, as other dogs do at such times. Instead, he continued to announce my presence with his monotone bark.

The dog was clearly a robot. Perhaps it was brought out of the kennel by a photocell located on the gate. A special mechanism located in its belly triggered a tape recorder with the recorded barking of a dog.

I stood patiently at the gate within range of the photocell. The electronic dog barked and barked.

Finally, the door of the barracks opened, and Miss Ala appeared in it, dressed in a white lab coat. She screened her eyes with her hand against the sun and looked toward the gate. She saw me and pressed a button next to the barracks door. The iron gate opened silently.

I entered the experimental facility. And when I disappeared from the sight of the photocell, the dog immediately stopped barking and retreated to its kennel.

"What brought you here?" Ala asked.

"The damned five cups. I have to hand them back. Director Marchak wants to send them back to Warsaw today."

"Oh, this will be tricky," she shook her head. "Come, you will see for yourself."

She shook my hand in greeting and then invited me into the barracks with a gesture.

The professor, the Master Engineer, and the rest of the staff left for Warsaw today," she explained. "I am almost alone here."

"*Almost* alone? What do you mean?"

"Well, there are some automata around. So, I can't say that I am completely alone."

"And where are the cups?" I inquired impatiently.

She didn't say anything. We entered a large room. I saw three control panels full of buttons, levers, screens, and they all flickered with all kinds of lights. I also saw a large TV monitor.

Ala slid a chair over to me.

"Sit down and watch," she said. And she approached the control panel.

"I did not come here to watch TV," I said firmly. "I need those cups."

"Well, just take a look. They are there," she pointed to the TV screen.

I sat down and took a closer look at the monitor, but I did not see the cups, only the undulating waves on the surface of the sea.

"I didn't come to watch a sightseeing documentary, either," I started again.

Ala turned some knobs on the control panel, and immediately

a new image appeared on the screen. I saw a sandy headland, and on it a tourist tent. And next to the tent stood... Valdemar Batura's red Mustang! After a while, I spotted the man himself. Stripped down to his bathing briefs, he was lying on the sand by the water, accompanied by thre buxom Miss Anielka, also in a bathing suit.

"What? What are we looking at?" I exclaimed.

"You are watching Valdemar Batura's camp."

"But what kind of a miracle is this?"

"I sent *ACE* along the bottom of the Bauda River," Ala explained. "ACE is underwater right now. Only one of his eyes is protruding above the surface. *ACE* is transmitting the image he sees back to us."

"I don't really understand..."

"Ah, it's rather simple. We are still experimenting with *ACE*. Yesterday, we wanted to see how *ACE* would perform underwater, and sent him out along the bed of the Bauda. And *ACE*'s cameras discovered Valdemar Batura and his camp. And, yes, I did see him handle five golden chalices."

"So you were not inside *ACE* when we met in the ravine?"

"Of course not. *ACE* is radio wave-operated. When you met *ACE*, I was here, and we talked to each other remotely."

"So, where are my silver goblets now?" I returned to the burning topic.

"*ACE* has them. In the box you gave me along with the cups."

"What do you intend to do with them?" I asked anxiously.

"OK. I think you need to be quiet now," hissed Ala. "Listen. I am about to turn on the listening apparatus installed on *ACE*'s dome."

I turned to the image on the monitor.

We saw a green Wartburg[15] coming towards the camp, bumping along a dirt track. It pulled into the campsite, and a young

---

[15] Wartburg was a car produced by East German car manufacturer VEB Automobilwerk Eisenach from 1956 to 1965.

man in dark glasses got out. At his sight, Batura and Anielka stood up. "There you are," I heard Valdemar Batura's voice greeting the young man. "You've finally made it!"

"I hit the road the moment I got your telegram," said the young man and bowed deeply to kiss Miss Anielka's hand. "What's the emergency?"

"We've got some hot goods for you. You must take them away from here as soon as possible. Take them to Warsaw—I can't keep them here or our friend Thomas is liable to bring the militia on our heads any minute now. We need to be as clean as a whistle."

"Makes sense," said the young man. "Let's see the goods."

Batura nodded and, with a beaming face, began rummaging in the sand near his tent. After a while, he pulled out a cardboard box—a box of the sort Cagliostro kept under his bed. I had seen Cagliostro give one such box to someone—probably Batura—in the Frombork harbor on my first night in town. I could easily guess what that box contained on that occasion: five silver cups that Cagliostro had brought from Warsaw. Those silver cups then ended up in Koenig's second cache.

But this box—the box Batura now held in his hand—very probably the very same box!—now contained five gold chalices.

"Look," he said to the young man in dark glasses, taking one of the goblets out of the box. "Every one of these beauties is worth a thousand times more than the five silver cups we bought in Warsaw. Look here. They are not only made of solid gold but are set with sapphires and opals. Think of that! What a trade!"

I must now quote Batura's words—even though it really hurts to do so.

"I never imagined that Thomas was such a sucker. He let himself be led by the nose like a babe in swaddling clothes. And, oh, the beauty of it! He probably suspects that we have made the switch, but he cannot say a word about it, or the suspicion will fall on him!"

"You are one devious mother operator, Valdemar," the young man beamed and adjusted his cool glasses.

Miss Anielka interjected.

"Don't forget to mention, Valdemar, that I, too, had my hand in tricking Thomas. I disguised you as the old man."

"Oh, yes. You were brilliant, darling," Batura agreed and kissed Miss Anielka's hand with great unction.

"I have worked as a make-up artist in the film industry for five years," Miss Anielka proudly declared to the man in dark glasses. "I am rather good at that work."

"Thomas is a babe," said Batura. "And we have our golden cups. Still, we must not rest on our laurels. The show is not over. We still have the rubies before us. Take these beauties away from here *ASAP*, amico. We must be prepared for every eventuality."

"Alright, but let me take a breather," laughed the young man with glasses. "I've driven all day."

"Fifteen minutes is all you got, my friend. Anielka, dearest, would you fix us a cup of coffee?" Batura said.

He put the cups in the box and put the box in his tent. Then, the three sat down on the other side of the tent, where Miss Anielka, screened from the onshore wind, was boiling water for coffee on a portable spirit stove.

The tent stood facing the river. Through an upraised canvas door, we could see its interior, the mattresses, and the sleeping bags. And the cardboard box left just inside the entrance.

I breathed a sigh of relief. I realized that Batura would not enjoy his booty for long. In just a few moments, I would speed off to Frombork and report the case to the militia. I would report the whole affair and provide the registration number of the Wartburg. The militia would telephone ahead to Warsaw and—just as our courier in cool glasses approached Warsaw city limits, he would be stopped and searched. And the five gold cups would go into militia custody until the affair got cleared up.

But just then, the plot took a totally unexpected turn.

"Hey, watch this, Mr. Thomas. I am about to perform a miracle," I heard Miss Ala say. "*Hocus-pocus dominicus, abra cadabra magicus*, as Maestro Cagliostro might say."

And Miss Al began manipulating the knobs on her control

panel.

Here, I owe you a slightly more detailed description of the place of action, so that you may visualize the whole event. The Bauda's current made a sharp turn here and then emptied into the lagoon. This meant that the current passed right by the tent, the shore was high, and the water deep. This allowed *ACE* to come very close to the camp while remaining fully submerged.

The image on the monitor now shifted—as if *ACE* had slightly leaned out of the water—while still remaining invisible to Batura and his friends because he was shielded not only by the tent but also by the high river bank. And now, we saw *ACE*'s two iron "hands" emerge on the screen, holding... a Cagliostro box. It was the box that I had given to Ala, along with the silver cups. *ACE*'s hands now carefully slipped into Batura's tent and, after a while, emerged holding... the other box.

"Oh God, what have you done?" I groaned. "Return those cups immediately! It's evidence! We can bust them for possession now!"

"Too late!" Ala replied with a mischievous smile.

And, indeed, it was too late to attempt a second swap of the boxes: Batura had risen from his seat behind the tent.

Ala quickly moved some lever on the control panel, and *ACE* submerged in the water. Batura walked forward, took out the box from the tent, and handed it to the man in dark glasses.

"Enough resting, amico. Off you go," he ordered.

The man shrugged his shoulders—the rush seemed completely unnecessary to him. Nevertheless, he drained his coffee, took the box, and carefully placed it in the trunk of the Wartburg.

I followed their movements with great suspense. All they had to do was look into the box again, and there would be trouble. But it didn't even cross their minds that another magical swap of chalices had just occurred. Their camp stood in the middle of nowhere; there were no other human beings for miles. Only a bird could have approached the tent unnoticed.

"Well, that's done then," enthused Valdemar Batura. "And

now the rubies and—we're done. It's been a long time since I have made such a killing. The game was well worth the effort, eh?"

"And it's been rather fun, too," said Miss Anielka. The young man adjusted his glasses, waved goodbye, and drove off.

Ala decided it was time to retreat. Looking at the monitor screen and turning the knobs on the control panel, she withdrew *ACE* from the mouth of the Bauda. We followed *ACE*'s entire return journey on the screen—it marched laboriously but persistently up the riverbed, then climbed up the bank and walked slowly through the forest toward the barracks. Finally, the gate of the experimental center appeared on the screen, and an electronic dog barked. Ala pressed a button and opened the gate. *ACE* pulled up in front of the building. A moment later, *ACE*'s iron hands took out the cardboard box with cups and placed it on the threshold of the barracks.

"Take them away," Ala said. "Give them to Director Marchak. You now have proof that the cache had been robbed."

I jumped in front of the barracks, bowed to the Iron *ACE*, grabbed the box, and brought it back in. I opened the box and, one by one, with extreme unction, began to take out the golden goblets.

"You beat them at their own game!" I exclaimed, laughing. "They swapped the cups, and you swapped them right back! That's very elegant, I have to say."

Miss Ala showed remarkable modesty.

"*ACE* did it, not me. And *ACE* was built by our professor and by your favorite Master Engineer. You should thank them. Though I suppose you could hug *ACE* in thanks."

"Oh, yes?" I said, and I thought of *ACE*'s steel hands. "I'd rather hug you, I think," I said, and I kissed her on both cheeks. Ala blushed and said something about having to summon *ACE* to defend her.

"What is the intended purpose for *ACE*?" I finally asked the question which had bothered me for a long time.

"I work at the Robotics Department, which means that we are involved in building all kinds of automata. One of them is *ACE*. What can it be used for? It will have all kinds of uses. It will work where it is too dangerous for humans to work, for example, in radioactive areas. In the future, robots like *ACE*, but far more versatile, will descend to the bottom of the ocean or fly to other planets. This one cannot do that, but we are testing it under different conditions to see how it can be used. That's why we brought it here.

"We are also working on other automata. Some of them may be useful to you, museum professionals, for securing museum halls. For example, we have an automatic lock that can be opened and closed by means of a photocell or even radio waves. All you have to do is attach this lock to the door..."

And she showed me a small automatic lock, which I was very interested to see. Such locks could indeed be helpful in securing museum halls from theft. After all, there was no shortage of thieves in the world ready to get their hands on the priceless works of art at our museums.

And then, Miss Ala escorted me to the gate of the experimental center. I walked through the forest, joyfully hopping and whistling. The land of *ACE* no longer seemed so scary to me. It felt friendly and full of the most delightful wonders of modern technology.

From time to time, I burst out laughing as I imagined the look on the face of the cool young man with dark glasses when, upon arriving in Warsaw, he opened the cardboard box and saw five silver cups. What would he do then? And would Batura believe him when he said that the cups just "changed" all on their own? Or perhaps he would think the young man tried to swindle him?

Oh, a nice quarrel among the villains would be perfect! The thought of the mutual accusations they would hurl at each other filled me with such wicked pleasure that, at one point, I stopped on the path and waved my fist threateningly in the direction of Batura's encampment.

"You just wait, Batura! You just wait! It's not over yet!" I called out.

CHAPTER 15: THE CANDLE IS TO BLAME

The mystery of the cardboard box. Director Marchak and bureaucracy. Trouble with the protocol. The candle is to blame. How magic shows are made. The cigarette and newspaper tricks. Cagliostro's props. What the chamois bag contained. Am I becoming clairvoyant?

I knocked on the door of Director Marchak's room, and when I heard a resounding "Enter!" I went inside and placed the box of cups on the table with great pride.

"Well, you finally brought them," the director stated gruffly. "You've been away for so long that I had to give up sending the cache today. The train to Warsaw has already left."

"I think you will find it was all for the better," I smiled. "My time was well spent. Just look inside the box."

"What for? You didn't swap the silver goblets for clay ones, did you? I've seen enough. Anyway, why did you borrow them in the first place?"

"I think you should take a look in the box," I said coyly.

Director Marchak carefully approached the box on the table.

"And no snake or rabbit will jump out of it?" he made sure.

"No."

"Eh, why do I feel that the boundless confidence I have in you will be grievously disappointed one day," Director Marchak sighed and opened the box with great care.

And then his eyes opened wide in amazement. He batted his eyelids and then howled:

"But these are golden goblets!..."

"And encrusted with precious stones," I added. "Sapphires and opals. These chalices are of very old manufacture."

Director Marchak furrowed his brow and pulled his eyebrows together in a stern frown.

"What does this mean, Mr. Thomas?"

"You asked me for proof. And this is proof, Mr. Director. The cache did not contain silver cups; it contained gold chalices."

The director stomped his foot.

"Not true! There were silver chalices in the cache. This is what is written in the minutes."

However, he couldn't help but take out the cups and study them with admiration.

"They are beautiful. Wonderful," he enthused, stroking them with his hand. "Very old, very wonderful work. Seventeenth century, I should say, this one is. And what wonderful stones."

But then he came to and looked at me sternly.

"Where are our silver chalices?"

"I exchanged them for these," I replied innocently.

"What?" barked the director in outrage. "Who gave you permission to swap them?"

"I made a spur-of-the-moment decision based on the assumption that such an exchange would serve our department and benefit the Nation. After all, Director, gold is gold."

And I told the director how the swap was made. Of course, I had to reveal the secret of the Land of the Terrible ACE, tell him about Ala and my acquaintance with her.

Director Marchak listened carefully, and when I finished, he said quietly:

"Do you know what you have done? In the eyes of the law?"

"I restored national treasures to the Nation and returned the thieves's property to them," I said.

"No. You robbed them. You made an exchange of gold chalices for silver ones without their permission. This is called theft, Mr. Thomas. And I cannot accept it."

"Why? These golden goblets came from Koenig's second cache. They belong to the Nation."

"You would have to prove it. An investigation should have been undertaken first. The law enforcement and judicial authorities should have returned the golden cups to us, not you. In the eyes of the law, you are a thief. Do you understand it? And what am I supposed to do with this now?" He looked in despair at the golden goblets. "After all, I have written in the protocol that we found five silver chalices in Koenig's hiding place. And do you imagine that I can now present to the treasury of the National Museum five gold chalices instead of the silver?"

"In that case, I'll take the gold goblets, go to Valdemar Batura, and try to settle the matter amicably. I will give him these, and I feel pretty sure that he will agree to return the silver ones in exchange."

And I took a box of gold chalices from the table. But Director Marchak sprang from his chair like a young buck. He grabbed the box and snatched it out of my hands.

"Oh, no, Mr. Thomas! Do you consider me a fool? These golden goblets are National property."

This said, Director Marchak placed his hand on the box and stated with unction:

"I take possession of these cups on behalf of Polish museums. As for the protocol..." he added with a sly smile, "I think we will find some explanation. Like... it was dark in the crypt, the candle gave so little light, it was easy to make a mistake. It's better to admit a mistake than to go on and on explaining stuff. In short, Mr. Thomas, we have erred. We thought we found silver chalices, while in fact, we found gold. I will add an addendum to the minutes: *On closer inspection, it turned out that the silver chalices were made of gold and set with precious stones.*"

"What?" I became indignant. "What an embarrassment! What will those who read this protocol think? That we can't tell the difference between silver and gold? My reputation as an art appraiser will be compromised! I protest against this solution."

But Director Marchak didn't listen to me. He took the protocol out of his pocket and made the annotation, which he then had me authenticate with my signature.

"That's right," he rubbed his hands together. "It was dark in the crypt, and that's why we made a mistake. And then, on closer inspection, the silver chalices turned out to be gold."

Disheartened, I signed the document.

"I know how you feel, Thomas," sighed the director hypocritically. "*Errare humanum est*, that is, to err is human. In other words, we made a mistake, but we corrected it in time. But for the future," he turned to me threateningly, "for the future, I say, I demand proof of the villains' guilt. I also hope that, as an honest citizen, you will immediately go to the militia and confess to exchanging the silver cups for gold and report the circumstances of the case."

"Absolutely," I nodded.

At this, the director left the room and, after a while, returned with Dr. Parsley in tow. The golden goblets were in a cardboard box on the table, so Parsley didn't at first see them. He didn't know why he had been summoned.

"Please sit down," said Director Marchak. "Just in case. And listen to me very carefully because the business I am about to unveil to you is of a very delicate nature."

"I see," Dr. Parsley nodded and made a very serious face.

The director continued:

"As you know, our colleague Thomas asked to examine the five cups we had found in the cache."

"Though it was completely unnecessary," Dr. Parsley said quickly. "I've inspected them and found that they did not represent much value. They were ordinary silver goblets from the end of the last century."

"*Hm*," grunted the director threateningly, dissatisfied with Dr. Parsley's statement. "Do not interrupt me, but listen carefully, Doctor. For the matter, I say, is of national importance. As you yourself know, Thomas borrowed these chalices from me. Now, after a thorough scientific investigation, he found, to his and my surprise, that these chalices are, in fact, made of gold and set with precious stones."

"What?" Parsley sprang from his chair.

"Oh, yes, Doctor Parsley," repeated the director. "They are made of gold, and this only adds to the splendor of your discovery and your reputation as the man who made it."

And Director Marchak reached into the box. He took out the five gold chalices and placed them on the table right in front of Dr. Parsley. Dr. Parsley looked at them and paled.

"They are made of gold, indeed," he muttered. "And these stones..."

Finally, he could stand it no longer and started screeching:

"But they are not the same goblets! Mine were made of silver!"

Director Marchak looked at him menacingly.

"Of silver, you say? And you continue to persist with the mistake you have made?"

"I don't understand any of this," whispered Dr. Parsley, a little frightened by the director's threatening tone.

"Let me clarify your mistake for you," Director Marchak said graciously. "It was dark in the crypt, yes?"

"Yes."

"We had to work by candlelight?"

"That's right."

"The light was rather dim?"

"Yes..."

"We could venture to say that the crypt was almost completely dark?"

"Er..."

"So, making a mistake in such circumstances would not have been unusual. We *thought* we had found five silver chalices in the crypt. But on closer inspection, it turned out that they were made of gold and set with precious stones."

Dr. Parsley reflected. And after a while, he said:

"It seems to me that you are right. In the dark, the goblets seemed silver to us, but they are, in fact, gold."

"Which is stated in the addendum to the protocol," the director added quickly and slid the document towards Parsley. "Please be kind enough to sign here, Dr. Parsley."

Parsley put a sweeping signature to the note. And then he breathed a deep sigh of relief.

"This dispels for good," he stated, "any suspicions that someone had pilfered something from the cache. I confess that the thought of these silver goblets did not give me peace. After all, why on earth would Colonel Koenig include such cheap silver goblets in the cache? And now that this misunderstanding has been cleared up, I am very happy about it."

I could guess what Dr. Parsley was thinking about this business. It was obvious to him that the gold goblets had come from Koenig's cache and that they had been exchanged for the silver ones he had found. His self-love, however, did not allow him to think that the cache had been robbed by Batura. He preferred to think that I had made the exchange of chalices and that Director Marchak then forced me to return the gold and take the silver back. But, because of the weakness he had for me, he decided to cover up the whole affair by making an amendment to the protocol.

I was very disturbed by this development.

But the game with Batura was not yet over. I felt that my honesty would eventually have to come to light and convince Dr. Parsley. I also hoped that I would be able to convince him that he had been a plaything in the hands of a clever villain.

Despite this, however, I had a strong sense of distaste. I left Director Marchak's room and marched to the militia station.

I was received by the commandant of the post, Lieutenant Yujinski, a forty-year-old man, thin and very tall: his long legs stuck out from under his desk.

"I have come to confess to theft," I declared boldly.

He glanced at me but, contrary to my expectations, showed little curiosity.

"Take a seat," he pointed to a chair in front of his desk. "When and what did you steal, and from whom?"

"I robbed a thief. I took the gold goblets he had stolen, returned them to their legal owner, and gave him back the silver ones that had belonged to him."

"Ah yes..." muttered the lieutenant. "In other words, you returned his property to him. This is not a criminal act, sir. It's even commendable—to return people's property to them. We do this, too. Among other things."

"But I did it against his will."

"Ah, yes... This changes the situation," he stated. And he looked at me questioningly.

I told him about coins, Koenig's caches, and silver and gold chalices. He listened attentively and took notes. In the end, I said:

"Director Marchak, my supervisor, believes that regardless of my good intentions, I nevertheless committed theft by taking the gold cups and planting the silver ones. In a word, I robbed a thief. I came here to confess my guilt."

"*Hm*," pondered the lieutenant. And after a moment, he said:

"Director Marchak is right from his point of view. But you see, for us, a theft exists insofar as, on the one hand, we have a person who stole and, on the other, the person or institution that was robbed. In your case, we have a person who states that he stole something—you. But who has been robbed?"

"Valdemar Batura," I replied.

He smiled.

"Are you sure that when we ask this Mr. Batura whether he was robbed of five golden chalices, he would confirm it?"

"No. He bought the silver chalices so he owns them. They remain in his possession. He stole the gold chalices, and I don't think he will confess to having done so."

"In other words, the second element is missing. And when the robbed person does not come forth, there is no thief. Since Mr. Batura won't confirm that he was robbed, you are not a thief. Shall we just forget about the whole business?"

"Yes," I breathed a clear sigh of relief.

"Very well. And now I will tell you briefly: you did wrong. Very, very wrong. Although you recovered the golden cups, which is a good thing, at the same time, you obliterated all traces of the crime committed by Batura. Your testimony about what you saw on the TV monitor cannot be admitted as evidence in the case of the robbery."

"So the criminal gets away with his theft?" I was outraged.

"Oh no, sir," the lieutenant shook his head. "We will follow up on Mr. Batura. But in order to arrest him, we must catch him in the act. What do you think: will Batura attempt to rob the third cache?"

"Definitely. Especially since he has just lost the golden goblets, and, by the way, I know where the third cache is," I added with pride. "Later today, I will inform Dr. Parsley about it. We will open the cache and take possession of the treasure. I expect Batura will attempt to beat us to it."

The lieutenant raised his hand in the air like a traffic cop stopping a car.

"One moment, please. Hold your horses."

"Oh. Do you have a suggestion?" I asked.

"Oh yes. Even a few. Please have confidence in us and don't do anything without consulting us first. Now, let's discuss this matter in detail."

Our deliberations lasted quite a long time. By the time we finished, I was totally exhausted. I returned to my room in the hostel, and not finding Cagliostro there, I lay on my bed and began to look through the book on magical tricks for relaxation.

Why did it interest me? No, I did not intend to become an illusionist. After all, I knew that magic tricks had to be practiced for weeks and sometimes for years, but I was curious to learn Cagliostro's secrets. It seemed to me that in this way, I might be able to protect myself from further surprises in my final showdown with Batura.

The trick of drawing mice and snakes out of the pockets of others relies completely on the dexterity of the fingers and the ability to distract the person who is about to become the object of the trick. Can just anyone, even by practicing for a very long time, put a mouse or a snake in someone else's pocket without being noticed? I do not believe it. To practice this kind of skill requires a very specific talent. No, not a talent. It requires artistry. The thing, after all, is to maintain extraordinary composure, to perform your movements with complete and utter smoothness while your mind is busy with the task of distracting your victim, lulling his vigilance, and directing his attention away from the business at hand.

And how to take a cigarette out of the pockets of a man who does not smoke and does not have them on him? How did Cagliostro find the cigarettes in Bashka's pocket?

It turns out that Cagliostro carried in his pocket a small flat box made of metal, so constructed that he could slide cigarettes out of it one by one with his thumb. The trick relies on dexterity and the ability to divert the attention of onlookers. First, the illusionist demonstrates his empty hands. Then, he sets about unbuttoning the pockets of his victim. While he does that, he quickly reaches into his own pocket, removes the box from it and—as they say in the language of the Illusionists, "palms" it. (*To palm* means to hold something in your hand in such a way that it is not visible to others). The rest is easy. The attention of onlookers is directed to the pocket in which the illusionist is rummaging. The illusionist then puts his hand in the pocket, pushes the cigarette out of the box with his thumb, and then takes it out to demonstrate it.

Why, some can even grab burning cigarettes from the air, but the cigarette in the box must be lit first. Illusionists usually do this when they have an assistant.

And the trick with the water that disappeared into the newspaper? The newspaper is "adapted": a plastic flat bag is pasted between its pages. When the illusionist leafs through the newspaper, no one is able to see the pouch, because it is pasted between two pages whose edges are glued together. Then, the illusionist rolls the newspaper into a tube while opening the edges of the pouch. He pours water not into the newspaper but into the pouch. He then shakes out confetti, which is in a different flat pouch pasted between two other pages.

And how simple the coin-counting trick turned out to be! Its secret lay in the tray on which Cagliostro had instructed me to lay out the coins as I took them out of the pouch. The tray had a secret compartment with more coins. When pouring the money from the tray back into the pouch, Cagliostro simultaneously poured out the coins from the secret compartment. And thus more coins were later found in the pouch.

I lay on my bed reading about other tricks—tricks with magic wands, tricks with strings, with cards, with pigeons and rabbits until late afternoon. Most of the tricks relied on dexterity, but others required special props, trays with latches, and hidden drawers.

I wonder, I thought, *does Cagliostro have more such props*? I rose from the bed and knelt down by Cagliostro's bedside. I pulled a cardboard box out from underneath. And what did I discover?

The folding miniature table with a concealed drawer hidden under the top. The drawer had two compartments, and the top had a latch. I found double-bottomed jugs and transparent pots so constructed that one fit perfectly into the other. I found some bizarre double-bottomed caskets with walls that opened with the squeeze of a hidden spring.

And just as I was looking at one such casket and pressed its spring, it unexpectedly opened its secret compartment and a chamois bag fell out. It fell on the floor with a rattle. I looked inside. It contained—gasp!—

rubies.

Yes, ten fake stones of the sort one sees in the displays of Jeweler's stores. None of them cost more than a few hundred zloty.

The sight sent a tingle down my neck. I was looking at the rubies that Batura intended to plant in place of the precious stones in Koenig's third cache! Did Batura know the location of the third cache already? Or had he stocked up on fake stones in advance?

I studied the fake rubies, and the tingle in my spine slowly went away. Suddenly, I laughed quietly. I hid the stones in the pouch and put the pouch back in the casket. Then, I carefully slipped all the boxes back under Cagliostro's bed.

I tucked the book on magical arts under my pillow, and cheerfully whistling, I left the room.

I filled my time until dinner with numerous activities. First, I paid a visit to the sexton and I tried to convince him of my innocence. I must have succeeded, for when I then asked him for the keys to the Copernicus Tower and several other rooms of the fortress, justifying my request by my work on the Frombork guide, he gave them to me.

I then visited the militia station again, and still later, I popped by my room. I returned the keys to the sexton and only then went to dinner.

I found Director Marchak dining in the company of Dr. Parsley, who had a very mocking expression. Marchak was clarifying something to him, which clearly displeased Dr. Parsley.

"I'm trying to persuade my colleague, Dr. Parsley," Marchak explained to me as I sat down at their table, "to combine the detective skills of the two of you in order to conclude the search for Koenig's stash all the more quickly."

"I would be delighted to cooperate with Dr. Parsley," I replied.

"But I refuse, Mr. Director," objected Dr. Parsley. "I have found the first two caches without anyone's help and I am sure I will find the third. Just give me a few days."

Director Marchak squirmed with reluctance.

"My duties call me to Warsaw, but I want to be at the opening of the third cache. And I feel that Thomas has found some kind of a clue."

"I don't want to hear about any leads from Thomas," Parsley said, covering his ears with his hands. "Have I disappointed your hopes, director? Haven't I discovered the first two caches? Give me some more time and a free hand."

"Very well, if you insist," sighed Marchak.

I said in deep thought, looking at the ceiling of the dining room:

"I sense that my colleague, Dr. Parsley, will find the third Koenig cache tomorrow night."

"How do you know that I will make the discovery so soon?" asked Dr. Parsley sharply.

"Oh, are you clairvoyant now?" Director Marchak glanced at me suspiciously.

"Er... Sometimes, I am able to predict the future. And here I see..." I said, still looking at the ceiling, "behold, I see Dr. Parsley discovering the cache of Colonel Koenig tomorrow."

"This is impossible!" barked Dr. Parsley, upset by my words, which he took for mockery. "I'm not on the trail of the cache at all."

"But you soon will be. You will soon find a clue," I declared firmly.

And until the end of our meal, even though they showered me with questions, I did not say another word about it.

CHAPTER 16: THAT A DETECTIVE NEEDS A MUSE

Director Marchak is angry. Eye to eye with the enemy. Gentlemen and adversaries. What a detective needs. A few words about museums. How Dr. Parsley became a genius. On the need for the philosopher's stone. Valdemar Batura's first defeat. Please help.

The glare of the setting sun shimmered on the Lagoon like molten metal. The sun itself was hidden from view by the forest on the Frombork hills, which closed off the horizon to the west and descended right down to the water, but the burning light reached around this obstacle and blazed on the sea. White seagulls sitting on the water rode the waves, swaying up and down like children on swings. A passenger ship sailed along the spit and, from a distance, seemed to be a huge white swan with its head tucked in under its wing. A cool breeze brought the smell of the sea, the coastal reeds rustled quietly, and white foam billowed at the rocky pier.

Director Marchak had invited me for a walk to the marina. We walked in silence for a while, each immersed in his own thoughts. We wandered all the way to the small lighthouse at the end of the breakwater. There, looking out toward the distant and barely visible Vistula Spit, Director Marchak asked me:

"Do you really think, Thomas, that I should stay in Frombork until tomorrow night?"

"Absolutely, Mr. Director," I replied politely.

"And tomorrow night, Parsley will discover the third cache?"

"Most definitely, Mr. Director."

"Clairvoyance, huh? Because, you know, even he himself doesn't know it yet."

"But I know it."

I had once known a certain individual who had spoken in a similar way. His name was Master Pyfello. Before the war, he advertised in newspapers as a clairvoyant and palm reader.

"Do you, Thomas, God forbid, also read from the palm?"

"I don't have any supernatural abilities, Mr. Director. Indeed, thus far, Valdemar Batura has beaten me at every step: he has foreseen my every move and has been able to counter it perfectly. I lost three rounds to him. This time, however, I am the one who knows: I know what moves he will make. What's more, I can provoke them."

"Could you initiate me into the arcana?"

"No, Mr. Director."

"You don't trust me?"

"Oh, that's not the point. I'm afraid that you wouldn't allow me to make certain moves, and without them, I won't be able to provide you with proof of Batura's guilt. Besides, I can't deny myself the pleasure of seeing the expression on your face when we finally get to Koenig's third cache."

"Oh yeah?" the director became angry. "You wish to amuse yourself at my expense? And this is my reward for saving you time and again from all sorts of trouble? I'll bear this in mind. I will not ask you anything again."

Exasperated, the director took one more step towards the water, slipped, and nearly slid down the wet concrete into the murky depths. Luckily, I managed to grab him by the arm, saving him from a full-body dunk. He glanced at me gratefully but then barked with menace in his voice:

"I don't care about you tattling on about Koenig's treasure. Tomorrow, we work on the guide. We haven't come here to take the sea air, you know."

Then he invited me for coffee at the port café.

We were just about to enter it when the red Mustang pulled up—with Valdemar Batura and Miss Ala in it.

"Ah, what a nice meeting!" cried Valdemar Batura with hypocritical joy. "Is there something very important going on in Frombork that even Director Marchak has come here?"

The director furrowed his brow, pretending not to recognize the man.

"Excuse me, do we know each other?" he asked.

"Yes, Mr. Director. I have even worked in your department at one time."

"Ah, yes, I remember you now. You were a very bad employee."

"Not true, Mr. Director. I was a very good employee but the salary was very bad: it only covered half my time. But we met again later, too, at a certain old mansion. I am told Thomas discovered a secret Masonic lodge in its basement."[16]

"Oh, I remember," said the director gloomily. "You received a suspended sentence for breaking into the manor."

"Yes, sir," bowed Valdemar Batura politely. "For I am the famous Valdemar Batura, the evil genius, the terror of all the museum workers of Poland, the cunning antiquities dealer. I am the man whom Thomas uses to frighten little children."

"And what brings you to Frombork?" Marchak asked.

"The same as you, Director. The Koenig Treasure. I decided to look into the matter."

"The Koenig Treasure, huh?" burst out Director Marchak, touched to the core by Batura's insolence.

But Batura only bowed politely and said:

"And since a common pursuit unites us, shall we have a little coffee together?"

"We are not in any way united. We have nothing in common," the director got angry. "Rather, everything divides us. Anyway, we will settle this business once and for all tomorrow."

The director suddenly stopped short and glanced at me with a bit of trepidation, realizing that he may have said too much. But I nodded my head and said:

"That's right. The day after tomorrow, we will all leave Frombork and leave you, Valdemar, to enjoy this lovely city in peace."

"In other words, you think you will uncover the third cache tomorrow?" Batura asked, and his face seemed to grow gaunt.

And now Miss Ala also got out of the red Mustang. She

---

[16] See Zbig Nienacki, *Mr. Wheels and the Mystery of Mysteries* (upcoming)

approached me and whispered to me under her breath:

"I was on my way to Frombork and met him along the way again. He gave me a ride and offered me coffee, so I agreed because I thought I might get something out of him about the third stash."

"I understand," I nodded. "And I am glad to see you. I will have to speak to you in private in a little while, OK?"

Meanwhile, Director Marchak and Batura had already entered the cafe. Ala and I tried to catch up with them but froze at the door at the sight of... Dr. Parsley sitting at a table in the company of Miss Anielka.

"Oh, please, do take a seat," Dr. Parsley rose from his chair at the sight of the Director and invited the two men to sit at his table. Parsley, who had only been working at our department for a short time, did not know Batura by sight.

Director Marchak glanced at Miss Anielka, then looked at Ala and said:

"I congratulate you, gentlemen. I congratulate you on your good taste and your extraordinarily good luck. You have managed to assemble the two most beautiful women in Frombork—at the same table, at the same time. You are clearly very talented men, although I confess that I would prefer you to think only about the affairs of our department day and night, even during off-duty hours."

We all sat down: Parsley, Anielka, Marchak, Batura, Miss Ala, and I. Soon, cups of black coffee and a large tray of pastries appeared on the table. There followed a flow of cheerful, casual banter. No one watching us from the sidelines would have guessed that we were fierce competitors engaged in a contest that was liable to break out in a sharp confrontation at the drop of a hat.

First, we talked about trivial matters, the weather, the beauty of the Frombork landscape, our holidays. Then Batura proposed:

"Let's take a sip of coffee in honor of Dr. Parsley's remarkable successes. The news carries that he has found Colonel Koenig's second cache. I heard this from the lips of the sexton of the Frombork cathedral himself."

"Ah, he's a talker," smiled Dr. Parsley modestly. "But, yes, that's right. I have managed to find the second cache."

Miss Anielka looked at Dr. Parsley with the expression of expression of complete and utter admiration in her huge black eyes.

"You are simply brilliant, Doctor. I knew it from the first moment I met you on the beach."

Dr. Parsley blushed all the way to the roots of his hair.

"Ah, you flatter me, Miss Anielka. Indeed, I have had some modest successes, but Thomas has had even greater successes in his time."

"Is that so?" Miss Anielka asked with a perceptible note of doubt in her voice. "Mr. Thomas looks to me like a man who is easily led astray."

"Or led toward the border," Batura added.

Only Ala and I understood Batura's joke. We both laughed. Sometimes, all you can do is laugh at your own stupidity. No one else noticed the joke. Dr. Parsley was so taken with Miss Anielka's admiration that he felt the soul of the company. He made a serious face and said:

"Unfortunately, I'm facing an extremely difficult task: I have to find the third cache."

Miss Ala squinted her eyes slyly and said:

"I have always been impressed by people with detective talents. I myself am an engineer and specialize in a boring field like automation."

A boring field, my foot, I thought, recalling both *ACE* and the electronic dog. But Miss Ala continued:

"Could you tell us how you made your remarkable discoveries, Dr. Parsley? What clues led you to the treasure?"

Dr. Parsley nodded in the direction of Miss Anielka and then ostentatiously bowed down to kiss her hand. He said with emphasis:

"Like every poet, every detective worth his mettle must have his muse. Miss Anielka has been my muse. It was in her company—as if under the glow of her charming influence—that the solutions to both puzzles suddenly occurred to me. Isn't that so, Miss Anielka?"

"Yes, it does seem so," Miss Anielka nodded, and again we saw delight in her eyes.

Dr. Parsley, meanwhile, mused about the happy moments.

"I remember," he told us, "that the realization that Koenig's map indicated the Frombork cemetery as the site of the first cache came to me when Miss Anielka and I first met on the beach. We were lying on the sand in the sun, looking toward the Vistula Spit. It was hot, so very hot. Miss Anielka said that she would like to be somewhere in the shade and that the Frombork cemetery was very cool because of the tall trees. And then she asked me how cemeteries were usually indicated on maps."

"Oh, did I say that?" asked Miss Anielka, surprised.

"And at that moment, I experienced a flash of revelation. Koenig's plan showed a rectangle with crosses—just the way cemeteries are marked on maps! And then it occurred to me that he had meant the Frombork cemetery!"

"And the second cache?" Ala asked.

"Why, it was all due to Miss Anielka again! I met her while walking through the cathedral courtyard. She had a frightened look on her face. I asked her what had happened, and she replied that she had been exploring the underground crypt and saw the Devil's Image there, which frightened her. 'A Devil's Image?' I thought. *Why, that's a* Teufelsbild—*that 'Teufelb.' from Koenig's map!* And so it was, ladies and gentlemen, so it was."

I nodded my head with complete understanding.

"Sometimes," I concluded, "an unusual coincidence can help us make a brilliant discovery."

"No, no. Those were not coincidences," insisted Dr. Parsley. "Those were moments of true inspiration! And I owe them to Miss Anielka."

"I hope," I added, "that your wonderful inspiration will not fail you on your way to the third cache."

An awkward silence fell, from which we were rescued by Miss Anielka:

"Dr. Parsley certainly overestimates my role in his remarkable successes. But it is very pleasant to be someone else's muse. And you?" she turned to me." Will you reveal to us the sources of your inspiration?"

I shrugged my shoulders.

"I have not had much fortunate inspiration lately. And now I know the reason for my failure."

"Ha! Of course! You need a muse!" chuckled Miss Anielka cheerfully.

Dr. Parsley, eager to bury me in the eyes of the company, said:

"Indeed, Thomas has not had much success as an investigator lately. But in the field of appraisal, he has proven to be downright brilliant."

"Really?" Batura feigned astonishment.

"And how! Imagine that in Koenig's second cache, we found five chalices. At first, we thought they were plain silver cups of little worth."

"And weren't they?" Batura asked.

"Well, hear this. This is unbelievable. When Thomas took them in his hands and looked at them carefully, it turned out that we had found not silver but gold chalices. And not just gold, but gold set with precious stones!"

I saw an expression of suspicion flash on Batura's face. It soon turned into concern.

"Is this true, Mr. Director?" he turned to Director Marchak.

Marchak grunted loudly. Then he took out a handkerchief and honked into it loudly as if he suddenly developed a runny nose.

"It was very dark in the crypt," he explained. "That's why we got the mistaken impression that the chalices were silver. But later, Thomas discovered that they were, in fact, made of gold."

Batura grimaced. It was not difficult to guess what thoughts were circulating in his head. From that moment on, he remained silent, glancing toward me suspiciously from time to time.

I felt Ala nudging me under the table. We were both trying to hold back laughter.

Meanwhile, the general interest in his person and the attention of the ladies had turned Dr. Parsley's head, and he began to perorate loudly about my person again:

"It seems that Thomas has lost his muses. He lacks inspiration. He, the man who had found the Dunin treasure,[17] the diary of a Nazi war criminal,[18] and the secret Masonic lodge, has turned out to be completely helpless in the face of the three puzzles posed by Colonel Koenig. To make matters worse, he fell under the influence of a suspicious individual—a certain Mr. Cagliostro, a maestro of black and white magic, and now he has convinced himself that he is clairvoyant."

At this point, I had to interrupt him because I didn't want Batura to learn that I had predicted Parsley's discovery of the third cache for the following night.

"Cagliostro has taught me some useful tricks," I spoke up. "While some people know how to turn gold chalices into silver goblets, I learned the much more difficult art of turning silver into gold."

"What do you mean by that?" Batura asked.

Director Marchak declared with directorial solemnity:

"Our department's payroll, dear Dr. Parsley, has no openings for muses to inspire our employees. Thomas' task has not been to search for Koenig's treasures but to compile a guide to Frombork. But if he really has possessed the skill of ancient alchemists and knows how to turn silver into gold, we can find a lot of work for him in our department."

Then, after a moment's reflection, he added mysteriously:

"We could also use a philosopher's stone."

"To turn silver into gold?" repeated Batura. "Gentlemen, forgive me, but I cannot believe in such tricks."

And as he uttered these words, a postman entered the café.

He stood at the threshold for a moment, looked around, and, noticing Batura, approached him.

---

[17] See *Mr. Wheels and the Island of Bandits* (upcoming)

[18] See *Mr. Wheels and His New Adventure* (upcoming)

"I think you are Mr. Valdemar Batura?" he asked.

"That's right."

"I noticed your car in front of the café and guessed you might be in. A telegram has come to you from Warsaw, so instead of going to your camp at the Lagoon, I brought it here."

And he handed an envelope to Batura. Valdemar opened it and ran his eyes over it.

Suddenly, he turned pale, and his expression became that of utter stupefaction.

"What happened?" asked Miss Anielka. And she took the paper from Batura's hands.

As she read it, I glanced over her shoulder and read:

"Silver in box. Where is gold? Stefan."

Batura rose from his chair. He looked at me and his eyes flashed full-on of rage for an instant.

"I am sorry, but I have to leave you. I must make an urgent phone call. We shall see each other again."

It was probably too much in his current mental state not to make those last words sound like a threat. He left the café hurriedly.

"Will you give me a ride home?" turned Miss Ala to me.

"Of course," I rose from my chair.

As we were leaving the café, we heard Dr. Parsley, who clearly had not understood much of what had just happened, speak affectionately to Miss Anielka:

"Although Director Marchak objects to the presence of muses in our department, I beg you not to leave me. You are an inspiration to me. You help me to come up with brilliant ideas. What can I possibly do without you?"

I saw an expression of great distaste appear on the lips of Director Marchak. And it was not because he did not foresee a full-time position for the muses. He was simply a very shrewd man. He had grasped perfectly the nature of Dr. Parsley's "inspirations."

"I think I can guess what was in the telegram," giggled Miss Ala on the way to the hostel where my vehicle was parked. "Mr. Cool-in-sunglasses discovered that the transmutation of silver into gold is a spontaneously reversible process. Batura is ready to believe in your magical powers."

"All credit goes to you," I said. "You made this miraculous switch. My God, what would I have done without you?"

"Oh?" said Miss Ala astonished. "You sound like Dr. Parsley. Do you want to make me your muse?"

"Alas, Miss Ala, alas. As you have heard, our department does not have such a vacancy. But I will have one more request for you."

"Do you want to hire *ACE* again?" she asked. "Unfortunately, that will not be possible. *ACE* goes back to the Polytechnic tomorrow."

"And you will leave also?" I frowned.

"No, I will stay here for a few more days to wind up our affairs."

I breathed a sigh of relief and made my request clear to her.

I think Batura would have given a lot to know what that request was about.

CHAPTER 17: EIGHTEEN BLUE ENVELOPES

The mystery of Copernicus' tomb. Which chapel? He who seeks, finds. An ultimatum for Dr. Parsley. Cagliostro's entreaty. Miss Ala fulfills my request. The blue envelope. Who doesn't like illusionists? A demonstration of the magical arts. Eighteen blue envelopes.

That day, which, as it turned out later, was to be fraught with dramatic events and bring our final showdown with the villains, began very uneventfully.

It had rained that night, and a drizzle continued until the wee hours of the morning. When the sky cleared a bit, Director Marchak took me out for a walk on the Cathedral Hill. He wanted to hear about another Frombork mystery—the mystery of Nicolaus Copernicus' tomb.

First, I showed the director around the huge interior of the cathedral, pointing out the epitaphs on the walls and the presumed site of the great astronomer's grave. Then we went out to the courtyard and again sat on our bench under the old oak tree. Here, I was able to unfold my tale:

"As you know, Director, Nicolaus Copernicus died in Frombork on May 24, 1543. The story has it that he received a copy of his privately printed *De Revolutionibus* on his deathbed—the book that was to cause such a stir across Europe only a year later. But, as he passed away, did the people around him realize what a giant he had been? They didn't. They thought he was merely one of the canons of the Frombork chapter. This is best evidenced by the fact that they did not even bother to record the date of his death. The chapter's annals recorded the day of his funeral as the date of his death! Only as his name became famous did the bishop of Varmia, Kromer, decide to fund a plaque commemorating him. By that time, thirty-eight years had passed since the astronomer's death, and no one in Frombork remembered the location of his grave. So, the epitaph was mounted on the first vacant dignified space: on the inner wall of the Cathedral, between the second and third altars. And from this many misunderstandings followed, for people who, many years later, tried to find the grave of the great astronomer were inclined to believe that the epitaph had been placed over his tomb. Then, as if to confuse things even further, this epitaph was displaced in 1735 during the construction of Bishop Shembek's chapel. It was decided that the old plaque was not worthy of the great astronomer, and it was taken down to be replaced with another. But, as often happens in life, money ran out before the new epitaph could be erected. In this way, Copernicus had no commemorative plaque for many decades."

"Well, things do seem to work that way a lot, don't they?" said Director Marchak with all the wisdom of ten years in middle management.

"Alas, Mr. Director, alas. Meanwhile, interest in all matters related to Copernicus was growing worldwide. In 1802, two representatives of the Society of Friends of Science, Thaddeus Chatski and Marchin Molski, arrived in Frombork. They suggested that a new epitaph be prominently placed on a cathedral pillar. They noticed the old plaque on the floor, and it made them think that its position marked the tombstone of Copernicus. They obtained the permission to open the grave beneath it and found human remains. As it turned out later, these were not the bones of Nicolaus Copernicus but of Bishop Fleming, one of the founders of the Frombork Cathedral, a man who had died two hundred years before the astronomer."

"Please go on, it is very interesting."

"Meanwhile, German researchers followed an older trail: they decided to excavate under the wall where the first epitaph used to be. After opening the floor, they found several old coffins. They studied the bones and transported the skeletal remains to Königsberg, where they were later buried. Their expertise report was, unfortunately, never published, and for many years, the guides to the royal Castle at Königsberg told visitors that the famous astronomer lay buried there.

"But the truth, Mr. Director, is that the astronomer's body is still in Frombork. You see, the searchers have not taken into account the fundamental issue: we now know from old documents that it was customary in Frombork for each canon to have his own chapel in the cathedral and to be buried in that chapel after his death. In other words, just as in the case of the Copernican Observatory, it was necessary to determine which altar in the cathedral belonged to Nicolaus Copernicus, for then we would know where to look for his grave."

"Fascinating, fascinating," muttered the director.

"Unfortunately, there was no document that might indicate which altar belonged to Copernicus. Historians, like detectives, searched for the slightest clue, a single scrap of paper, even the shadow of a clue. And finally..."

I stopped for dramatic effect.

"And finally, what?"

"In an old folio containing documents on the chapter's administration, a note was discovered. It said that a certain canon named John Zanau had been assigned the chapel at the fourth pillar. And we knew from the chapter's list of canons the names of canons who followed Zanau. You see, there were sixteen canons and every time one canon passed away, another was appointed *in his* place. That canon would then take over his predecessor's curia and his chapel. And, well, according to one of these lists, John Zanau was Copernicus' predecessor. The astronomer would have taken over his curia, his chapel, and his seat in the chancery. So, since John Zanau had held the chapel at the fourth pillar, it had to have also been the chapel of Nicolaus Copernicus and the place where he was most likely buried. Finding his corpse will not be so difficult, for according to the chapter's records, the astronomer was buried forty-eight years after the death of his predecessor, and the next burial in the chapel did not take place until sixty-five years later. So, in the space of one hundred and thirty years, the body of Nicolaus Copernicus was the only one laid to rest near the fourth pillar. The techniques of modern science allow us to identify the coffin and the remains of Copernicus using this information. It is only necessary to organize a proper scientific team, get permission from the church authorities, and remove the floor at the fourth pillar—and maybe one more Frombork mystery will then be solved?"[19]

I finished my story by saying that I intended to include it in the guidebook. Director Marchak seemed lost in thought. Perhaps in his mind's eye, he was already completing a team of scholars and sourcing the finances needed for this kind of research. After a moment, he rose from the bench.

"I have to return to Warsaw tomorrow morning. Are you sure that we will have the solution to Colonel Koenig's latest mystery by tomorrow?"

"Yes. I swear by it," I replied with all seriousness.

We returned to the hostel and went into the dining room since it was already lunchtime.

We saw Cagliostro and Dr. Parsley dining at the same table. Dr. Parsley was eating his soup, but time and again, he glanced suspiciously at Cagliostro, or more precisely, he studied the maestro's pockets, fearing that a snake's head might peek out from one of them.

At the sight of us, Cagliostro got up from the table and, bowing low, said:

---

[19] This excavation did not take place until 2005. Thirteen skeletons were discovered near this altar, including one belonging to a male aged between 60 and 70 years. This particular skeleton was identified as the closest match to that of Copernicus. The skull of the skeleton served as the basis for facial reconstruction. In addition to morphological studies, DNA analysis is often used for the identification of historical or ancient remains. A significant challenge lay in identifying a suitable source of reference material. There were no known remains of any relatives of Copernicus. In 2006, however, a new source of DNA came to life. An astronomical reference book used by Copernicus for many years was found to contain hair among its pages. This book had been taken to Sweden as war booty following the Swedish invasion of Poland in the mid-17th century. It is currently in the possession of the Museum Gustavianum at Uppsala University. A meticulous examination of the book revealed several hairs thought likely to belong to the book's primary user, Copernicus. The DNA extracted from the hairs was compared with the DNA from the teeth and bones of the discovered skeleton. The mitochondrial DNA from the teeth and the skeletal sample matched those of the hairs, strongly suggesting that the remains were indeed those of Nicholas Copernicus.

"I have the honor to invite you to a great illusionist show today. The event will start at six in the evening. I will demonstrate all my prodigious powers at the event."

Director Marchak waved his hand as if chasing away an intrusive fly.

"I'm not familiar with the magical arts, and I don't like them. No, I don't like them," he declared categorically.

"And you?" the maestro turned to me.

And at this, an almost satanic plan was born in my head.

"I'll think about it," I answered evasively.

We sat down at the table. The director spoke to Dr. Parsley, and a kind of steely firmness resounded in his voice:

"Tomorrow morning, I return to Warsaw. Please find Koenig's third cache by tonight."

"What?" Dr. Parsley was so surprised that he pushed his soup away. "It's impossible, Mr. Director! I have not yet come up with a single clue to the third cache. You promised to leave me both a free hand and some time to find it."

The director shook his head.

"Let's stop playing games. I'm sure Thomas knows the location of the third cache. If you, Dr. Parsley, cannot manage by yourself, Thomas will help you. It's a pity to waste all this time in Frombork. New, serious tasks await us."

Dr. Parsley looked at me with great reluctance.

"Thomas, have you really solved the mystery of the third cache?" he asked.

"Yes."

"No, no, I don't want to know your solution!" exclaimed Dr. Parsley. "I wish to discover the cache by myself, and I swear that I will do it by tonight. Just leave me time to think about it. Anyway, I don't believe you have the solution. You have a conjecture, at most, and that's not enough. You're probably on a false trail again. And because of your conjecture, our Director gives me this ultimatum!"

I got up from the table, went to my room, and returned to the dining room, carrying a sealed blue envelope in my hand. I placed this envelope on the table next to Director Marchak's plate.

"Mr. Director," I said solemnly. "This envelope contains my guess as to the location of Colonel Koenig's third cache. Please, at any moment you see fit, open it and proceed to recover the treasure. If, on the other hand, you decide to give Dr. Parsley more time and he gets to the third cache before you, I will at least have the satisfaction that I was on the right track."

Marchak took the envelope from the table and put it in his jacket pocket.

"All right," he said graciously. "Dr. Parsley, I'll give you your chance. You have until 10 am tomorrow morning. If you haven't found the cache by then, I'll open the envelope, and if Thomas has indeed solved the mystery, I'll take the treasure to Warsaw. We don't have time for a longer stay in Frombork. I need you in Warsaw as well."

We finished our soup in silence. At the second course, Cagliostro renewed his invitation. But the director said with irritation:

"I've told Thomas in the past that I don't like magic arts shows."

"Ah, what a blow it is for an artist when someone doesn't want to see his work!" sighed Cagliostro sadly.

Dr. Parsley lost his appetite completely. The thought of the director's deadline paralyzed him. The evil serpent of ambition devoured him on the inside.

As I looked at him, I felt a great urge to inquire about the whereabouts of his muse and to console him by telling him that he was guaranteed to be soon visited by a new inspiration. But I feared that this highly ambitious man would take my words as derision.

Which, I guess, they would have been.

I went back to my room, and after a while, Cagliostro came in.

"Mr. Thomas," the maestro folded his arms imploringly, "do something for me, will you? Director Marchak is an influential figure in the ministry and a good friend of the director of the events department. I have already told you about the trouble I am having finding a permanent job. If Director Marchak likes my show, maybe he can put a good word about me with his colleague in the events department, and then all my troubles will be resolved."

"Very well, " I agreed. "I will try to persuade the director to come to tonight's performance."

At this, the maestro rubbed his hands together, then embraced me, hugged me, and said:

"If you manage to arrange this and bring Director Marchak to my show, I will gift you my snake."

"Oh, no!" I cried out desperately. "I will do it out of the goodness of my heart. Please, no need for bribery, Mr. Cagliostro."

The thought of acquiring Peter frightened me so much that I mulled not just giving up on bringing Director Marchak to the Cagliostro show but, in fact, forbidding him outright from going there, should he suddenly develop an urge to do so.

We heard a knock on the door, and Waltzing Zosha and Bashka entered. They brought me an invitation to the evening campfire event.

I looked at the invitation. There was not a word in it about either Cagliostro or black magic.

"Would you please take this invitation to Director Marchak," I said to my young friends. "And whatever you do, do not mention that there will be a magic show at the bonfire. Director Marchak is very fond of the Scouts and will probably be happy to go to the bonfire. But be careful because he hates illusionists."

They went to the director's room. Leaving Cagliostro full of hope that he would have Director Marchak at his show, I hurried to the courtyard of the cathedral.

On a bench under the oak tree sat Miss Ala. She had with her a bag of rather large size.

"Well?" I inquired impatiently.

"I arranged everything as you asked. And here is the apparatus you asked me for," she passed the surprisingly heavy bag to me.

I knocked on the sexton's door and, pointing to the camera that Ala had brought me in her bag, asked for the keys to the towers. I explained to the sexton that I wanted to take some pictures for my guide. Half an hour later, I gave the keys back to him and took Ala for a walk around Frombork.

I realized that this was my last day in this charming town: on the following day, we would all return to Warsaw.

"Are you sure that things will go as planned?" Ala asked.

"They better. I can't keep on failing, can I?" I laughed. "If Dr. Parsley is allowed to experience his moments of inspiration regularly, then I, too, should be able to hope to come up with a good idea from time to time."

I felt optimistic, but the wait made me restless. I looked impatiently at my watch, anticipating the coming of the evening, which was to bring the final showdown with Valdemar Batura.

Until now, he had dealt the cards, keeping the best for himself, but now our roles reversed. I would call the tune and he would dance the dance. But would he? Would he do what I wanted him to do? What if the magical exchange of cups had warned him to be cautious? Maybe he won't let himself be led into the snare I had set?

I tried to think it through:

Even if he feels suspicious, Batura has to accept the hand I have dealt him. He has no choice. Parsley has been given until 10 am the next day. If Batura wants to use him as his dupe, he has to raid the third cache tonight. And when people are in a hurry, they don't look carefully enough to see where they tread. Then, it is easy to spring a trap.

The sky brightened over Frombork. The clouds moved away to the north and hung over the Vistula Spit. The sun became the usual harsh, hot August sun.

"*ACE* has left today," Ala said.

"And we, will we see each other again?" I asked.

"Well... it's up to us, right?" she replied.

I nodded, and we smiled at each other. I really liked this young lady, who, barely out of the Polytechnic, was already an assistant to a great scientist—and in such an interesting field, too. I was passionate about works of art, treasure hunts, lost museum collections, and such. And she—she was interested in automata. And yet, I felt that our interests did not divide us. On the contrary, I found a great understanding for my passions in her, and I thought I understood hers.

We went for a long walk—all the way to the Frombork Hills—from where we could see the lofty structure of the old cathedral full of all kinds of mysteries.

We returned to the PTTK hostel before 6 PM. I invited Ala to dinner. The four of us ate together: Ala, Director Marchak, Dr. Parsley, and I. Dr. Parsley was thoughtful, eating absentmindedly. His mood indicated that perhaps he was already on the trail of the third cache.

Director Marchak accepted the Scouts' invitation. Dr. Parsley, on the other hand, when I asked him if he would go to the bonfire, contemptuously curled his lips and shrugged his shoulders. He said he had an appointment with Miss Anielka. I guessed that the expected inspiration was about to strike.

Then, the three of us went to the Boy Scout camp near the port. There were already a lot of scouts there, and a large number of guests had arrived, too. Waltzing Zosha and Bashka led us to the seats of honor—right in the front row.

I won't describe the performances to you because each of you, my readers, has participated in similar events. I will only say that when the scout in charge of the bonfire announced the performance of Maestro Cagliostro, Director Marchak tried to get up from his seat, and I had to restrain him by force.

"What? Black magic?" fumed the director, outraged. "And such drivel is fed to our youth? I do not agree with this. I protest!"

But he calmed down a bit when Cagliostro began to demonstrate his skills. And no wonder because the maestro showed us some real wonders.

First, there was a trick with cards, which he would take blindfolded out of the deck after asking us what card we wanted to see. When we asked for the ace of clubs, he took out the ace of clubs; when asked for the queen of spades, he pulled out the queen of spades. Then he showed us tricks with a string, which he cut with a miraculous magic wand and then reunited into a whole using the same instrument. We saw him put a white bunny into a box on the table, wave his wand, and disappear the bunny without a trace. And a second later, he pulled a snake out of the same box, then a mouse, then the bunny again.

The tricks were so clever that even Director Marchak forgot his dislike of illusionists and warmly applauded the maestro's performance. And perhaps Cagliostro would have achieved his goal—that is, gotten Director Marchak to whisper a good word to his colleague, had it not been for something that happened at the end of the maestro's performances.

Because now, you see, Cagliostro went too far. He announced that he would show the audience a strange trick with envelopes and invited Director Marchak to participate.

"Me, why me? Please invite someone else," the director defended himself when Cagliostro pointed him out.

"Because you are an unbeliever. You do not believe in my miraculous powers," replied the maestro.

The scouts began clapping their hands, and Director Marchak, joyless, willy-nilly, got up from his seat and approached Cagliostro. The maestro took out of his pocket seven identical blue envelopes.

"Ladies and gentlemen," he declared, showing his envelopes. "You can see that I have only seven envelopes in my hand. I put these seven envelopes in the pocket of the director's jacket. Just like that..."

And Cagliostro put seven blue envelopes in the director's jacket.

"How many envelopes are in the director's pocket?"

"Seven!" cried the audience.

"Eight," said Director Marchak, as he remembered my envelope with the solution to the riddle of the third cache.

"Neither seven nor eight," declared Cagliostro, "but seventeen!"

And he asked Director Marchak to take out the envelopes. Marchak reached into his pocket and, to his surprise, pulled out eighteen envelopes.

"Eighteen, not seventeen," he corrected Cagliostro.

"Sorry, I was mistaken," stated Cagliostro. "The honorable gentleman had his own envelope in his pocket."

And he returned one blue envelope to the director.

This was the last number in the performance of Maestro Cagliostro. This was followed by the demonstrations of various scouting games. The bonfire ended at eight in the evening. We left the camp along with the rest of the guests. The three of us—Director Marchak, Miss Ala, and I—went to the café for an evening snack. I gave a sign to Waltzing Zosha and Bashka to come along.

Our great adventure was about to reach its grand finale.

CHAPTER 18: THE SUPER-ULTRA-HIGH FREQUENCY RADIO PLAY

Very strange radio broadcasts. Are there super-ultra-high frequency waves? Conversation of villains. Where is the treasure? The cache. We wait for the sexton. A misadventure on the way to Tolkmitsko. What the blue envelope contained. In the tower. Dr. Parsley on the trail. True or False. The final disclaimer.

In the café, punctually at ten o'clock, I looked at my watch and said to Director Marchak:

"Would you like to listen to an interesting radio program in my room right now?"

"A radio program?" Director Marchak seemed reluctant. "Our radio pays way too little attention to national monuments."

"But this will be a very special broadcast. It is entitled *How Colonel Koenig's third cache was robbed*," I explained.

"What's that? You are up to something, Mr. Thomas. I'm sure that if I looked up the radio schedule, I wouldn't find such a program."

"The national radio broadcasts only on low, medium, and high frequencies. However, the broadcast I'm recommending to you will be on super-ultra-high frequency waves."

"Are there such waves?" Bashka asked, puzzled.

I pointed to Miss Ala.

"This kind lady brought a special receiver to my room. The broadcast promises to be interesting and on a topic of interest to us all."

Waltzing Zosha got up from her chair, performed a small arabesque, and repeated the title aloud:

"*How Colonel Koenig's third cache was robbed*. Is that really the title of the broadcast?"

"Yes," I nodded.

"Well then, let's go," said Director Marchak and summoned the waitress to pay for our cakes and tea.

We headed back to the PTTK hostel. I hurried the group along because I was afraid that the performers of our broadcast might, out of sheer artistic eagerness, start the show early.

We entered my room. I seated everyone at the table and took out a miniature receiver from under my bed. Miss Ala immediately set to turning its knobs, but only a slight static issued from its speaker.

"The actors have not yet entered the studio," Ala said.

"So it's going to be some live show," said a somewhat disappointed Director Marchak.

"More like a live reportage. I hope to record the crime live," I consoled the director.

"I don't understand any of this," said Waltzing Zosha. "But I'm sure it will be the coolest broadcast I've heard all summer."

"Or is this some kind of a magic trick?" wondered Bashka.

These words have awakened the director's concern.

"Has living together with Cagliostro had such a huge impact on you, Thomas? Since I've arrived in town, all I ever see is *hocus-pocus*. I warn you that if you attempt to introduce these new illusionist practices into our department, it will not meet with my approval."

And the noble director suspiciously looked around the room, expecting to see snakes and lizards crawling out from behind the furniture.

But the friendly animals, which I confess I had come to like a little, were probably out and about with Cagliostro. The maestro of black and white magic has not yet returned from his performance at the bonfire.

"Attention!" hissed Ala. "Something is beginning to happen..."

A loud rasp was heard in the speaker as if of someone opening a rusty iron door. Then a male voice, immediately recognizable as Batura's, commanded:

"Lock the door. Where's the flashlight?"

The transmitting apparatus was located somewhere underground. The actors' footsteps became louder and louder as they approached the device.

"Here, shine your light on this wall," Batura ordered. There was a long moment of silence as (we imagined) the light of the electric flashlight swept the wall of the underground chamber. After some time, Cagliostro's voice came through:

"There isn't anything here. The walls are just brick and stone."

"And what's that thing?" Batura said. "It doesn't look like this room has ever had a chimney. Yet, there, right at the ground level, there is a door that looks like an ashpan."

"We don't have a tool to open it."

"The pliers, man, the pliers."

We heard the quiet rasp of iron against iron. Then something creaked.

"It's open," Cagliostro said. "But it's all bricks behind."

"Well, take out the bricks!" Batura ordered again.

There was the sound of someone gasping; then something thumped several times. Someone was throwing bricks on the stone floor. And after a while, we heard Cagliostro's voice full of joy:

"It's here! Valdemar, it's here! It was behind the bricks!"

Batura began to order him in a feverish voice:

"Step aside, Cagliostro. Let me get to work. We need to find a box or a bag of rubies among these things. We will leave everything else alone."

Again, there was a moment of silence, and then we heard Batura's voice:

"There. Look at this tin tobacco box. See?"

"My goodness. These are gorgeous. And huge!"

Another moment of silence and then Batura's voice:

"Yes, these are rubies, my friend. Rubies."

"Let me see, let me see," Cagliostro asked.

"Forget it. This is not the time for gem appreciation. The sexton will be back at any moment and then Parsley will arrive. Now, let's have the fakes. Hurry up. There, put them in the box. Now, these go into the pouch. Yes, like that. Give it here."

Director Marchak slammed his fist on the table.

"The scoundrels!" he yelled. "They are switching the stones!"

Now, the clatter of bricks sliding back into the ashpan, then the rasp of iron against iron: Cagliostro closing the door. Still later, we heard footsteps moving away and the loud noise of the door opening.

But just at this moment, Batura and Cagliostro must have seen something or someone in the open doorway because we heard them both cry out in unison:

"Geezus!"

The broadcast was interrupted. A profound silence fell in our room. We had just witnessed the discovery and pilfering of Koenig's third cache. It was now obvious to everyone that the first and second caches had been robbed in the same way. I had provided Director Marchak with the proof he had so strenuously demanded from me.

But, surprisingly, Marchak was not at all thrilled by this. A menacing frown furrowed his brow.

"You knew about this all along, Thomas, haven't you? You knew where the third cache was!" he asked me in an ominous tone.

"Of course. I made a note about it and gave it to you this morning," I said unconcernedly.

"You knew where the hiding place was," Marchak repeated. "You put some kind of broadcasting apparatus there. You also knew that the bad guys would go there and carry out the robbery. In other words, knowing that they would rob the cache, you not only did not prevent it, but you made it into a radio program, exposing the Nation to a potential loss!"

"Oh, we'll recover those rubies," I replied carelessly. "But I must object, Director. I did not enable the crime. You did. You led the crooks to the third cache."

"Me?" outraged the director.

"Yes, Mr. Director. I entrusted you with an envelope containing the location of the cache. I confided in you."

I did not finish, for, just at that moment, the door of the room flew open, and—tense like a bomb about to go off—Dr. Parsley rushed in. His hair was tousled, his eyes wide open.

"I know, I know!" he shouted hysterically. "I have the solution to the mystery of the third cache! The eight angles on Koenig's plan indicate the Octagon: the octagonal tower of the Frombork fortress! That's where the third cache is!"

"Is that so?" Director Marchak asked grimly.

"Yes, Mr. Director! It was brilliantly simple. But simple solutions are the hardest to think of. Miss Anielka, seeing my despair, asked me about the cipher to the third locker. I told her about the eight corners on Koenig's plan. "Eight corners," she repeated. "Eight corners." And then I remembered the Octagon!"

Dr. Parsley interrupted his speech to catch his breath, and then the index finger of his hand pointed in my direction:

"And now, Mr. Director, please open the envelope that Thomas has given you. We will see if he has also come up with the same solution to the puzzle!"

Director Marchak reached into his jacket pocket and took out the blue envelope. He tore it open and took out a piece of paper. He looked at it for a moment, then turned it around for all of us to see.

It was empty.

"So that's it, then!?" roared Parsley with disdain. "Thomas has fooled us, Mr. Director!"

But Director Marchak did not say a word. He remembered my words that he had revealed Koenig's third cache to the villains. He also remembered the envelope trick played on him at the scout campfire. Angrily, he crumpled up the piece of paper and threw it into the trash.

"Can a radio broadcast be evidence in a court of law?" he asked me.

"No, Mr. Director. The broadcast was for you. It was the proof you had demanded. But even if we had recorded the broadcast on tape, we would not have been able to present it in court, where a tape recording cannot be used as evidence in a criminal case. Criminals will always be able to say that they wanted to do me a favor and, at my request, *played* their roles."

Dr. Parsley did not understand anything.

"What are you people talking about?" he asked.

With an accusatory gesture, the director pointed to the small receiver on the table:

"This small radio has just broadcast the voices of two villains who sneaked into some underground chamber and removed a tin box of rubies from a secret compartment. And in their place, they put fakes."

"Does this have anything to do with the Octagon?" howled Dr. Parsley.

Director Marchak rose slowly from his chair.

"I'm afraid it does. I also fear that we have underestimated Thomas's multiple talents. It turns out that in addition to his detective vein, he has a talent for directing theatrical performances."

"And he cheats, too!" Parsley added, recalling the blank piece of paper in the blue envelope.

Director Marchak waved his hand.

"Let's go see the third Koenig's cache. And to you," he threw me a threatening look, "I leave the matter of recovering the real rubies."

Dr. Parsley became embarrassed.

"We must wait for the arrival of the sexton. He has the key to the Octagon door. Unfortunately, he had received some telegram in the evening and took the 8:20 ferry to Tolkmitsko. I think he will return to Frombork by the last ferry. That will be—" he looked at his wristwatch—"in five minutes."

We left the hostel, heading for the marina.

"Wow, that was a great radio program!" giggled Waltzing Zosha.

Bashka had an embarrassed look on his face.

"How will you get the real stones back?" he asked.

Ala also spoke up with sincere concern:

"It seems to me that you have overplayed your hand, Thomas. You should not have allowed the villains to replace the rubies. How will you get them back now? I fear that Batura has already left for Warsaw."

Dr. Parsley still understood nothing of our conversation.

"What are you people talking about? What does Batura have to do with this case? Is he really that dangerous? He made a sympathetic impression on me."

We now found ourselves in the old moat of the Cathedral Hill. It was a bright, moonlit night. After the morning rain and the heat of the day, the trees gave off an intoxicating fragrance.

From the direction of the port came the loud toot of a siren. It was the last ferry from Tolkmitsko entering the harbor.

"Let's wait here," said the director.

Ten minutes later, fast footsteps sounded on the empty street. It was the sexton hurrying home. He walked quickly as if rushing in great anxiety. He was muttering to himself.

We surrounded him and explained to him that we needed the key to the Octagon tower, as that's where the third treasure cache was hidden.

"The key? The key to the Octagon?" burst out the sexton. "Imagine that! I lost the keys to *my apartment*!"

And leading us to his home in the fortress, he told us an astonishing story. In the evening, at about 8 pm, a man claiming to be a postman brought him a telegram saying:

Please come immediately to Tolkmitsko. I will meet you at the marina. Very important.

"I asked the letter carrier if he knew how to get to Tolkmitsko at that hour. He replied that a ferry was leaving the port in half an hour. I was curious about the message, so not thinking much, I locked the apartment and went to the harbor. I arrived in Tolkmitsko, got off, and began to wait. But no one was there! I waited there like a fool. And, of course, I returned to Frombork on the next ferry. On the way back, I discovered that I did not have the keys to my apartment. I think I lost them somewhere."

"And as you boarded the ship to Tolkmitsko, didn't a man with a beard bump into you?" I asked unexpectedly.

"You mean the illusionist?" asked the sexton. "But how do you know? That's exactly what happened, sir. He pushed me aside because he was in a hurry to get on the ship. But as soon as he did, he turned around and got right off. Were you there to see it?"

"No, sir. But I find I am acquiring the powers of clairvoyance."

We did not inquire more of the sexton. For all of us—with the exception of Dr. Parsley—the meaning of the scene at the harbor was quite obvious. Cagliostro had pilfered the keys from the sexton's pocket, then he and Batura opened his apartment and "borrowed" the key for the Octagon. That had been the whole point of luring the sexton to Tolkmitsko: with the help of a fake telegram, they got him out of the house. The telegram had not been difficult to forge—in provincial towns, they write out telegrams in pencil: it is enough to take a blank sheet from the post office.

The sexton's keys were in the door of his apartment.

"Oh God," he marveled. "I was so preoccupied trying to imagine who was waiting for me in Tolkmitsko that I absentmindedly left the keys in the lock!"

None of us said anything about it. The meaning of this was also obvious: the villains had left the keys in the lock to cover all traces of their crime.

The key to the Octagon was not there.

We headed through the dark courtyard to the squat octagonal tower. On our way there, we came across Miss Anielka, Batura, and Cagliostro. They were standing surrounded by several militiamen, led by Lieutenant Yujinski.

"What's happened?" asked Dr. Parsley, approaching Miss Anielka.

She shrugged her shoulders.

"I was arrested. This is some kind of misunderstanding."

"Is that so?" interjected Lieutenant Yujinski. "I don't think the two gentlemen," he nodded to Batura and Cagliostro, "will try to deny that they were caught red-handed while robbing Colonel Koenig's cache. As for you," he bowed to Anielka, "you will be charged as their accomplice."

Dr. Parsley froze as if struck by lightning. He was unable to squeeze a word out.

Director Marchak nudged him on the shoulder.

"We're going in," he said. "The main thing is to find and secure the treasure."

Dr. Parsley seemed to awaken from deep sleep. With a dazed expression on his face, he walked over to the Octagon and tried the door: it was unlocked, and the key was in the lock.

"We will also take a look at the treasure," Lieutenant Yujinsky said and followed us to the tower along with the other militiamen and the arrested three.

The sexton lit thick candles, and down the winding staircase, we all descended into the basement.

"Where could the cache be?" pondered Dr. Parsley aloud, looking around the arched ceiling of the rather large room.

"The ashpan. Go for the ashpan," said Director Marchak impatiently, arousing Dr. Parsley's delight.

"The ashpan? You are brilliant, director! You immediately spotted the place. Of course, the treasure must be there!"

"Okay, okay," muttered the director. "Open that ashpan and let's have the treasure."

As Dr. Parsley struggled to open the ashpan, Miss Ala went into a corner, recovered a small apparatus from a pile of rubble, and tucked it away in her bag. It had already served its purpose and was now superfluous.

"Here is the treasure!" whispered Dr. Parsley suddenly. And he opened the door of the ashpan.

In silence, holding our breaths, we watched as he slipped his hand into a compartment of the ashpan and took out one by one: a tin box, four beautiful silver-wrought reliquaries of very fine workmanship, and two embroidered infulae encrusted with precious stones.

"Everything checks out," triumphantly declared Dr. Parsley. "No one has been here before us or taken anything from here."

"And the tin box?" asked the director.

Dr. Parsley opened the tin box and began counting:

"One, two.... five... eight... ten rubies."

Marchak angrily took the box from him and, without even looking into it, declared:

"This time, I won't be fooled, Dr. Parsley. These rubies are fake!"

Dr. Parsley took the box from the director and began studying them.

"They are real, Mr. Director," he said after a while. "I know a little bit about stones. These are real stones."

Director Marchak took the box from Dr. Parsley again. Without looking inside, he began waving the box until the stones rattled like dice.

"These rubies are fake, Mr. Parsley. Batura switched them. We all heard him switch them."

I took the box out of the director's hands, opened it, and looked inside. And what I then said sounded to the director—and to my friends—like a cannon shot:

"These rubies are real, Mr. Director."

"What the...?" choked out the Director.

"What?" I heard Batura's astonished voice.

"For real?" gasped Cagliostro.

I nodded and passed the open box to the director.

"Take a look at them, Director. They are the truest of the true."

But instead of the director, Batura grabbed the box. He greedily looked inside. I saw his eyelids flutter violently with shock and amazement. He simply could not believe his eyes.

"These are real stones!" he whispered and looked at Cagliostro. And the maestro answered him with a puzzled look.

Director Marchak took the box from Batura and only now began to look carefully at the stones.

"Yes, indeed..." he whispered. "They look real to me. How did this happen, Thomas? After all, we heard the radio broadcast. I am confused!"

"I don't understand anything, either," muttered Batura grimly.

I bowed to Cagliostro.

"It is to you, maestro, that we owe the *hocus-pocus*."

"Me?" said Cagliostro, surprised.

"Yes, you. You see, I discovered Koenig's third stash yesterday. I took the real stones out of it and took them to my room. I took the fake rubies out of your chamois pouch and put the real ones in it. Then, I placed the fake rubies in this box and replaced it in the ashpan. You did the rest of the work yourselves, gentlemen," I bowed again to Cagliostro and Batura. "You, gentlemen, put the real rubies into the box and stole the fake ones. The world is an illusion, Maestro."

Director Marchak grabbed his head.

"Oh God, I'm going crazy! Fake, real, real, fake. In the end, where were the fake and where were the real rubes?"

I exchanged glances with Lieutenant Yujinski. It was he who, at my request, allowed me to plant the real rubies on Cagliostro. Ever since I had disclosed the matter of robbing the caches, the militia kept an eye on both Batura and Cagliostro. I asked the lieutenant to authorize the swap because, as sometimes happens to me, I like to stage dramatic turns at the end of an adventure.

Meanwhile, Director Marchak hastily drew up a protocol of the opening of the cache. And when he gave it to me to sign, he said quietly:

"You saved your skin. Nothing from the cache was lost. But I can't forgive you for making a buffoon out of me. I should have recognized real rubies."

I pointed to the candle in the sexton's hand:

"It's dark in here, Mr. Director. In fact, it is *very* dark in here. And it's easy to make a mistake in the dark, isn't it?"

HERE ENDS BOOK 2
OF THE ADVENTURES OF
THE LEGENDARY POLISH DETECTIVE
MR. WHEELS

I hope you enjoyed this wonderful book. It has been a great pleasure to translate and publish it for you. If you like my taste in books and the way I publish them, you may be interested in other books I have published.

Joe Alex
The Ships of Minos

This five-volume series tells the tale of a 1600 B.C. journey of exploration: Minoan adventurers sailing up the river systems of Eastern Europe in search of the sources of amber. The book, stylized after the *Odyssey* and the *Aeneid*, imagines the world of Eastern and Northern Europe as it must have been three and a half thousand years ago. This epic tale, written by a great translator of English literature and the only man in the world to have translated all of Shakespeare, was first published in 1975. It has since acquired in Eastern Europe a fan following a little akin to that of Tolkien's cycle in English.

Arkady Fiedler
The White Jaguar

In 1726, a Polish-Virginian renegade fleeing the law joined a Stone Age tribe on the Orinoco. This tale of pirates, castaways, runaway slaves, and a European man becoming a full-fledged member of a Latin American Indian tribe is based on a few mentions in old Spanish chronicles and oral traditions preserved among the Arawak of Guyana and Venezuela. Its author, Arkady Fiedler, was a traveler and a best-selling writer with special love and experience of the Amazon region.

Witold Makowiecki
Fleeing Carthage

Written during the dark days of German occupation, the two volumes of tales about the adventures of Greek youths set in Greece, Italy, Asia Minor, Carthage, and Egypt in the middle of the fifth century B.C. draw a wonderful, entertaining, and humorous picture of the Mediterranean world in the Classical Age. Their literary accomplishment and historical accuracy have made them part of the school curriculum. Pick up your copy today and enjoy the nefarious political plots, mysterious Oriental priests, Olympic games, runaway slaves, garrulous merchants, chases at sea, and the heroism of war.

Jacek Bocheński
The Notorious Roman Trilogy

Jacek Bocheński's great trilogy, set in the waning decades of the Roman Republic and the first decades of the Roman Empire, is arguably the most important literary work to emerge out of Eastern Europe since World War Two. Written in a beautiful experimental style reminiscent of Kazuo Ishiguro and Orhan Pamuk, the books have not merely served to delight. Its first volume--on the career of Julius Caesar--was taken by the communist authorities as a criticism of the system and banned, causing a furor and turning the book into highly sought-after contraband; it also set its author on the unintended career of a political dissident which was to make him one of the leading figures of the Solidarity movement.

Aleksander Krawczuk
Aleksander's Antiquities

Aleksander Krawczuk (1922-2023) was an institution: a scholar, professor at the Jagiellonian University in Krakow, minister of culture of Poland (1986-1989), and author of over 30 immensely popular books on Graeco-Roman antiquity. His delightful, accessible, conversational, highly readable style, addressing complex topics in an approachable manner without ever dumbing them down, made antiquity come alive to both professionals and fans but also to ordinary readers who normally take no interest in the period. International best-sellers in Eastern Europe, his books have shaped three generations of antique lovers, but, as a consequence of Soviet cultural policies, they appear in English only now.

Maria Rodziewiczówna
The Wonderful World of Maria Ro

Maria Rodziewiczówna (1864-1944) was a daughter of Polish gentry in today's Belarus, then Russian Empire. Dispossessed by Russians and exiled with her family to Siberia as a child, she was entirely self-taught. Orphaned, she returned to Poland aged 18, where she inherited a badly mismanaged estate of over 6,000 acres, cut her hair off, donned man's clothing, and took over the management of the property. She proved an excellent farm manager and tough but fair leader of men. She paid off debt, introduced modern agricultural techniques, built roads, hospitals, and churches, led the Boy Scout movement, propagated Theosophy, and wrote over forty books. She was one of the most successful authors of her time and most of her books remain in print today. Hated by the right for her unconventional lifestyle (she was a lesbian and lived in a menage a trois with two other women) and by the left for her staunch anti-communism and her commitment to traditional forms of religious piety, she remains one of the best known and widest-read Polish writers forty years after her death.